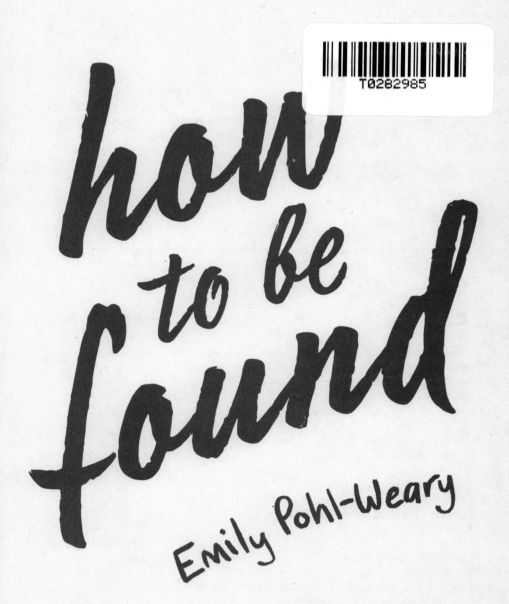

how to be found

Emily Pohl-Weary

ARSENAL PULP PRESS
VANCOUVER

HOW TO BE FOUND
Copyright © 2023 by Emily Pohl-Weary

ARSENAL PULP PRESS
Suite 202 – 211 East Georgia St.
Vancouver, BC V6A 1Z6
Canada
arsenalpulp.com

The publisher gratefully acknowledges the support of the Canada Council for the Arts and the British Columbia Arts Council for its publishing program and the Government of Canada and the Government of British Columbia (through the Book Publishing Tax Credit Program) for its publishing activities.

Arsenal Pulp Press acknowledges the xʷməθkʷəy̓əm (Musqueam), Sḵwx̱wú7mesh (Squamish), and səlilwətaɬ (Tsleil-Waututh) Nations, custodians of the traditional, ancestral, and unceded territories where our office is located. We pay respect to their histories, traditions, and continuous living cultures and commit to accountability, respectful relations, and friendship.

This is a work of fiction. Any resemblance of characters to persons either living or deceased is purely coincidental.

Cover and text design by Jazmin Welch
Cover art by Jazmin Welch
Edited by Catharine Chen
Proofread by Alison Strobel

Printed and bound in Canada

Library and Archives Canada Cataloguing in Publication:
Title: How to be found / Emily Pohl-Weary.
Names: Pohl-Weary, Emily, author.
Identifiers: Canadiana (print) 20230211216 | Canadiana (ebook) 20230211259 | ISBN 9781551529356 (softcover) | ISBN 9781551529363 (EPUB)
Classification: LCC PS8631.O35 H69 2023 | DDC jC813/.6—dc23

For my families

Of course we can solve mysteries
as well as grown-up detectives.

—CAROLYN KEENE, *The Nancy Drew Sleuth Book*

CHAPTER I

Planning the Perfect Crime

Trissa tucked her breasts back into her fuchsia sports bra and pulled up her hot-pink sweater with rhinestones along the neckline. She flicked a red curl out of her face, popped the tip of her middle finger into her mouth, and sat there beside me, chewing on the stubby fuchsia nail and flipping the bird at the world. Trissa was the queen of not giving a shit.

"Juicyyyy," said Red. "My mouth is watering. Gimme a bite."

"So gross," I snapped.

"Shut up, Michie." Red's real name was Rocky, but nobody called him that. His orange armpit hair had earned him the nickname when it first grew in. Since he was the one who dared Trissa to flash everyone, he was obligated to act excited, even though he probably hadn't seen much of anything. He was sitting on the far side of our circle of friends.

The only light in the abandoned apartment came from a handful of candle stubs in the middle of the circle that I'd picked out of the nearby Greek Orthodox church's garbage. They were nicer than phone lights, but at this point, they were burning dangerously low. Wouldn't last more than a few minutes.

"Doink, doink!" screeched Red's little brother, Timbit, and his auburn curls bounced all over the place. "Laser beams shooting from her nipples. Doiiink. Hypnotized."

"C'mere, Trissa Baby," said Red. "I'm hungry. Mmm. Top sirloin."

Trissa's heel shot across the circle and connected with his shin. He yelped and rubbed the spot, even though it probably hadn't hurt much. Trissa's only response was to remove her middle finger from her mouth with a soft popping noise and hold it closer to the light so there was no mistaking her message.

"You gonna take that disrespect?" jeered Anton, who was sitting on Trissa's other side. He raised two beefy hands to encircle her neck like he wanted to strangle her. "You've gotta show a bitch who's boss."

Red snickered.

I shook my head in disgust. "Nice. Joking about a serial killer."

The West End Strangler had been targeting girls our age for over a year. Police knew very little about him except that he was good looking enough to pick up victims on dating sites. He drugged his victims, choked them to death, cut their bodies into pieces, packed them in cheap cargo bags, and tossed them into the lake. Body parts kept washing up, and girls were scared to walk alone at night. Or at least more scared than they'd been before.

Trissa chewed her bottom lip. "I heard the Strangler snatched someone a few blocks from Club Jelly last weekend."

The air left my lungs, and for an instant, I couldn't inhale. She was talking about the exclusive nightclub downtown where she worked as a cage dancer on Friday and Saturday nights. "That's eight girls now."

"That we know about," she said.

"Gotta admit, he's effective," said Anton, cracking his knuckles.

I couldn't figure out what Trissa saw in Anton. He treated her like gum stuck to the bottom of his shoe, but she always messaged him when we were meeting up. It felt like he'd always been around and always would be, bringing my life down a couple notches. He acted like the leader of our group just because he was a couple years older, and he always needed someone to pick on. He usually focused on Timbit, because he wouldn't fight back, or Trissa, because she was bright, shiny, and mouthy. Plus it was easy to press her buttons.

Anyway, in my opinion, Red deserved to be kicked for comparing Trissa's breasts to steak. On my left, Timbit was still shaking his head, as if he was having trouble clearing his brain from the mesmerizing effect of nipples. He was a year and a half younger than most of us, only fifteen, but we let him hang because he'd found the master key card that let us enter this unit. It was probably owned by a real estate investor waiting for the right time to sell. Also, Timbit and Red's parents owned a condo right across the alley, and if we froze him out, he'd just rat to his scary dad. Not like we did much in here—there was no electricity, running water, or furniture—but we didn't want to lose the only private space we had. I felt kind of sorry for Timbit too—most of us did, except Anton, who didn't experience human emotions—because he didn't have his own friends.

To be honest, it was so dark that me and Anton were the only ones who could see anything more than Trissa's general shape. The candles barely illuminated our faces, and Trissa was sitting back a ways. The shadows pressed inward, thick enough to touch. Anton didn't seem particularly interested. And it wasn't like her body was anything new to me. We'd grown up in the same house and started playing doctor at the age of five.

I squinted across the candles at the other two people in the room: my childhood friend Anwar and his perfect girlfriend, Kelli D. Anwar's dimly lit face didn't give anything away, but he wasn't laughing. I could sort of make out the outline of Kelli D's body melded into his side. I didn't need light to know how perfect she looked. Her skin was smooth, her straight brown hair silky, and her green eyes flawlessly lined. Her skin and face and all the other parts of her body were perfect too.

My hair was a rat's nest of over-bleached frizz. My skin was pale, even after a summer spent outside, and my breasts overflowed from a double-D BuyMart special. The underwire jabbed painfully into my armpits, and if I didn't keep my back straight, my fingertips tingled. I should have gone up a cup size but was terrified to find out what the size above double D was called. E for Epic? Enormous? Elephantine?

Anton's bulbous nose and heavy black brows flashed into sight when he used the screen of his phone to roll a joint with some sativa I'd stolen from my mom. She smoked cannabis to keep her lupus symptoms under control. Though she was legally allowed to have four plants in the basement, she actually had more than thirty and sold the extra weed for cash.

I stared at the sputtering candles, forcing myself not to fixate on Anton's dead-fish eyes. He was clearly bored of Truth or Dare. The rest of us were too, but used the game as an excuse to pass the time together. If you hung out with the same people every day and nobody had much money, sometimes you had to get creative.

Anton sparked up his vintage *Clockwork Orange* lighter. He lit the joint and inhaled a few times before passing it across the circle to Red with a grunt. Red puffed hard on it, then handed it to his brother. Timbit inhaled quickly about five times, then tried to hold all that smoke in his lungs for maximum effect. He started to hack and almost dropped the lit joint. Getting Timbit high was a disaster. He was annoying enough when he was sober.

"Guess it's my turn to dare," said Trissa, tilting her head to peer sideways in my direction and grinning in an evil way.

Timbit cleared his throat to let me know the roach was coming to me. I waved my hand to pass, then changed my mind. If Trissa was planning something evil, I might need help surviving the next few minutes. I took it, smooshed the soggy end to my lips, inhaled long and hard a couple times, then passed it along to Trissa.

She took her time smoking, savouring the tension she'd created. "Truth or dare, Michie?"

"Dare."

"You sure about that?" she asked, passing the joint to Kelli D, who was on the far side of Anton.

I shrugged.

Trissa cupped her hands around her mouth and leaned closer. A wave of jasmine oil washed over me, and a stray curl tickled my nostril, making me feel like I was going to sneeze. Her lips brushed my ear. She was wearing sticky lip gloss. I wondered if she was going to suck on my earlobe—she'd done that earlier—although she was just as likely to bite it.

"Make out with Anwar," she stage-whispered, loudly enough for everyone to hear.

I jerked away but didn't get far. Timbit was too close. His breath smelled like skunk and sour cream and onion chips. Yuck. I scooched back a bit, out of the circle. Why were we all squeezed in so close? There was plenty of space here.

"With tongue," Trissa added.

Kelli D swore at her.

"Jealous much?" asked Trissa.

"No way," I said, before Kelli D could answer. "Not happening."

Trissa laughed, a sharp barking sound, then full on cracked up and toppled backward, kicking her feet up into the air with glee. "You know you want to, Michie."

My face lit up, red as a tomato. I cursed my skin for flushing so easily. Hopefully nobody could see my cheeks in the dark.

Anwar used to be my best friend. Just a couple days ago, Trissa had complained that he'd dropped us like a couple of over-microwaved Pizza Pops after surgically attaching himself to Kelli D this past summer. She didn't live in our neighbourhood, but she was always here. We'd barely seen him alone for months. Before that, it'd been the three of us against the world. Well, more like me and Trissa, and me and Anwar. I was the pivot between their opposing personalities. Trissa was a bouncing rubber ball. Anwar was a sensitive artist with a chip on his shoulder.

"Do you forfeit?" demanded Red.

"Bawk bawk bawk," squawked Timbit, right in my ear.

"Why are we packed in like sardines?" I grumbled. If I refused to go through with Trissa's dare, everyone would put their minds together and come up with something much worse. Those were the rules we played by.

"Go do it outside, where nobody's watching," said Trissa.

"Anwar's not objecting," drawled Anton. "Notice that? Only you, baby girl."

Red rubbed his hands gleefully. "Time to figure out something even worse."

Anton was right. Anwar wasn't making a peep, but that wasn't out of character. Anwar could be chatty one-on-one, but he hardly ever spoke up in the group unless he had something important to share. I switched my phone to flashlight mode and pointed it at his face, giving him the chance to object. He only held up a hand to shield his eyes from the light.

Trissa leaned toward me again and whispered, a little more quietly, "C'mon. I'm giving you a free pass."

I shoved her hard. She fell back again, and her knee banged into Anton, causing him to drop the roach. He swore, then fished around for it between his legs with one hand, holding Trissa away from him with the other one.

She was now giggling compulsively like this was all a big joke.

Anton found the joint, jammed it between his lips, and inhaled a lungful, shaking his head as if to say she was a lost cause.

I turned off my phone light. Trissa had a vindictive streak—she'd shaved the heads of all my dolls when we were seven because I wanted to read instead of playing Barbies—but this was so much worse. I wasn't quite as bad as Timbit, but I didn't have very many friends, mostly because I was sick a lot and there weren't that many people I could stand. I didn't want to permanently lose one of them to a dare.

"Why are we even playing this game?" I asked. "We're not kids."

"Michie's a pussy," Timbit squealed.

I pinched his thigh.

He squeaked.

"Don't be sexist," I mumbled. "You're better than that."

"Michie only likes *girls*," said Red, referring to my last turn, when Timbit dared me to put my hand down Trissa's pants. That was no problem. Trissa had taught me everything I knew about sex.

"I hate you," I hissed at her.

That made her giggle again.

"Frigid?" taunted Anton.

I didn't respond, knowing that would bother him more than if I got pissed off.

"We know she's not," said Anwar, finally breaking his silence. "She's had three boyfriends and a girlfriend in the past year."

My jaw dropped. Now he decided to weigh in? Why wasn't he refusing the dare? To my surprise, he stood up and started walking toward the sliding balcony door. Kelli D made an angry choking noise.

Trissa clapped excitedly. "Yeah! They're gonna do this."

The dark room went fuzzy white for a moment like it was filled with a dense fog. I blinked to clear my vision and took a slow, calming breath. Trissa elbowed me. I sighed and grabbed my teal vinyl jacket and began to crawl after Anwar, making sure my knee landed on Trissa's fingers as I passed. She yelped and whacked my ass. It was worth it.

Outside, the city lights were dazzlingly bright, even though we were overlooking an alleyway. The autumn night was cool and humid, like it might rain. I pulled on my jacket just in case. Anwar was already climbing down the fire escape ladder—apparently, he was serious about getting privacy. A floor above street level, he dangled down and dropped to the pavement. I followed, even though I only had socks on, lowered myself off the bottom of the fire escape, let go, and landed right in a puddle. Yuck.

"You could stand on that," suggested Anwar, pointing at a concrete traffic barrier that had been colonized by weeds.

I scurried over to it, ignoring my cold feet, and took several deep breaths of polluted air. As I willed my heart to stop racing, I searched the sky for any stars that dared to shine through the smog. If I could find just one, it would help. No luck, but I did find an airplane headed somewhere away from Toronto and wished I was on it.

Whenever I got too stressed, my heart murmur acted up, and if I didn't chill out, I might actually faint. It had happened before. Cardiac arrhythmia and asthma were two of the four million health issues I'd been born with. My chest was already tightening, my head beginning to pound. I cursed myself for forgetting my pills at home. Actually, I should have just stayed home along with them.

Trissa could handle this sort of thing. She fell in love when the wind blew. Her heart was broken all the time, and she was always ready to give it away again. Mine had remained relatively intact. What Anwar said about me having relationships was the truth, but none of them had lasted more than a few weeks. I had enough problems. Didn't need more drama in my life. Plus, I couldn't be bothered with anyone who wasn't 100 percent worth my time. So far, nobody had been. Except Anwar. And sometimes Trissa. But mostly Anwar.

He was less than a step away from me, and his expression was oddly calm.

I hid my terror behind directness. "Are we really going to do this?"

His eyes shifted downward to my lips, and he nodded, a minuscule movement. I shuddered. This was Anwar: the boy I'd pushed down the slide at the playground when we were five years old and who had to get stitches above his right eye as a result. The scar was still visible now—a faint silvery line on his forehead. I had an urge to touch it.

"We've hardly talked in months," I whispered.

Anwar's Adam's apple bounced. He licked his lips.

"Maybe we shouldn't do this, An. What about Kelli D?"

His eyes flicked upward to the balcony, then settled back on my mouth. A little fire started to burn in my abdomen.

"You guys better actually go through with this," yelled Trissa from inside the apartment. "I'll be able to tell if you don't."

One of my hands reached for Anwar's purple shirt with graffiti-style Arabic writing screened down the left side—he told me once that it was a special prayer for the dead, for his little sister Nadia, who had left us almost four years ago. I pulled him forward, a bit too hard. His chest smashed into my breasts and made my breath catch. My other hand snaked through his short black hair. I tugged his head downward.

His nose bumped my cheek. The smell of deodorant and the hair oil he'd been using since he was twelve—spices and baby powder—wafted over me and made me nostalgic, even though he was standing right in front of me. I'd missed him.

My lips brushed against his. He opened them to let me inside.

Even with my eyes closed, I could see every detail of his face: brown skin, hazel eyes with long black lashes, wide mouth slightly too big for his narrow chin. His expressions usually echoed whatever was in my head. We knew each other so well that we could practically read each other's minds. At least, we used to. I wondered if we still could.

Forget all the weirdness this year. Forget Kelli D. Trissa was right. I wanted him. Bad. I flattened against him and deepened the kiss.

CHAPTER 2

Identifying Your Target

The balcony door slid open above us, causing Anwar and I to spring apart like the wrong sides of two magnets.

Kelli D and Trissa were staring down. Trissa's face shone with pure delight. She screeched and clapped a hand over her mouth. Kelli D, on the other hand, looked ready to murder someone. Probably me. I couldn't blame her. My mouth still tasted like Anwar. A pang of excitement mixed with guilt shot through me, immediately followed by an intense wave of jealousy. All I had was that kiss. Kelli D had him.

She ducked back inside for a moment, and I wondered if she was going to huddle in a corner and sulk, but then she reappeared, wound up her arm, and threw a high-heeled wedge. It sailed through the air, smacked Anwar in the shoulder, and bounced on the cracked pavement. Her other shoe followed a second later. I ducked, but it was also aimed at Anwar, who smartened up and leapt aside just in time.

Kelli D started climbing down the fire escape. "You were *enjoying* it."

It was time to get out of there. "My shoes!" I yelled at Trissa.

She dove inside and came back a second later to hurl them down at me. I jammed on my first sneaker just as Kelli D hopped off the ladder, caught her footing, twisted, and lunged … at Anwar, not at me. She walloped him in the gut before he realized what she was going to do. He doubled over, gasping for air. Kelli D's enraged scream filled the air, then she bent over to slide on one of her high-heeled sandals. Was she planning to come after me or keep attacking him?

I didn't want to wait around to find out. My second shoe was on now, so I took off down the alley.

"Michie, wait for me!" called Trissa.

At the end of the alley, where it connected with the street, I paused to watch Trissa swing over the second-floor fire escape railing and jump to the ground, ankle boots dangling from one hand. She barrelled in my direction, still roaring with laughter. She fed on chaos. I loved her, but she had the social skills of a feral cat.

Trissa could run a lot faster than me. She caught up quickly, tugged on her boots, grabbed my hands, and started a wild victory dance. As she spun me around like a floppy doll, I could feel strangers watching us, but focused on gulping mouthfuls of air and calming my racing heart.

"Stop," I pleaded, but I never could stay mad at her for long.

"Fine." She dropped my hands abruptly, as if she'd just remembered my heart. "But you kissed him, Michie! What was it *like*? Oh my god, you've wanted him forever."

"Shut it," I wheezed, reaching out to clamp a hand over her mouth.

She danced away from me, cackling in bursts that reminded me of seagulls squawking.

I peered back toward the alley just as Kelli D launched herself in our direction. She looked like a prancing show pony on her ultra-high heels, but she made pretty good time. If she wiped out and broke an ankle, I'd feel awful.

"We'd better keep moving," I said, beginning to speed-walk but keeping an eye on Kelli D.

"I bet he'll finally dump Little Miss Perfect," Trissa said, "now that he's had a taste of his one true love."

Behind us, Kelli D's ankle wobbled, and she fell to her hands and knees. Her micro-miniskirt flipped up over her moon-white ass cheeks. Oh crap. I'd willed it to happen. She struggled to stand up but couldn't get traction and ended up flapping around like this betta fish I used to have that would jump out of its tank.

"Painful," I said, wincing.

Trissa laughed even harder at the sight of Kelli D upside down, flapping her arms.

Meanwhile, the boys had caught the scent of blood and surged down onto the sidewalk. Anwar looked horrified. Timbit was hooting. Red had his phone out and was filming. Anton looked irritated.

"Rotten turd!" I yelled at Red.

He gave me a thumbs-up but didn't lower his phone.

"I've never understood why people wear G-strings under minis," I muttered. "Things like this always seem to happen."

"That's *why* we wear them," retorted Trissa, flouncing up her own skirt to show off hot-pink lace.

I had never understood those games—my mom always told me there were better ways to attract attention than wearing sexy clothes. When I was young, she refused to buy me bikinis, micro-miniskirts, see-through shirts, or high heels. Trissa had all those things. If I asked to borrow something, she'd dress me up like Canada's Next Top Model.

Anwar flipped Kelli D's skirt down and hauled her onto her feet. As soon as she was stable, she punched him again—in the arm this time. That would leave a nasty bruise.

Trissa dragged me forward, still hopping with excitement. Before we made it to the corner, my lungs gave up. I leaned forward, hands on my knees, and heaved oxygen into my lungs. Trissa skidded to a halt a few steps ahead and turned to check out the show behind us.

Kelli D wasn't following anymore, but she yelled something I couldn't quite make out. It sounded like "fake feminist traitor." Her shoes were off again, and she whipped them in our direction. One of them smacked the hood of a Tesla, setting off its alarm. Then her shoulders started to shake. Was she crying or laughing? Bawling.

Anwar kept a safe distance, uncertain whether he should try to comfort her.

"You're … the wicked … bitch of the north," I gasped at Trissa.

"Pssht," said Trissa, waving my words away. "You gotta live more."

"I don't."

"Yeah, you do. You never grab what you want, not even when it's within reach. Like Anwar. You're totally in love with him. Happily-ever-after storybook shit. Admit it. He waited for years, but you were always, like, separate from us, wearing your weird baggy clothes with your nose in the air, alone in your room or the backyard, acting like everyone else was the subject of some detective story investigation. You have to make a move, force change, even if you're scared. You should be thanking me right now. It might be my last chance to give you a shove."

I straightened up. Was she planning on going somewhere? "What does that mean?"

"Nothing," she said. Her attention was focused up ahead now, on the corner that led to our street. "Use your puffer. You sound like a bulldog with sinus problems."

"Left it at home," I wheezed. "Kelli D is never going to forgive either of us."

Trissa threw up her hands in frustration. "You're pathological with that hos-before-bros stuff—it doesn't apply here. That girl is so shallow she cares more about her makeup than Anwar. She just likes the way they look together. She talks about you behind your back, stole the guy you love, and you *still* worry about her feelings?" She smacked my cheek with her free hand, not gently, then started marching up the hill toward home. "Toughen up, Michie, or the world will eat you alive."

"Being your friend toughens me up," I heard myself saying, and I knew it to be true.

She snorted. "Hardly. You still hear voices in your head? Still feel like you're floating above everyone when you're stressed? You're not tough, Michie."

I sniffed and stared at the sidewalk. She was being nasty, bringing those things up now, but I didn't want to show her how much it hurt. Not long after Anwar's sister was killed, my mom sent me to a psychiatrist because I was talking to imaginary friends. The doctor met with me three times, took a lot of notes, then informed me that Nadia's death and the repressed trauma of spending my first five years in and out of the hospital had resulted in something called "dissociative disorder." He gave me a prescription for pills that made me feel like my head was full of cotton balls and my feet were heavy blocks of cement. I only took them for a couple months before refusing to touch them. There was still a bottle of them in my underwear drawer three and a half years later, gathering dust.

Trissa pulled out her phone and tapped the little screen. A video message wiggled. I couldn't see what she was watching, but I could tell how long it ran because the light on the screen changed. Maybe fifteen seconds. Her expression got serious, and she started walking faster. I couldn't keep up without my lungs burning and my heart starting to skip around uncomfortably. It wasn't like her to forget about my health.

By the time Trissa reached our house, I was trailing almost half a block behind, and I'd decided she wasn't going anywhere. She was just being dramatic. Everything was life or death to her. She could be having a one-girl party, then suddenly fly into a rage and then seconds later burst into legit tears.

The big old brownstone was the only home either of us had ever known. Trissa and Charlene had the top two floors. Mom and I lived on the first floor and the renovated basement—mostly because Mom loved to garden, so we had easy access to the yards. Back when our mothers bought this place together, before either of us was born, Parkdale wasn't quite so gentrified. It was still a hub for newcomers and people who worked part-time or dangerous, illegal jobs, couldn't afford their own apartments, and needed somewhere to crash. But beneath all the bug-infested skyscrapers were a few old brick houses like ours that had survived almost a century and a half. It took a certain mind to see past the superhighway that sliced us off from the lake, the chaotic traffic, the businesses constantly going out of business, the pimps hovering on street corners, the people camping out in the shadows, the rooming houses, and the outpatients from the nearby mental health hospital. Of course, things had changed in the last few years. Gentrification and the onslaught of hipsters and suits. These days our house would probably sell for ten times what the mothers had paid for it.

Although the moms owned it fifty-fifty, Trissa's mother, Charlene, was the one the bank decided was responsible enough to carry a mortgage, thanks to her long-time job as the assistant to a city planner. My mom, Rachel, barely scraped together her half of the mortgage payments, but she was great at fixing things and tending the yards. Plus, they were best friends, or sisters, in the sense of that old Aretha Franklin song, "We Are Family," which was practically an anthem around our house.

We headed up the stone front walk, hemmed on one side by hedges and on the other by rose bushes so tall they rivalled the brambles that protected Sleeping Beauty. Trissa made it to the door first, of course, waved at my paranoid mom's infrared camera, and swiped her hand over the lock pad. The heavy wooden door swung open.

Inside the foyer, we kicked off our shoes and tossed our jackets onto overloaded wall hooks. To my surprise, Trissa put her finger to her lips and tiptoed after me into my apartment on the first floor. Mom's sleepy voice called out from her bedroom. I was still buzzing from all the excitement and the smoke, so it was hard to focus, but she seemed to be mumbling that it was past my curfew and she had to get up for work in a few hours. Ever since a falling out with her boyfriend, Franklyn, all she did was work, go to political meetings, take care of her plants, and complain with Trissa's mom about how much men sucked.

"Sorry I'm late! Love you, Ma," I called back. Mentioning love was my standard way of dealing with any contention. There was no way she could find fault with me loving her.

She sighed loudly. "Love you too, sweetie."

"G'night," I said, as Trissa and I crept into my room. Once I'd locked the door behind us, I took a few puffs of the inhaler on my bedside table, then swallowed a heart pill. Trissa shucked her miniskirt, tossed her pink sweater in a ball on the floor, shimmied out of her bra, and dropped it on top of the sweater. Half-naked, she hunted around in my drawers for a tank top, pulled it on, and flopped down on my rumpled bed. I turned away, more self-conscious than she was, and put on a nightgown before awkwardly removing my clothes underneath it.

"Can't believe you still use these." She was referring to my pillow-case and sheet set. Each pillow had a character from this old cartoon called *Jem and the Holograms* that used to be on TV when my mom was a kid, but they'd been washed so many times their faces had nearly faded to oblivion. And they were a thrift store find to begin with. Still, I refused to get new ones.

"They protect me while I sleep," I said, plumping up Raya and sliding under the comforter. When we were little, Mom gave us a complete set of all the episodes, and we watched them so many times we practically memorized them. We played Holograms all the time. Trissa was the perfect Pizzazz, lead singer of the Holograms' rival band, the Misfits, while my blond hair and blue eyes made me perfect for Jerrica/Jem.

Our friend Jimmy Salmon made the best Aja—even looked a little like her—but his family suddenly moved out of town.

Trissa crawled underneath the comforter and slid sideways until our elbows were touching. Her fingers gently rubbed my thigh and slid my nightgown upward.

My skin tingled, but I brushed her hand away and flicked on the bedside lamp. I was still kind of pissed over the Anwar thing, and my disintegrating copy of *A Girl's Guide to Murder: How to Get Away With the Perfect Crime* was waiting for me on the table. On the sparkly pink cover, a hand with rainbow nails clutched a dagger. It was the single most crucial source of knowledge in my universe. I'd discovered it in the dollar bin at BuyMart just after Nadia died. It had been peeking out at me from beneath a photo book on grooming angora bunnies and the FA to FLE volume of an encyclopedia set. The people who worked at the store clearly had no understanding of true value. I used two dollars of my birthday money to buy it.

By now, I'd read it a trillion times. I flipped to Chapter 11, which was all about surveillance, and pretended to be deeply engrossed in author Lacey Milan's words of wisdom. "When it comes to getting information about your target, nothing beats making friends. These days, the easiest way into a person's life is through social media."

Trissa nestled her head into the Jerrica pillow and mumbled, "You're so harsh, Michie."

"Ew. You sound like Anton. Plus you probably ruined any chance I might have with Anwar for the rest of my life. To be his friend or more than that."

"Oh please. He had fun. We both love you." She rolled away and fell asleep within seconds.

One of Trissa's most annoying abilities was that she could sleep anywhere, anytime. Not me, though. I lay awake, staring at the two-page section of *Girl's Guide* on analyzing body language but thinking about the kiss with Anwar. Would he avoid me even more now? Kelli D definitely would. Were they still a couple after this? It was going to be awkward between the three of us at school tomorrow. They were both in my homeroom. Anwar had seemed to enjoy the kiss as much as I did …

*

I must have finally fallen asleep, because I woke up just before three, still thinking about Anwar, and noticed that the other side of the bed was empty. Trissa must have crept out—maybe she was annoyed that I kept tossing and turning—and the bedside lamp was turned off.

A little disoriented, I turned it on again so I could hunt through my sock drawer to find the half of a sleeping pill I'd stolen from mom's prescription bottle. Kissing Anwar in front of his girlfriend counted as an emergency, in my opinion.

The mirror over my small dressing table was covered in lipstick. Trissa had used my Fairy Pink to draw a heart with A+M inside it. Underneath, she'd scrawled a crude picture of a chicken saying, "Bawk, bawk, bawk." That was going to be fun to clean off.

I crawled back into bed and slept through until morning.

CHAPTER 3

Feigning Innocence

My alarm didn't ring at seven-thirty, like it was supposed to, and Mom didn't wake me. Weird. On school days, she normally dragged me out of bed by the foot if I hit the snooze button twice. In the past, she'd poured a glass of water on my head—okay, just a few drops from the bottom of a glass—and another time, she sang protest songs through her megaphone. Yes, she has her own personal megaphone. Uh-oh. Maybe she'd decided to go on strike. She pulled that move whenever I took her for granted. Women's work was under-recognized labour, she would say, then threaten to bill me for all the hours she'd put into cooking and cleaning throughout my life.

As I yanked my hair into a chaotic topknot, reality swam into focus, and the sensation of kissing Anwar rippled through my stomach. I shivered and shoved that thought aside, then realized our apartment was silent.

My memory started working. It was Friday morning, which meant Mom had left super early for a dog show where she sold buttons and magnets and other stuff—that was why she had been in bed so early last night. She needed to get her table set up before the hordes arrived at ten. Seven or eight times a year, she rented tables at festivals and events and went on binges making buttons with activist slogans and jokes on them, laminated coasters, silkscreened T-shirts, and art made from Lake Ontario driftwood that she'd painted to resemble various famous people. Her side hustle supplemented her sales of medical-grade organic cannabis and kept our fridge stocked with Danish cheese and antipasto.

I needed to leave in six minutes if I wanted to make it to school on time … where I'd have to face Kelli D and Anwar in homeroom. Arming myself with clothes that helped me feel confident would help. I hurriedly shook out my leopard-print miniskirt and a low-cut black crop top. Before pulling them on, I sent Trissa a bus emoji and a question mark, like I did every weekday morning. I didn't really expect a response. Up until a few months ago, we'd taken transit together every morning. Then something changed. Lately, we only rode together a couple times a week. I wasn't sad about it today—she was still on my shit list—but I wasn't angry enough to break our routine.

I swiped on eyeliner, mascara, lip gloss and tried to make my hair look like it was on-purpose messy, tossed a granola bar and a banana into my bag along with the binders and books, and laced up my black high-tops. I couldn't find my teal jacket, even though I was pretty sure I'd left it on a hook in the lobby last night. It must've gotten buried in other coats this morning. I snatched up my second-favourite coat—lavender faux fur— and jogged to the bus stop. At least it wasn't raining.

The bus was full and stuffy. Someone stood up as I approached, so I slid into their seat and hefted my heavy book bag onto my lap. I'd just started munching on the granola bar when a familiar man got on and stopped to hold a pole nearby.

Mr. Booger was what Trissa and I called him. He must have lived nearby, because he travelled this route back and forth all morning, every morning, when the buses were packed to capacity with the high-powered suits and skirts who were gentrifying our neighborhood. I didn't particularly like the way things were changing—everything was getting so expensive—but Mr. Booger hated them with a passion. His routine was to wait until one of them was crammed up in his face, then make eye contact, sneeze aggressively into his hand, and lick it clean.

This morning, his target was a man with a tidy beard and a handlebar moustache. The guy wore a tailored black jacket and carried a leather shoulder bag that probably cost double my entire wardrobe.

I deliberately kept my eyes on my phone, but a couple seconds later, I heard a small explosion and smothered a giggle. A wave of bodies made room for the hipster, who pressed through to the back of the car, shaking his head in disgust and trying to wipe wet droplets off his chest. Trissa thought Mr. Booger was hilarious. I had never been able to figure out how the guy managed to store up so much snot and then sneeze on command. Ground pepper, maybe?

Once the bus arrived at the station, I took the train three stops, then jogged past expensive homes with tidy lawns to my school, which was filled with kids whose parents were mostly lawyers and business people who drove luxury SUVs. Somehow, I managed to get my butt into my seat just before the morning bell finished ringing. My history teacher shot me a disapproving look as the morning announcements started broadcasting over the PA.

Anwar was sitting behind me. His head had bobbed up when I entered, so I knew he'd seen me, but I didn't meet his gaze. Kelli D was shooting daggers with her eyes in my direction. Normally, all three of us sat together, but today she was across the room with the other perfect girls.

The rest of the class was populated with people who weren't as pretty as Kelli D, but had pricey salon haircuts, brand-name clothes, got shiny new cars for their sixteenth birthdays, and had boyfriends or girlfriends who looked just like them. At least that was how it felt. There *were* a couple weirdos—Jack hadn't washed his hair yet this term, and Lauren sat up front near the chalkboard, picking her zits compulsively. And then there was me. Depending on which PP (perfect person) you asked, I was either a weirdo (fine with me), a slut (highly debatable and also sexist), or a loser (because I didn't waste my time being default friendly to the PPs).

Knowing that Kelli D probably felt terrible right now made it harder than usual for me to carry my head high in this school full of rich kids. I felt myself curl protectively over my desk and desperately recalled the words of Lacey Milan in Chapter 16, The Aftermath: "Feeling guilty may project to other people that you're a conscientious friend, co-worker, or boss, but it won't help you get away with murder. To achieve your ultimate goal—protect Number One, stay out of suspicion—you must rid yourself of the emotion."

Nine months and eight days to go before I would be gone from this place forever. Transcripts from this school would set me up for the university of my choice, but it had sucked the life out of me since the day I entered its doors. Soon enough, though, I would never have to speak to any of these people again. Except Anwar. Hopefully, I'd still be speaking to him.

At the end of class, the teacher called me aside, told me I seemed to be distracted, and tried to pretend he was concerned about my well-being. Really, he just wanted to get me alone so he could put his arm around my shoulders and pull me against his side. It was horrid, but I knew if I played along, he wouldn't record me as late. History was my least favourite class, and I didn't get great marks, but I'd made sure it was my homeroom for two years in a row. Since he would try to hug me anyway, why not have a spotless attendance record in exchange?

Second period was advanced calculus. Kelli D was in that class too, but Anwar took visual art. When I entered, Kelli D was sitting in my spot, flanked by a couple of PPs. There were only two empty seats left: right up front, or far back, in a dark corner. I humped my knapsack to the last row, slid into the school desk, took out the homework I hadn't even opened last night, and completed a few calculations before the teacher arrived.

On my right was Vee Leung, an outsider like me but a much more confident and stylish one. They had stubby, short baby bangs and a ragged bob dyed the greyish purple hue that everyone wanted, and they were always dressed to be noticed. One day, it might be a yellow-and-white tutu with a neon-yellow shirt, the next a pair of farmer's overalls, scuffed boots, and a battered straw hat. Today, they wore a dark, shimmery minidress that changed colours when they moved. It reminded me of an oil slick.

Vee leaned across the aisle to whisper, "What happened between you and Barbie? She's, like, *this* close to leaping over the desks and clawing your face off."

I made a sour face. "I kissed her Ken doll."

"Anwar?" Vee's eyebrows shot up, and they waved their hand to indicate I was on fire.

"It was a dare. He's my friend."

"Kelli D and her posse will never forgive you. You realize you're socially dead now?"

"Already was." I grimaced. "I hate all the PPs anyway."

"Peepees?" they asked.

"Perfect people. That's what I call everyone who looks like they popped out of the same plastic mould."

Vee snorted, causing a small group to turn and stare. "PPs. Love it! I'm going to steal it, okay?"

I shrugged and grinned.

"Ugh. I live for the summers," Vee hissed. "The instant exams are done, I head up north and disappear into the bush."

"Summer's a long way off," I grumbled. "It's not even October."

"True. I'm counting the days, though. I've got a job lined up cooking for a camp of tree planters. I make good money."

"That's got to be hard work."

"I'm tougher than I look." They flexed a bicep to prove it, which cracked me up, reminded me of the conversation with Trissa last night, and earned us another dirty look from Kelli D's friends.

Just then, Ms. Lasowski, the math teacher, entered the room and barked at everyone to open their textbooks. Lasowski had short grey hair and huge round glasses that magnified her hyper-alert dark eyes. When she focused intently on someone, she looked like an owl spotting prey. She began explaining a new concept, and I quickly scribbled down a few more calculations from our homework so that I could raise my hand a few times. Back in grade nine, I'd figured out that if I volunteered in class and it looked like I was paying attention, teachers wouldn't randomly call on me. It was a good technique for keeping my grades up while doing as little as possible.

Vee, on the other hand, was openly doodling caricatures of other students in the margins of their notebook. So, of course, Ms. Lasowski called on them to share their work, probably hoping to catch them off guard. Instead, Vee sashayed to the chalkboard, effortlessly copied the equation onto the board, curtseyed to the class, and returned to their seat. Lasowski tried really hard but couldn't find a single mistake. Somehow, Vee never seemed to be paying attention but was always prepared.

After class, Vee decided to stick around me for some reason. I was relieved, because it was lunch period, and entering the cafeteria by myself would have been brutal. It seemed like getting on Kelli D's bad side had gained me a new friend. I picked out french fries and an apple while Vee poked around for the least wilted tempeh salad. We headed outside to sit on the grass and eat. It was chilly enough that most students were staying indoors, except for a few soccer jocks kicking a ball around the field nearby. I noticed Red over there, along with a guy named Chad who'd hit on me at the only high school party I'd ever gone to, with Trissa.

When Chad "accidentally" kicked the ball in our direction for the second time, missing us narrowly, Vee's back stiffened, but they ignored it. They clearly understood what it was like to be a target. A couple minutes later, the ball came whizzing back toward us. I raised my hands involuntarily, positive I was going to be hit in the face. Someone intercepted it. Anwar.

He turned, gave Chad the finger, and dropped the ball. Then he yelled at Red to stop being an ass or he'd tell his father. Red looked a little embarrassed, shrugged, and said something under his breath at Chad, then sat down to eat his lunch on a nearby bench. Chad didn't look apologetic. He gestured for one of the other boys to retrieve the ball. Vee waved cheerily at the jock who loped over and blew the guy a kiss.

"Finally found you," Anwar said to me.

"Thanks for saving us from the dickbags," said Vee, flapping their fake eyelashes flirtatiously. "You're my new hero."

"Anytime," said Anwar, grinning. "Can I sit with you two?"

"Sure."

He deliberately turned his back to the soccer guys, letting them know he wasn't concerned about them, and sank to the ground right beside me.

I stuffed a handful of fries into my mouth, swallowed without chewing, and nearly choked.

Vee gave me a meaningful look. *Go for it*, they were saying. What did Vee expect me to do, jump him right here on the grass? Not my style. Anwar meant too much for me to mess things up even more.

"How's the yearbook looking so far, Vee?" asked Anwar, pulling out a sandwich his mom had probably made.

"Awesome."

"How could it not be, with you as the editor?"

Vee fanned their face as if the praise was making them hot. "Oh, stop flattering me."

"What are your plans this year?" I asked, trying to keep any safe conversation going.

"I'm organizing the book around the four seasons," said Vee.

"Cool," I said, "how does that work?"

"Instead of grouping all the clubs together and such, we're arranging it according to when things take place during the year, so everything that happens in fall will come first, then winter, then spring. It might be a little confusing for some people, but too bad. The class photos will still be at the end, because they happen in May. It makes sense to me."

"Need an extra set of hands?" I asked, thinking this might be my ticket to having company at lunch every day. "I'm an okay writer, think. At least I want to be. And Anwar's art is beyond amazing."

Vee winked at Anwar. "Oh, believe me, this boy has already promised me half a dozen illustrations."

Anwar laughed. "Vee's got serious plans for me."

"You bet I do," they teased.

The nearby doors banged open, drawing our attention. A gaggle of PP girls swept out of them. Kelli D was among them and immediately fixed her glare on us. She'd already known we were out here. Anwar muttered something I didn't quite catch and dropped his head to stare at what was left of his sandwich. I wasn't smart enough to do the same. Kelli D sneered at me, tossed her hair, and linked arms with two of her friends. As they passed us, one of her friends said, "Loser alert."

"Sheep alert," Vee snapped back, forking up a big mouthful of salad, then chewing and *baa*-ing with their mouth open and tongue lolling around.

Anwar and I cracked up.

"You two are totally gonna be featured on Kelli D's next airhead video," said Vee. "And everyone at school streams those because she loves humiliating people."

"She can be kind of mean," Anwar admitted.

"It took you how long to figure that out?" asked Vee. "She must have kept you seriously distracted. That girl is pure evil genius."

Anwar shrugged. "She's not evil, Vee. Just insecure, thanks to over-achieving moms who expect her to be flawless."

Vee sucked her teeth. "You can't convince me she has human emotions."

The PP girls had reached the sidewalk now. They stopped and turned back to stare at us, whispering to each other. My temper flared, but I wasn't about to pick a fight with Kelli D over Anwar. Hos before bros, I repeated silently to myself. I could practically write the lecture my feminist mother would give me if she found out I'd made out with someone who was in a relationship. Plus, a tiny part of me still felt sorry for Kelli D. She was being nasty to make the betrayal sting less. Better to just tune her out.

The three of us finished our food and walked to a coffee shop. I got an iced mocha loaded with whipped cream and chocolate sprinkles, and Anwar got a bottle of water. Vee ordered a unicorn slush that streaked their tongue green and purple. We chatted about yearbook stuff—now that I'd offered, Vee had decided I would take over writing the short paragraphs about all the different student groups. Just when I started feeling relaxed about having Anwar so close, he looped his baby finger around mine. I started freaking out and pulled my hand away, then regretted it. What was going on?

The rest of the school day unfolded without incident. Thankfully, I didn't have Vee, Anwar, Kelli D, or any of her best PPs in my afternoon classes. Besides, nobody could ruin drama or sociology for me—they were my favourite classes. When the end-of-day bell rang, I considered checking in with Anwar to see if he wanted to head home together, then decided I needed more time to process things. I sent him a text that said, *Promised Trissa I'd help her with something at home. TTYL.* It was a complete lie, but it sounded good. Then I turned off my phone and put it away.

Avoiding the crush of students on transit, I walked home through High Park, a massive plot of land modelled after Manhattan's Central Park that separated my school's rich neighbourhood from Parkdale and the lake. It took me an hour to get home, but by the time I opened the front door, I felt more settled. I didn't have to be terrified by the fact that my relationship with Anwar might be changing. If I acted super weird and standoffish, I would jinx everything before we had a chance to see how things went. I shouldn't worry about getting bored of him, like I had with other pseudo-relationships, and we had enough history to stay friends even if a relationship didn't work out.

I still wasn't quite ready to face him though, so when I turned my phone back on I didn't open the message he'd sent me, instead flopping down on my bed and messaging Trissa to see if she wanted to stream a few episodes of *Stunt Girls*. She'd never responded to me this morning, I realized. What the hell. Normally, she would write back to say she wasn't ready to leave yet. Had I upset her last night?

I went out to the lobby and banged on her apartment door. There was no answer. I could have unlocked it, since their lock was programmed with my handprint as well, but if she was home, she'd have answered. So I headed to our kitchen, made myself some microwave popcorn with tons of butter, and munched alone in front of my battered tablet. It wasn't as fun as watching with Trissa, but at least *Stunt Girls* shut down my brain.

At some point, Mom messaged to say she wouldn't be back from Woofstock until ten-thirty or later, but there was a freezer pizza and a bag of salad I could have for dinner. I added extra handfuls of mozza and Parmesan to the pizza and slid it into the oven to cook. By the time I'd eaten, my head was sagging. It was still early, but I was exhausted and a little dizzy. The fluttering in my chest told me I needed rest, so I changed into pyjamas and climbed into bed.

Trissa still hadn't texted. Maybe she was at the club? It was Friday night, so probably. I wrote to tell her she was a dick for not messaging back, then fired off a note to Timbit, who went to Trissa's alternative school, asking if he'd seen her today. A couple minutes later, he wrote back that she hadn't shown up, but that was the norm these days.

I got a notification that Kelli D had posted a new video rant about "sleazy boys who cheat with sluts." In it, she looked slightly less immaculate than usual—the heart on her necklace was off-centre, and the pink blush on her cheeks was too heavy—and she went on and on about how self-respecting girls should never believe it when their man called another girl his "best friend." I clicked the little thumbs-down icon and left a comment: *Fighting with another girl over a boy is TOTALLY anti-feminist.*

I decided to send Vee a message too, thanking them for keeping me company at lunch and repeating my offer to help out with yearbook by doing whatever they needed. Too tired to even plug in my phone, I shoved it under my pillow, picked up *Girl's Guide to Murder*, opened it randomly to Chapter 17, and read the first sentence: "When it comes to managing an authority figure who has the ability to toss you in a cell and throw away the key, remember: comply now, contest later."

Good advice from Lacey Milan, I decided. Then I passed out.

CHAPTER 4

Evading Police Suspicion

Loud pounding at the front door rattled my bedroom walls. I jolted awake to find the bedside light shining directly into my eyes. It was still dark outside my bedroom window. The page of *Girl's Guide* I'd been reading when I fell asleep was stuck to my cheek with a bit of gluey drool.

Groggily, I pulled it away, smoothed it out, and replaced the book on my bedside table. I should be taking better care of it. Reading it was my ninth-level cleric protection spell against the extreme crappiness of life. I'd tried searching for a backup copy online, but there was no record of it or Lacy Milan even existing.

A few bars of "Rudolph, the Red-Nosed Reindeer" rang out in all the electronic doorbell's tinned glory. When Trissa got bored, she'd cycle through tones to find the most irritating one and crank the volume way up. So annoying.

I clamped the Aja pillow over my head. Her face was nearly translucent, yet she still had the power to make me stronger.

More banging. It was the middle of the night. One of the cabaret of misfits who lived here should have given the person a piece of their mind by now. Eavesdropping on that conversation was almost worth waking up for.

The banging continued. I couldn't fall back sleep until the person went away, so I gave up and rolled onto my feet. My phone slid off the bed and plunked to the ground. When I scooped it up, I noticed the battery was in the red zone, it was just after three in the morning, and there were two new messages. Anwar had written not long after I'd fallen asleep, asking if he could come over and talk. Vee was definitely going to take me up on the offer of helping with yearbook and asked whether I could start coming to their weekly lunch meetings on Wednesdays. Still nothing from Trissa.

Where was my mother? Her activist paranoia should have clicked in by now; normally, she'd be threatening the person at the door with my bantam bat, which she kept beside her bed in case of situations like this. It was possible she'd taken a sleeping pill so the noise hadn't penetrated her foggy brain, but she didn't need them as much these days.

I yanked an oversized sweatshirt over my nightgown, grabbed my nearly dead phone, and padded down the hall to the apartment door. The cracked vinyl flooring was so cold it made the bottom of my feet tingle. September was too early in the year to feel a wintry chill. We needed to turn the heat on.

Prepared to unleash a can of whoop-ass, I pulled open the apartment door, flicked on a light in the entryway, and froze. Through a window, I could see two police officers standing on the porch. They weren't wearing uniforms, but they were obviously cops. A tall, skinny guy with thinning blond hair was peering up at the wooden second-floor balcony, which was so decayed that it was a shocker it hadn't fallen off yet. He was clearly nervous about standing beneath it. The woman beside him was short and stocky, with dark-brown hair pinned in a sleek bun. She noticed me hovering and crooked a finger to indicate I should hurry up.

Dammit. I'd been considering a stealth recoil. Along with a bunch of stuff about the beauty myth, Mom had pummelled into me at a young age that I should never let cops get me alone. She didn't trust them and was a teeny bit overprotective—an instinct probably ingrained in her when I was little and my health was fragile. But also, she and Charlene had gone through some terrible experiences when they were young activists living in New York City.

It was probably for the best that neither of the mothers had answered the door. Mom was a live wire, and Charlene got robotic around cops. Charlene disguised herself as a harmless city planner assistant these days, but she was hard core. She and Mom had met in the 1990s while they were working for women prisoners' rights. Charlene got renovicted, and my mother, who was squatting in an abandoned building, suggested she come live at the squat. They went through all kinds of stuff back then, including having their activist group infiltrated by undercover police, getting beaten up at protests, and even being hauled off to jail twice.

Mentally, I reviewed Lacey Milan's tips in Chapter 9 for handling antagonistic police: "Keep your phone fully charged, your finger on the Record button, a lawyer on speed-dial. Make sure you're not carrying anything that could justify a search, and keep your hands visible at all times." As if on cue, my phone beeped to let me know the battery was critically low. Great. I tucked it under my arm and lifted my fingers to my hair—making a show of keeping my hands in sight—to tidy up my sloppy bun. As soon as our apartment door locked behind me, I moved forward and opened the front door just wide enough to speak through.

"Hey," I said.

The woman detective's eyes narrowed. She glanced down at a page of the lined notepad in her hand. "Michelle Gold?"

"Michie," I said automatically. "Yeah?"

"We need to ask you some questions."

A blast of cold, damp air swept right up my nightgown, making me shiver. "Go ahead."

"First," said the man, with a wide grin he probably thought came across as friendly, "why is your bell playing 'Jingle Bells' in the fall?"

Okay, Lacey Milan had a whole chapter on the different tricks law enforcement uses to gain your trust—this guy was either playing the Friendly Neighbour or the Safe Everyman.

"Rudolph," I corrected him, then shrugged. As if I was going to tell him about Trissa changing the tones. Or anything else.

"I'm Detective Lorenzo," said the woman, "and this is my partner, Detective Wilson. We'd like to ask you some questions about your friend Teresa Taylor."

"Trissa? Why?"

"Is your father home?"

"Don't have one."

She frowned, and her face tightened judgmentally.

"Test-tube baby," I said, feeling panicky. "Tell me what's going on with Trissa."

Lorenzo's frown deepened. She checked some scribbled notes on her pad, then casually rested a paw on the door, not so subtly pushing on it to widen the gap. She wanted to get inside the foyer, but I was a step ahead of her—I'd positioned my bare foot against the door as a stopper. If she wanted to get inside, she'd have to remove a pound of sixteen-year-old girl flesh. Although my can of whoop-ass would remain closed, I wasn't going to let them in.

"Go get your mother, then," Lorenzo commanded. "Since you're a minor, she should be present for questioning. We need to talk to her too."

Mom really wouldn't want to talk to them. Did they know about her side hustle? She'd been charged with dealing a few years ago, when she branched out to GHB and ecstasy in order to afford my braces. The judge had let her off with a light sentence and court-ordered community service, but the police probably still kept tabs on her. She didn't use anything but cannabis these days, which was legal—just not in the quantities she grew. She'd also kept a few bags of mushrooms, because she was proud of herself for getting them to fruit consistently.

"She's asleep. Tell me why you want to question us about Trissa."

Lorenzo didn't respond.

"Can we come in?" asked Wilson.

"Everyone's sleeping," I said. "I should be in bed. Not feeling well. Come back tomorrow." I rested a hand on my chest and fake-coughed up a lung—I've had a lot of practice acting like I'm on my deathbed. My mom blames herself for my health issues because she smoked, drank, and took ketamine before figuring out she was pregnant. Having me straightened her out, got her life on track or whatever. Anyway, I was an expert at pulling off sickly.

The cops exchanged a look that told me they weren't falling for my excuses. For some reason, they wanted to talk to me *now* ... and they wanted to look around. Lorenzo had already decided I was a juvenile delinquent. She was attempting to hide it, but I was pretty good at reading people's faces. No way was I going to speak to either of them alone, even though I hadn't done anything wrong. It would be guilt by association with my own mother. Or with Trissa.

"We're here now," said Wilson. "Can we just come in for a little chat?"

I shook my head and started to shut the door.

Lorenzo stopped it with her polished black boot—one of the uses of reinforced toes. "Why don't you want us to enter?" she demanded, eyes darting around, trying to see past me.

When I continued to hesitate, she shoved the door really hard. The bottom of it scraped across the bridge of my foot. I yelped and hopped out of the way, allowing the detectives to come into the foyer. If I hadn't, they probably would have plowed me down. I looked down and saw some blood bubble out of the scrape on my foot. It stung.

Lorenzo pulled out a phone, lifted it to chest height, and slowly turned in a circle. There wasn't much to see here, just a jumble of shoes and boots on a giant plastic mat and too many jackets and coats loaded on half a dozen hooks. The only decor was a dusty Chilean arpillera wall hanging that showed women bustling around a small town.

"What are you looking for?" I asked.

Lorenzo tilted the phone so the camera was aimed at my face. "A teenage girl has gone missing, and we're searching for her."

My mouth went dry. "What girl?"

"Teresa Taylor," she said. "We understand that she lives here and you were probably the last one to see her, just over twenty-four hours ago."

Memories from two nights ago came flooding back: the dare, kissing Anwar, Kelli D's meltdown, Trissa's hand on my thigh in bed. She must have woken up really early and gotten into a fight with her mom or something. She would have gone somewhere to cool down. That happened sometimes. Trissa was fiery. Charlene was calm but stubborn. "She's probably at a friend's place. Or the club where she dances."

"What time did you last see her?" asked the giant detective, his head tipped slightly to one side as he peered down at me. He was trying to figure out what game I was playing.

"Um, maybe midnight? She stayed over, and I had trouble sleeping, but I think that's when I passed out." My foot was throbbing now. "I didn't hear her leave, but I woke up again around three, and she was gone. Trissa kind of does whatever she wants. Is Charlene really worried?"

He glanced at Lorenzo, who raised an eyebrow. That silent exchange told me that I should take this seriously. Trissa wasn't okay. Might never be okay again. My heart started fluttering. The West End Strangler popped into my head. He usually snatched his victims a little closer to downtown, but they were all around our age. I took a long, slow breath before asking, "Do you think it's the Strangler?"

"The majority of these sorts of cases resolve quickly," Lorenzo said, holding up her palm as if to say *whoa there.* "Don't jump to conclusions."

"What conclusions shouldn't I jump to?" I demanded, getting even more worried. "That Trissa was choked to death, cut up, shoved in a cargo bag, and dumped in the lake like all those other poor girls?"

They glanced at each other again, but neither of them spoke.

Shit. I should never have gone to sleep pissed at her, no matter how irritating she'd been. That was a mantra my mother had drilled into me: never go to sleep mad because you don't know if the other person will wake up. Morbid, and she mostly used it to manipulate me into chilling out when I was angry at her, but she had a point.

"Uh, I'm going to wake up my mom," I said.

Before they could follow, I slipped back into our apartment, closed and locked the door, and raced down the hall. Mom's bedroom door was ajar. Her bed was empty, still made. I didn't hear her moving around anywhere. That meant she'd never come home. Maybe she was at Franklyn's place, her on/off boyfriend. She normally only did that on the weekend though, and she would have messaged me first. Where could she be? Was Charlene out too? Was that why nobody had answered the door?

I sent both mothers a message telling them that detectives were here. Were they out looking for Trissa? Did the police already know the mothers weren't home? Was that why they'd shown up now—to deliberately catch me alone? I headed back to the foyer, heart and mind racing.

"She's not here," I told them.

"That's all right. Just walk us through your evening together," Wilson prompted. "This isn't a formal interview, but the clock is ticking if your friend's in trouble."

I told them how Trissa and I hung out with the same friends we'd known since we were kids—Anwar, Kelli D, Red, Timbit, and Anton— in an empty apartment that was safe and private. We'd been doing that about three times a week over the past few months and would continue to do so until someone moved in or changed the lock on the door. I decided not to mention Trissa's dare, smoking my mom's weed, or the drama with Kelli D. Those things were none of their business. Trissa and I had left our friends just before eleven and come straight home. My mother was already in bed, so she didn't know Trissa had decided to sleep over, though that wasn't unusual. We stayed over in each other's rooms all the time. I finished up by saying I wasn't sure any of that would be helpful.

"Anything might be," said Wilson.

"We really need to take a look around," said Lorenzo, holding the phone in my face.

"Don't your body cams record everything you see?" I asked.

She didn't lower the device.

"We need to bring you down to the station to make an official statement," said her partner.

That was the last thing I wanted to do. It could go very badly. I'd seen a lot of people in this neighborhood get bullied by cops like these two. Where the hell was my mother?

My phone beeped. Mom's brief message said only, *Sorry for scaring you, Sweetie. Back ASAP. Will explain.*

Struggling to keep up with what was going on, I shoved my feet into a pair of pink sneakers, ignoring that it made the cut angrier, glanced at the apartment doors to double-check they were locked, and pushed through the front door. Outside, everything was quiet in the apartment towers and historical manor homes that had been chopped into breadbox apartments and rooming houses.

Wilson and Lorenzo's squad car was halfway down the sidewalk, facing the wrong direction on our one-way street. I glanced down the street and noticed an unmarked cruiser parked under a street lamp in front of Anwar's building. He hadn't visited much lately, but if Charlene was panicking, she'd have given the police contacts for all the friends. Were there detectives at Red and Timbit's house too? Anton's? Kelli D's?

I sent Anwar a quick message asking if his mom was okay. Amina would be terrified to find police at the door in the middle of the night. She'd lived through a nightmare four years ago, when Nadia was killed in that hit and run.

But if this was a big deal, my mom would have woken me up or at least messaged to tell me about it. Maybe I should relax. Our moms had raised us to keep our eyes open and be street-smart. When Trissa and I snuck out in the middle of the night to keep Anwar company after his sister died, the mothers grounded us both until we'd read an entire stack of non-fiction books about catfishing, child trafficking, and other potential dangers. Then they registered us in Saturday-morning self-defence courses for girls. And I'd shared every single tip in *Girl's Guide* with Trissa.

But that wasn't how it worked, was it? The Strangler was supposedly an expert at getting girls into his car after first dates—even the ones who didn't normally trust strangers—and then they were never seen again.

I headed back inside and kicked off my shoes. Lorenzo was rattling the door to Trissa and Charlene's apartment.

"I'm pretty sure you need permission to enter," I muttered.

"This is Teresa's place?" she asked.

I nodded.

"If you know the code, let us in. The first hours are crucial in cases like these."

My heart sped up, thumping weirdly inside my chest. "Cases like what?"

Neither of them responded. Apparently, that was their number one technique.

A dizzy spell came over me. I leaned against the wall. "When I think about it, maybe Trissa—Teresa—was acting a little off last time I saw her."

Lorenzo's eyebrows raised expectantly. "How so?"

"Moodier," I said, meaning bitchier. "She mentioned she might not always be around for me. At the time, I assumed she was just saying that to make me appreciate her more."

Lorenzo's eyebrows wiggled like they were trying to commune with her hairline. "Was she upset about something in particular?"

I had no clue, so I shrugged helplessly.

"We really need to take a look around," growled Wilson. "Before it's too late for—"

"For what?" I demanded. "You've gotta know I'm not the person who's been murdering all those girls, and I'd never hurt Trissa. Besides, my handprint's not programmed in their lock." I was lying, but there was no way I'd let them upstairs without Charlene and Trissa around.

"Fine. We'll look around your apartment first," said Lorenzo.

While this seemed like a situation in which my fear of police could be set aside—Charlene had clearly told them Trissa was in trouble—my brain was running through all the times they'd done awful things to people in this neighbourhood. With no witnesses. Then there was the list of things in our apartment that my mom wouldn't want them to see. Like the professional food scale and the pile of tiny baggies ready to be filled with cannabis and mushrooms for customers. Or, uh, the massive grow op in our basement.

"I need to call my mom before you come in," I said, eventually.

Lorenzo's eyes narrowed to slits. "What are you hiding?"

"Nothing." I didn't tell her that the last time cops had entered our place, they charged my mother with possession with intent to sell, and she spent the night in a holding cell at the local station. Charlene bailed her out as soon as possible, but Mom lived with restrictive conditions for almost a year and couldn't leave the house alone, until a judge stayed the charges in exchange for the promise she would limit herself to four plants and attend some bullshit professional retraining program.

Wilson grunted and took a step toward me. Then another. He was not only tall, I realized, but built like a tanker truck. He took up enough space for two men. Suddenly, the foyer felt tiny.

Not wanting to find out what would happen when he reached me, I twisted just enough to press my hand on the scanner that unlocked our apartment door. I silently prayed that they'd head to the farthest room first. Mom didn't keep anything dubious in the kitchen, and on the way past, I could grab my backup battery from my knapsack.

Instead, they immediately spotted Mom's rolling papers and bong on the table beside the couch and entered the living room. Nothing worse than that was visible, but I cringed at her giant poster of two generals sitting behind a table of homemade pies, cakes, and cookies with the caption, "It will be a great day when public schools have all the money they need and generals need to raise money for weapons by throwing bake sales."

My phone battery died, and the screen went black. "Uh, I'll be right back."

I dashed to my room so I could get the power pack. While there, I found an old Band-Aid in the drawer of my bedside table and slapped it on my scraped foot. I tugged on a pair of wool socks and jeggings and traded my pyjama shirt for a tee with a sparkly airbrushed leprechaun napping on a cloud at the end of a rainbow.

I'd failed my mom by letting them inside the apartment, but it wasn't like I had a choice. If only she and Charlene had come charging in while I was stalling them outside. Even better, I wished Trissa would come flouncing through the door, dressed for clubbing and laughing about how worried everyone was that she'd slept over at some guy's place.

CHAPTER 5

Collecting False Evidence

As I hurried back to the living room, I powered up my phone and felt slightly less panicky. Wilson was already pawing through a drawer of old board games and puzzles. Lorenzo had taken some books off a shelf to see what was behind them. Nothing but painted drywall. She picked up a dusty hardcover, turned it upside down, and riffled through the pages to see if anything might flutter out before shoving it back in haphazardly. What could she possibly think might wedged in there?

"I never gave you permission to search our place," I protested. "Isn't there a law about that? Like, you need some kind of warrant, or ..." I cut my own sentence short, wondering if that was only an American thing I'd seen people say on TV.

Neither detective stopped what they were doing.

I sent a message to Mom. *Cops are searching the place. Want to go upstairs. Where's Charlene?* Before hitting Send, I added Charlene and Trissa to the recipients. Then I sent a second message: *COME HOME NOW!!!*

"How is this going to help Trissa?" I asked the detectives.

"We're looking for information," grunted Wilson, slamming a desk drawer.

"You want to find your friend or not?" asked Lorenzo.

I shook my head, then changed the movement to a nod. "Of course, but how do you know she's not just at a friend's or something?"

"Her mother called us to report her missing," said Wilson.

"Teresa's personal effects were abandoned in an alley," said Lorenzo, at exactly the same time.

"What are you talking about?" I wailed, confused.

Lorenzo glanced at Wilson for confirmation. When he nodded, she continued, "Someone found a bag with her phone, passport, a couple changes of clothing, and over two thousand dollars."

Before Trissa started dancing at the club in June, she used her bank card to pay for everything, like most people. Now she always had crisp twenties and fifties on her. Since she was underage, the club's owner paid her under the table. Why were the detectives acting like I was a possible suspect or something? Did they think the Strangler had snatched her and maybe I was some kind of Karla Homolka wannabe, capable of conspiring to rape and kill my chosen sister?

My phone dinged with a reply from my mother: *Char's with me. Five min away.*

Lorenzo's eyes darted toward the phone, but instead of asking me who it was, she started sifting through a stack of unopened bills.

They're tearing the living room apart, I texted Mom.

My heart was skipping erratically and so strongly I could almost hear it beating. I needed to take a pill, but the bottle was in the bathroom cabinet, and I didn't want to leave the cops alone again. What would Lacey Milan have suggested? To call a good lawyer immediately. The police wouldn't listen to me, but they'd have to listen to a lawyer, right? Mom's on/off boyfriend, Franklyn, was an activist criminal lawyer with a gambling problem who took on cases nobody else would touch— because the clients had no money or their cases were impossible to win. Living that way meant Franklyn had trouble paying his debts, but his conscience was clear.

Getting close, Mom responded.

Wilson lifted one of the couch cushions, flipped it over, and ran his hand in the crack behind the cushions. He came up with a flattened Swedish Berry, a couple coins, some popcorn kernels, a pen, a bunch of dusty hair, and a handful of crumbs.

On the other side of the room, Lorenzo dumped the contents of a desk drawer on the floor. Pens and paper clips and Post-its splayed out all over. She reached for the side drawer that contained mom's stash, yanked it out, whistled, and held it up for her partner to see: lots of empty baggies and a dozen filled with various quantities, obviously not intended for personal use. There was also a small food scale, a dozen cheap lighters, matches, bongs, and an old pill bottle filled with hash. Wilson's expression told me he wasn't surprised to see it.

They didn't say anything, just snapped a whole lot of photos of Mom's stash, then moved on—leaving a huge mess—down the hall to my bedroom, where we all crowded into the small space. Lorenzo's eyes narrowed at the lipstick message on the mirror. Why hadn't I cleaned that off?

Wilson picked up *Girl's Guide* and pawed through a few pages. I already knew the headings that would catch his eye. Chapter 3: Preparing the Murder Scene, and Chapter 5: Planting Seeds of Deception. Sure enough, he waved Lorenzo over to record it. She grunted and took a look. For the first time, I understood what a mouse must feel like when they see an eagle swooping toward them. My legs began to shake.

"It's just a book!" I heard myself squeak, picturing Wilson in an old-timey costume, tossing it onto a bonfire.

Lorenzo sneered and dropped it on the floor.

I scooped it up, clutched it to my chest, then carefully put it back on the table.

Next, she opened my closet and began to sweep her hands along the ground beneath my dresses, disrupting piles of dirty clothes, half-filled diaries, and other stuff I didn't want any human being to see.

"You're not going to find her in there," I cried, darting over and grabbing a handful of underwear. I tossed it into a nearby laundry bin.

"Get away from me or I'll light you up," growled Lorenzo, her hand on the taser clipped to her belt.

I squeaked in shock and leapt back. My hip smashed into a corner of the peeling dresser I'd had since I was a kid. I rubbed it absentmindedly and glared at her. "Just so you know, I have a congenital heart defect. That would kill me."

Lorenzo raised her eyebrows to let me know I'd better not try anything. She wouldn't care if I had a heart attack in front of her.

Wilson bent over and reached for the pile of laundry I'd just moved so he could search it carefully. So embarrassing. My cheeks burned as his fingers sifted through the items of clothing.

Please just let Mom get home before they find the door to the basement. I wanted nothing more than to huddle under the blankets and sob. My heart was skipping around dangerously. Having the police around brought back memories. Terrible ones. Of mom getting arrested and taken away. And of Nadia's death, when they canvassed our street and put her face into heavy rotation on the news. For weeks I couldn't go on the internet without melting down in tears. The police chief had even given press conferences, appealing to people to call Crime Stoppers if they had any information. Reporters followed us around, hoping we'd talk to each other privately and let some little tidbit of information drop. Some clue to finding the reckless driver.

Was that going to happen with Trissa? Was I going to see her face on the news as the latest victim of the Strangler? My chest felt like it was caving in. For a moment, I thought I might faint. "I need to get some medication from the bathroom."

Lorenzo didn't look like she believed me but waved for me to go ahead. She followed me to the bathroom and watched me open the cabinet. Inside, there was a full shelf of prescription bottles for both my condition and Mom's various lupus symptoms, but my emergency pills were right at the front. Lorenzo grabbed the bottle out of my hand and read the label, peering at it as if she'd be able to tell whether the contents matched the name, then handed it back to me.

I popped the lid and swallowed one dry while she pawed through the small shelves, turning all the tiny bottles to face forward so she could see what they were. She'd effectively blocked me from leaving, so

I slumped down on the toilet seat, waiting for the medicine to hit my bloodstream. After a few moments, she presumably decided my health issue was real and wandered back to join her partner.

I remained sitting there, my head in my hands, not wanting to see what they were doing in my room. The apartment door slammed open. Mom and Charlene were finally home. I shoved myself to my feet and made my way down the hall to fling myself into my mother's arms. She held on to me but steered us to the doorway of my room.

"You have no right to be in our house," Charlene said to the officers.

The detectives moved toward her, side by side. I saw her through their eyes: a mixed-race woman with light-brown skin, wild eyes, and a splotchy face, her hair coming loose from a scarf.

The sight of Charlene rattled me even more than the police's behaviour. Maybe Trissa really was in trouble. Charlene was normally so put together. As a child, she'd been adopted by a middle-class white couple who raised her to fit in with their lifestyle. Since her adoption records were sealed, she didn't know exactly what her heritage was, but the police would only see a hysterical person of colour.

"Searching our place and harassing my underage daughter is shameful," added Mom.

"Calm yourselves," said Lorenzo.

"You calm yourself," snapped Charlene. "My daughter's missing. Don't you understand that?"

Lorenzo's hand dropped to her taser—she was just dying to use it on someone. "We're doing our job here, ma'am. Trying to find Teresa."

"If you have nothing to hide, there's nothing to worry about," added Wilson, smiling so wide I could see his molars. I trusted him even less than his partner. He was having fun now.

The two detectives moved past us, farther into the apartment. Charlene was right behind them. Mom stayed with me, put her arm around my shoulders, and made sure I was supported by the wall. The door to the basement was after her room, before the kitchen. They wouldn't miss it. Her weed supply had nothing to do with Trissa, but she did have that trafficking charge on her record. They wouldn't let her off with community service this time.

I couldn't deal with this a second longer. I broke away from my mother and ran through the messy kitchen. One of her favourite mottos was, "There's always something better to do than housework," and nowhere in our apartment was it more evident than in this room. The brick-red vinyl flooring could have used a good scrub. There was a stack of dirty dishes in the sink, some shrivelling fruit in a bowl on the counter, cans and boxes of dried food overflowing from shelves, and the front of the fridge was plastered with cards, coupons, silly magnets, and political stickers. There was even a birthday card I'd made for her in grade three.

I flung open the back door and stumbled out onto the wooden deck, then kept going right into the yard. Cold grass squelched beneath my feet, and mud oozed up through my socks and between my toes.

Those detectives were more interested in finding out what we were hiding than in looking for Trissa. Maybe it was part of their process of gathering information, but it was pretty extreme to systematically toss the house. It was possible that they knew things they weren't sharing with us. Crucial things.

I really should have stopped to grab some shoes. The grass was numbingly cold. Actually, I should have put on warmer clothes too, but there was no way I was going back inside.

Trissa *had* to be okay. She could take care of herself. She'd run away before. When we were kids, she used to get into arguments with her mom and then decide to run away, packing her Hello Kitty knapsack with the change from her piggy bank, clothes, and a giant bag of freshly popped popcorn. I don't know why popcorn. Maybe it was just that she knew how to operate the machine. But she always came home after a few hours—hungry, exhausted, and ready to try again with Charlene.

It upset me that she hadn't replied to my message, even if she was avoiding Charlene. That was definitely not normal. Then again, the cops had found her phone in that knapsack. No way she'd forgotten to take it with her. She would have gotten it surgically implanted under her skin if she could. What if she was in serious trouble and had no way of communicating with us?

At the far end of the yard, I wedged myself into my favourite hiding spot on an old tree stump hidden between our rusty aluminum shed and the back of the solid brick house behind ours. I curled my knees up into my chest, tucked my feet under me, and stretched my sweatshirt down.

This was my quiet place. It was autumn, so all the flowers and plants in the garden were beginning to disintegrate, making everything heart-breakingly beautiful. All the love inside my mother came out in this yard, which burst with colour from the moment purple glory-of-the-snows, yellow daffodils, and pink crocuses peeked out in the early spring through to the dark-red and orange leaves of fall. She'd planted my all-time favourite flower, the death-white lily of the valley, along the entire fence on one side, even though it was only around for two weeks in May. Its tiny fragrant white bells hid in the moist shade beneath bigger, gaudier plants and smelled amazing.

Trissa is fine, I repeated to myself. *She has to be*. We completed each other. Without her, I barely had a life. She was the exciting one. She danced and sang and yelled. She dragged me into impossible situations. Without her, I would just watch and read and listen.

The red leaves of our giant maple tree swayed in the wind. A few tall blades of grass flapped beside me, tall enough for me to touch. It was my job to cut the lawn, but I'd been slacking. I yanked the closest blade out of the ground, cupped it between my thumbs, raised it to my lips, and blew a high note. Mom had taught me how when I was little. The rhythmic inhale-exhale soothed my lungs. Plus, it made a strangled whistling noise.

How could Trissa have disappeared into thin air? Someone had to know where she was. Even when she'd run away before, she'd told me ahead of time because she knew I'd worry. Why hadn't the mothers woken me up before heading out to search? I would have helped. Mom protected me too much because she worried about my health.

I thought about Anwar's mental state. It wasn't like I could pop over and check on him right now. His mom, Amina, would be losing it. At least she still had Anwar. Even though I used to be like a daughter to her, I hadn't seen her in almost a year.

After Anwar's sister died, he used to climb into my room through my broken window screen every night after Amina fell asleep. The doctors gave her some heavy-duty sleeping pills because otherwise she wouldn't have slept at all. Anwar didn't want to talk much in those days, but he needed company, so he would just fall asleep on my bed, close enough that we were touching, and sneak back home at dawn so his mother wouldn't know he'd been gone. Just thinking about that time made me ache.

Amina's reaction to bad things was to disappear into her own mind. That was pretty different from the arguments between my mother and me, which could get heated. But when Trissa and Charlene fought, they shook the house. For Charlene to deal with the police at all meant that she was really scared about her daughter. In this neighbourhood, cops treated everyone who didn't look like a suit or a hipster as if they were criminals and deadbeats. One time, I saw a man overdose right in front of an officer, who was sipping a coffee and did absolutely nothing until I screamed at him to radio an ambulance. Another time, they smashed down the door of an old lady who lived alone in a boarding house on our street and spent her days feeding crumbs of Wonder Bread to the pigeons in a nearby park. They'd been looking for a dealer who used one of the rooms, and when they smashed down her door, she was standing behind it and got hit in the head so hard she blacked out.

I felt safe sitting out here by myself, but it was a waste of time. I could hear Charlene yelling at the detectives now. Taking a deep breath, I got to my feet and headed back inside. Trissa needed to be found, and I needed to help.

I went to my room to grab a new Band-Aid and dry socks and put them onto my frozen feet. In the living room, I discovered the two mothers had locked arms in front of the couch and appeared to be in some kind of standoff with the detectives. Mom's cannabis baggies were littered across her desk. Lorenzo was taking more photos of it all. Were they going to arrest her again? How could this be helping Trissa?

Charlene waved her arms in front of Wilson's phone. "You found my baby girl's wallet filled with money but all you care about is Rachel's stash? Un-fucking-believable."

"Where exactly did they find Trissa's stuff?" I whispered to Mom.

She kept her eyes on the cops but whispered back, "Behind the club where she dances. Her backpack was stuffed with clothes like she was going on a trip."

Charlene jostled Lorenzo's arm, almost making her drop the phone. Lorenzo growled. Literally. This was the first time I'd ever seen Charlene out of control—she was normally unflappable. My mother hovered beside her, shifting from foot to foot, trying to figure out how to both protect and calm her down.

Wilson and Lorenzo had both turned toward Charlene, livid, and while their guns, tasers, cable ties, and clubs were still put away, we were all aware they could use them with no consequences.

"I have lupus," blurted out my mother suddenly. Maybe hoping to defuse the tension.

"Cannabis is her medicine," I added.

Wilson glanced at Mom, pointedly looked down at the pile of baggies and the mushrooms, and cocked his head to one side, as if to say *let's hear you try to explain that.*

"We've seen enough here," snapped Lorenzo. She circled around to stand behind the moms. "Upstairs. Now. Let's go."

Wilson moved forward. Charlene shuffled away until her calves bumped against the couch. The detectives clearly hoped to find something much worse than some illegal weed in her place. Wilson moved forward again.

Charlene made a strangled noise, threw her hands in the air, then led the two detectives out of the apartment. Mom and I went to follow, but Lorenzo held up an arm to block us. "You two, don't go anywhere. We're taking you down to the station for statements as soon as we're done here."

"But—" Mom managed before the door swung shut behind them. She visibly shrank, then sank down on the couch springs—the cushions were still on the floor—and buried her face in her hands. I patted her shoulder, knowing nothing would really help. I checked my phone, still plugged into the backup power bank. It was up to 18 percent now. I dropped them both into my shoulder bag along with my wallet, my medication from the bathroom, an inhaler, and *Girl's Guide*, and slung it over my shoulder. In the kitchen, I added a granola bar and my water bottle to the bag. If they were planning to take us to the station, it wouldn't hurt to have some essentials ready. I hadn't eaten since dinner.

Back in the living room, Mom hadn't moved. She looked like a statue, listening to the detectives bang things around upstairs. I picked up one of the couch cushions and slid it back into place, then I sat down and hugged her. Hard. Mom roused enough to shift a little closer. "It's so awful, Michie. All night I was thanking the goddess it wasn't you. That's awful, isn't it?"

"It's normal," I said, but her words chilled me. I curled into her, and we sat together in silence until Mom heaved a sigh, stood up, and began to tidy her desk. I put the rest of the cushions back on the couch, then started sliding books back onto the shelves.

*

We'd finished putting the living room back together and were working on the kitchen cupboards when the detectives rapped at our apartment door. Mom hurried to open it, with me right behind her. Wilson and Lorenzo had been joined by more officers, who were in the process of carrying cases of what must be crime-scene-processing equipment upstairs. I noticed a couple large briefcases and some lights.

"Time to go," said Wilson, waving for us to come out into the foyer.

Charlene stuck her head around the corner. "This is bullshit. My baby girl is out there somewhere, in trouble, and they're searching my freezer for body parts."

"They're trying to help," said my mother, though she didn't sound convinced.

"Ha. What they're trying to do is build a case that she ran away. Or that I ..." Charlene's voice caught in her throat, and she choked. "I'd never hurt Trissa."

"None of us would," said Mom, patting her on the back.

The detectives' behaviour didn't surprise me, given that they'd tossed my dirty laundry hamper and threatened to use a taser on me. It didn't give me much hope that they'd find any information about Trissa. The contents of her abandoned bag seemed much more likely to tell a story. What kind of clothes had she packed? I couldn't think of a single reason for her to have two thousand dollars in cash, let alone to drop it in an alley and not come back for it. Where would she even have gotten that kind of money? What about her bank card, bus pass, and ID—were they in her wallet? She wouldn't have gone anywhere without those things.

"The Strangler took a woman from one of the alleys near Club Jelly," I said to the detectives. "Maybe you should be looking into that angle?"

Once again, they ignored me.

"You come in here and treat us like criminals," said Charlene, "when my daughter is—"

"Ma'am, calm down," said Wilson, stepping toward her. "We're trying to—"

"What you're doing is harassing innocent people!" Charlene yelled. She was shaking. I'd never seen her like this.

"And she has now verbally assaulted two officers of the law," said Lorenzo to Wilson. "I want to get that on record. She's obstructing this investigation. Let's take her in and continue the search."

"Obstructing!" screeched Charlene. "How? By telling you to stay out of my refrigerator?" For a moment, it looked like she was going to lunge at Lorenzo, but instead, she spat on the floor near the woman's foot.

Lightning fast, Wilson grabbed Charlene's arms and twisted them behind her back, then shoved her face first against the wall. Another officer who was on his way up the stairs came barrelling back down to support him. But Lorenzo was already on Charlene's other side, holding her head against the drywall.

Charlene tried to squirm, but couldn't move. "Ow! You're hurting me."

"Show some compassion," begged my mother, still trying to figure out how to defuse the situation. "Please, she's very worried about Trissa."

"Not another word," said Lorenzo. "From any of you."

Wilson shoved Charlene toward the front door. "We're all going down to the station."

"What if Trissa tries to get in touch while we're gone?" asked my mother.

Neither detective even looked at her.

Lorenzo and Wilson pulled Charlene up by the hair and wrists. Once on her feet, Charlene howled and smashed her head backward, narrowly missing Wilson's chin. Suddenly, she was flat on her stomach with the two officers on top of her. She rocked from side to side, attempting to get free. Wilson jammed his knee into her spine and leaned his weight on it while pulling one of her arms upward at an awkward angle. Charlene's face turned bright red. It looked like he was going to squeeze her insides out, all over the linoleum flooring.

I took a step forward. "Get off her!"

"Back up!" hollered Lorenzo.

"I can't feel my arm," sputtered Charlene.

I took another tiny step toward them. Lorenzo leaned back on her heels and brandished her taser in my direction. At least she was off Charlene's neck, but there was nothing more I could do without making things worse. Wilson secured Charlene's hands behind her back with a plastic tie.

"This is so messed up," I mumbled, feeling dizzy.

"You're going to break her arms!" said Mom.

Wilson hauled Charlene to her feet, then held her upright because she was so stunned she would have pitched right over. She made an outraged gurgling noise and then fell quiet.

I hurried into the living room to sling Charlene's purse on top of my canvas bag. She'd left it on the coffee table. Her phone was probably inside, so at least Trissa could reach us if she was able. Mom and I followed the procession, with Lorenzo bringing up the rear. I barely managed to slide my feet into a pair of black platform sneakers. They had lights that twinkled each time I took a step. Mom grabbed my faux fur jacket and shoved it at me to put on. The new officer decided he wasn't needed and continued upstairs. What was he hoping to find?

The cruiser parked out front had brought neighbours outside to gawk. I wasn't sure if they were eager to witness our shame or hoping we were okay. Maybe a little of both. Something set Charlene off again, and she started screeching and flailing again. She managed to land a backward kick on Wilson's shin. Lorenzo's hand went back to her taser, but she didn't use it. Instead, she smirked as Wilson yanked Charlene's arms upward hard enough that something popped in her shoulder. She hollered in pain, then subsided into sobs.

Without Trissa around, I had no clue how to navigate this situation. She always had my back. She'd been gone only a few hours and already everything was garbage. Charlene was spinning out, and Mom was weirdly quiet, her mouth clamped shut and her face stony. Normally, she was the feisty one who Charlene had to calm down.

Ahead of me on the sidewalk, Wilson shoved Charlene into the back of his cruiser. She did a face plant into the hard plastic seat and lay there with her hands up in the air behind her back. Mom slid in and levered her upright. Charlene didn't acknowledge Mom's help, just leaned against the far window and rested her forehead on the glass.

"You next," Wilson commanded me.

I hurried to get in, and he slammed the door shut. Reflexively, I reached for the handle, but there wasn't one. The world's most effective kiddie lock. Fury rose up in me, but I clamped it down hard—it wouldn't help at the moment. At least my heart seemed to be behaving, thanks to the pill I'd taken.

Lorenzo slid into the driver's seat, attached her phone to a charging station, and pressed a button to connect it to the car's system. Wilson took the passenger seat and immediately began pushing keys on the touch screen. I shifted, hoping to see what he was doing, but with Mom beside me, the headrest blocked most of my view.

The cruiser bounced off the curb, lights silently rotating on the vehicle's roof. It took only five minutes to get to the station from our house, but it felt like a lifetime. Everyone we passed peered through the window, assuming we'd done something terrible. I'd read *The Scarlet Letter* in English class. We were being paraded through the neighbourhood like Hester Prynne.

CHAPTER 6

Catching Flies with Honey

Lorenzo pulled the police car into a spot behind the squat red-brick station. The detectives got out and opened the back doors so Mom and I could exit into the busy parking lot. Charlene refused to make eye contact or speak but wiggled across the seat and allowed Wilson to hoist her to her feet. Since she couldn't get out without the use of her hands, she had no choice. To my surprise, he also released her hands from the restraints and stood aside so she could walk ahead of him. Her face was pale, and she cradled her left arm to her chest.

The detectives led us through a set of glass doors and into a large waiting room with beige walls and ass-sized moulded seats covered in brown and green vinyl. In each corner, there were metal chairs set apart from the rest, with a large iron ring welded on either side so handcuffs could be attached. Clearly the Toronto Police's interior decorator was skilled at creating unwelcoming spaces that could be hosed down when necessary. Like the airport, in this room no one could possibly fall asleep or get comfortable.

My friends were already here, I realized. They were scattered around the room, separated from each other by unhappy strangers.

Wilson and Lorenzo took off without a word. A burly desk sergeant squinted at us and picked at a computer terminal in front of him. Charlene was still cradling her arm, and her face was tight with pain. The mothers chose a spot next to Amina, who barely acknowledged their presence. Somehow, Anwar's mom managed to look totally put together, despite having been woken up in the middle of the night. She wore an elegant dusky-gold head scarf that brought out her brown eyes and somehow had a full face of makeup.

I squeezed in on the far side of Anwar, who was in grey sweatpants and a forest-green hoodie with a grey elephant stencilled on it. Any interaction with him would only confirm Kelli D's hate-on, so I inched away to make sure we weren't touching. He frowned, but nodded to acknowledge me. Amina continued to stare straight ahead, lost in her own private nightmare.

Kelli D and her moms—not surprisingly also PPs with long straight hair—were on the opposite side of the room. All three of them looked irritated and wore matching pink-and-white OrganikNaturalz track suits. Expensive. The two older women both had their hair pulled back in scrunchies, faces free of makeup, and foreheads that shone with heavy night cream they hadn't had time to wipe off. I knew one of them was Deputy Minister of Unemployment or something and the other was a history professor. Kelli D's back was stiff, and she wouldn't look over. Not that I wanted her to after the way she'd acted at school. That reminded me to message Vee about the yearbook. I added a video clip of the waiting area and the bulldog of a desk sergeant to show them what was going on.

Red and Timbit were sitting nearby, separated by their burly father, who wore an old baseball shirt with a faded hardware store logo on it and work jeans stained with grease. He worked at an auto shop that repaired European luxury cars. His muscular arms were crossed tightly, and he looked livid. Red was leaning against the cement wall with his arm covering his face, trying to nap. Timbit looked small and miserable.

Anwar elbowed me, then jerked his head to indicate the four security cameras mounted on the ceiling, showing different angles of the room. Did the police really think we'd incriminate ourselves? Maybe some people did, I realized, when a man a few feet away who'd been snoring loudly started to talk in his sleep. Waves of alcohol wafted in my direction.

I leaned over to whisper in Anwar's ear. "How's your mom dealing?"
Anwar whispered back, "Shit."

I shot him a knowing look. Years ago, when the police told her they had no real leads on Nadia's hit and run, Amina had crumpled up like a tissue, stopped cooking, cleaning, washing her hair, everything. She hadn't been able to function, let alone go to her job in a genetic research facility. By the time of Nadia's memorial service, Amina had been laid off without pay, and Anwar was forced to find a part-time job stocking groceries to make sure they could pay rent.

Our family had helped however we could. Trissa and I packed snacks for Anwar. My mother made extra dinner so I could feed him when he visited late at night, and Charlene sent Trissa to school with a second lunch. We all went to the same middle school back then. Up until that point, we'd pretty much shared the same experiences—except for the racism, which Anwar got bad. Most people couldn't even tell Trissa's mom was a person of colour. And I was paler than a naked mole rat. Eventually, things eased up for Amina, but she never totally recovered; it was as if her fight, flight, or freeze instinct was on overdrive. She still only worked for short stretches and panicked if she couldn't reach Anwar.

"They brought Anton in to be interviewed first," Anwar told me, then leaned back against the cement wall, crossed his arms, and shut his eyes. Apparently, he wasn't fully awake. Or maybe he was just stressed and worried.

"It's going to be okay—your mom and Trissa." I said. "We'll get through this."

The muscles in his jaw bounced, and he peered sideways at me from beneath his long black eyelashes. So hot. I pictured the way he'd stared at my mouth before kissing me. Was that only twenty-four hours ago? Then I noticed the worry in his eyes, and my hormones calmed. Now was not the time to fantasize.

"You don't know that, Michie."

He was right. I nodded reluctantly.

Charlene was quieter, but she was staring straight ahead like Amina. I had no idea what to do for her. I just couldn't bring myself to consider that Trissa really was missing ... or even dead. How would Charlene cope with that? How would I? The police knew enough to be concerned. Why else would they have hauled us all down here?

Kelli D had noticed me sitting close to Anwar and looked like she was going to explode. I wondered whether their relationship was over.

Had he ever opened up to her about his sister's death? They started seeing each other long after Nadia was gone, so I wasn't sure what she knew. Talking about his sister threw Anwar off, sometimes for days. He didn't often bring her up anymore.

It was hard for me to think about Nadia too. She was pure joy, a sparrow of a girl who had flitted around, worshipped her big brother, and constantly annoyed me and Trissa with questions about nature and why things were the way they were. Back then, our mothers were all closer, so we spent a lot of time together, and Anwar protected her fiercely. The day she was killed, he was inside watching TV while she rode up and down the driveway on her brand-new bike.

Like us, Trissa had lived through the aftermath of that death. She knew how it affected all of us; no one was the same after Nadia was killed. There was no way Trissa would make us worry needlessly.

*

Detectives Lorenzo and Wilson returned to announce they were ready to record statements. Wilson led Charlene away, and Lorenzo came over to ask my mother if we were ready, like there was any free will in this scenario.

We stood up and followed the detectives through maze-like corridors with doors that all looked the same until we got to a small cement box of a room painted a noxious dirty yellow. There was a metal table bolted to the ground, four wooden chairs, and a video camera on a tripod. On one wall was a mirror—TV crime shows told me it was probably one-way glass for observational purposes—and on another were fraying posters with police warnings, including one about the West End Strangler. I tried not to look at the composite illustration of a handsome man with a square jaw and brown hair curling under his ears. Beneath his face, it said, "He could be your boyfriend, neighbour, friend. Have you seen this man? Call our tip hotline or visit this site!"

Lorenzo gestured at the far side of the table—she wanted us over there so we would be directly in front of the camera—but didn't utter a word until we were settled and she'd pressed Record. "Detective Amelia Lorenzo. I will be asking questions of Michelle Gold to further the Trissa Taylor investigation. Her mother, Rachel Gold, is present."

"You didn't ask permission at home," I said.

She blinked but otherwise remained stone faced. "This is an official interview, which may be used during court proceedings. Your legal guardian must consent to allow you to be recorded."

My mouth went dry, and my stomach suddenly cramped. Why did I feel like I was walking into a trap? We were supposed to be here to help the police. Beside me, Mom looked more angry than nervous. A quote from *Girl's Guide* Chapter 18 sprang to mind: "Never utter a word more than necessary when answering questions, or you will provide investigators with a rope to hang you. Remember what you have revealed. Even record the interrogation yourself, if possible." I put my phone on the table in front of us, pulled up my recording app, and hit Start.

Lorenzo didn't look pleased, but she didn't object. I wondered if she would try the technique Lacey Milan called "pouring on the honey" to make me feel like we were on the same side, or whether she was going to "freeze" instead and stop talking long enough that we would rush in to fill the silence. She did neither, just turned to my mother and said, "You will need to state your consent out loud. Please say your full legal name, as well as your daughter's."

"I, Rachel Chaya Gold, give permission for myself and my daughter, Michelle Rivka Gold, to be interviewed in the hopes of bringing our Trissa home."

Lorenzo peered at me. "All right, Michelle, this is important. Tell me everything you and Trissa did on Thursday. Walk me through it again."

On Thursday, I'd gotten home, made a cup of hot chocolate, done some math homework, then messaged Trissa to see if she wanted to watch an episode of *Stunt Girls*. She'd been streamed into a school focused on kids who had trouble with academics, and she never seemed to have much homework. We microwaved some MegaMeat stew and watched the show for a while. Around six, Red messaged her to say everyone was getting together.

Lorenzo leaned toward me. "Who's 'everyone'?"

"Um, me and Trissa … Anwar, Kelli D, Anton, Timbit, and Red. All the people in the lobby."

"And did you meet up?"

"Yeah. You already know that."

"Where?"

"We hang out in a building near our place. Nobody lives in one of the apartments, and the door's, uh, never locked."

"Give me the address."

I did, even though it meant we'd have to find another spot to gather, and I could feel my mom watching me closely. I had no idea where she thought we all met up, but probably not an empty condo. She was the kind of mom who thought she knew everything about my life. She knew more than most parents because she was pretty cool, but I still had some secrets. I was pretty sure the others would be asked the same question and made a mental note to tell them I'd snitched, just in case. Lorenzo might decide to search the place. She'd probably ask the super to let her in, and then the lock would be changed. I told her we'd spent the whole evening there and recapped the details, but omitted the same things as before.

"How did Trissa seem when you got home?" Lorenzo asked.

"Same as always. A little worked up, maybe."

"In what way?" asked Mom.

"She's such a drama queen. Said she might not always be around to take care of me."

"Was she threatening suicide?" asked Lorenzo.

"No! She was making fun of me because I, uh, have a crush on someone but never do anything about it. She was being a bitch, trying to push me into telling him how I feel." Who I had a crush on wouldn't have been a secret to my mother, even though we'd never talked about my feelings for Anwar. She was pretty perceptive. I could feel her peering at me, and a flush rose up my neck.

Despite the camera, Lorenzo was writing furiously in her notebook, but now she paused, lifted her head, and tilted it to one side. "So you say she wasn't suicidal or going on a trip, but she mentioned not always being here, the same night we found a packed bag with her passport and money behind the club where she works."

I shook my head. "I have no idea. Maybe she was planning to go away for a few nights. She doesn't tell me everything."

Lorenzo raised her overly tweezed eyebrows, encouraging me to continue.

"Her vibe was strange, though. Amped up."

I finished my summary of events as quickly as possible: Mom was in bed when we got home, so we didn't ask permission for Trissa to sleep over. She passed out quickly—at least I thought she did—and I read for a while, then fell asleep too. When I woke up around three, she was gone. Then I dozed off again and overslept.

"Tell me more about the abandoned condo," said Lorenzo. "What were you doing there?"

"Nothing much. Talking. Playing Truth or Dare."

"Truth or Dare?"

I glanced sideways at Mom, not wanting to reveal the kiss. "Yeah. You know, it's a game where you dare people to do things that are uncomfortable. Anwar dared Red to pull his pants down. Red dared Trissa to flash her boobs. Stuff like that. Everyone was having fun, except Kelli D, I guess. She got really pissed."

"At who?"

"Me and Anwar. They're a couple. Or they were." I took a deep breath. "Until Trissa dared him and me to make out."

Beside me, I could feel Mom's eyes boring a hole into my head. So awkward.

Lorenzo cleared her throat. "You said that she seemed different and mentioned suicide?"

I gritted my teeth. Was she trying to trip me up? "No, not suicide. I just assumed she was making me feel bad because I was pissed about her dare."

"But she said something about not being around forever," said the detective. "Couldn't that imply she was going to end her life?"

"I'm pretty sure it was hypothetical. She might have been talking about, like, taking off to Mexico for two weeks." I realized I'd fallen down a rabbit hole and needed to climb out again. "See, me, Trissa, and Anwar have been friends since we were kids, so it was totally awkward that she made us kiss. Especially considering his girlfriend was there. Trissa wasn't planning to jump off a bridge in the middle of the night or anything … It was more like she was going to remove herself from my life if I didn't appreciate her more."

Lorenzo dropped the pen and stretched her right hand.

"I don't know," I said. "It's only now she's missing that it seems like she knew she might be going somewhere."

She picked up the pen and jotted a note. "Where do you think she might have gone in the middle of the night?"

"A walk, or Club Jelly. She dances there. Or maybe a friend's place."

"Was she dating someone?"

I shrugged. "Trissa's always seeing someone. She doesn't really stick with anybody for very long. In the past week, she mentioned there was some hot guy at her club, two cute girls at school, that Anwar and Anton are hot, and that Red's cute in a brotherly way … Those last two are seriously ew, by the way. And I've probably forgotten a couple." I realized I was talking too much again, but I was relieved to be off the topic of me and Anwar. "The only person I know for sure she's not sleeping with is Anwar because he's not like that. And they're basically brother and sister."

"Rocky, Timothy, or Anton?"

I threw up my hands. "That's not really my business."

"You're best friends." Lorenzo waited to see if I'd offer more. I didn't. "Tell me about Trissa's relationship with her mom."

"What would Charlene have to do with this?" my mother demanded.

"Ma'am, we need to follow every lead."

I didn't want to offer any insights into the mother-daughter dynamic that could get Charlene into trouble, so I just shrugged again and stayed silent.

"Okay. Tell me about Trissa's drug problem," Lorenzo prodded.

"Trissa doesn't have a—" I was having trouble stemming a rising tide of anger. The police obviously had a theory about what Trissa was like. "She might smoke weed and drink sometimes, but she doesn't do hard drugs—nothing bad."

Lorenzo glanced at Mom. "Ma'am, can you tell more me about your side business?"

"I make buttons."

"And sell homegrown cannabis."

Mom crossed her arms. "Look, you already tore our house apart. I'm not implicating myself. Weed is legal."

"You need a business licence to profit off the proceeds." Lorenzo turned back to me. "According to our records, complaints were lodged on two separate occasions about domestic altercations in your house. I assume that wasn't you and your mother?"

"Of course not," interjected Mom before I could respond.

"Trissa and Charlene argue," I explained. "Trissa gets pretty emotional."

"So you've witnessed physical altercations?"

"No. Just arguments. Why are you trying to make it seem like Charlene is violent?"

The detective snorted as if the answer was obvious and wrote something down. "Would you agree that Trissa's substance abuse makes her behave erratically?"

"Stop making it sound like I agree with you about anything."

She levelled an exasperated look at me. "We found evidence of her drug use."

I was flustered by that news but didn't let it show. "You're lying."

She removed a small stack of printed photos from the back of her notebook and slid them across the table. The first one showed a large hiker's backpack wedged behind a dumpster. The next few showed its contents laid out on the pavement: Trissa's phone, which I recognized because it had a sparkly pink case; her wallet, which contained a thick wad of cash and a fake ID; makeup and toiletries; two brand-new dresses; some skinny jeans that definitely didn't come from BuyMart; sexy lingerie; a bikini with a matching wrap; and several pairs of socks and T-shirts.

I handed the pictures to my mother, who studied each one, then looked up at Lorenzo. "These are Trissa's things that were found behind Club Jelly?"

Lorenzo nodded.

"Maybe someone stole the bag from her dressing room," I suggested.

"The person who called it in worked at the club," said the detective. "He noticed it when he went out back to toss a garbage bag."

She gestured for us to look at the remaining photos. "Those were taken off the phone."

The first one was a selfie of Trissa and another dancer. I recognized the other girl but couldn't remember her name. They were both wearing dance outfits—basically gold string and feathers that covered a few key inches of their bodies. Trissa's wild curls were pulled back in a slick ponytail. Her eyes were unfocused, and her cheeks were flushed. In another photo, someone had captured her splayed out on a couch in the club's backroom beside a table littered with half-full glasses, a giant bowl of jelly beans, an ashtray full of cigar stubs, and a handful of tiny baggies. I had to admit, she looked out of it.

"We know Trissa was dealing," said Lorenzo, gathering up the photos. "And we also know she got her supply from you, Rachel, so you can both stop pretending that Trissa wasn't involved in *extracurricular* activities at the club."

"Excuse me?" my mother said. "I sell a little weed, and sometimes mushrooms, which I grow and dry myself. That's it. No chemicals. And I definitely don't get teenage girls to move my product."

Lorenzo tapped the photos and acted like Mom hadn't spoken. We all knew she was thinking about mom's previous charges. "What was she selling for you there?"

"I'd know if Trissa were selling drugs," I cried. "She's my sister."

Lorenzo exhaled dramatically. "You're not related, Michelle. And I'm very disappointed in you. You said you wanted to help us find your friend and now you're lying to cover up illegal activities."

"I am not. You're just trying to bully my mom into admitting she deals hard drugs ... which she doesn't. Neither does Trissa. Look, Jellybean would never let her do anything like that at his club. He runs it like the Godfather. He'd never risk his business licence. And Trissa would definitely flash that kind of cash in my face if she had it. She wouldn't be combing the sale bins at BuyMart. She'd probably get the fantasy hair extensions she's been wanting ... and a tattoo sleeve or something. She's an open book. She's got no secrets."

"Then you're aware she was having sex for money in the backrooms of Club Jelly?"

"What?" My face scrunched up reflexively. Once, Trissa had brought me and Anwar back to the VIP room so he could meet his favourite artist, Jordan Watanabe, who was in town from New York to paint murals featuring cartoon animals at a local kids' television station. Another time, she told me that rival hip hop artists had shown up with their entourages and started rap battling there. She would have slept with any of them for free just so she could brag about it. "Sometimes Trissa parties with VIPs, but they don't pay her."

Lorenzo could see that she'd gotten under my skin, so she just raised an eyebrow and waited for me to keep talking.

"Okay, she likes to have fun and she's not, like, saving herself for marriage. But Jellybean keeps a close eye on everything that happens at his club. He's very protective of the dancers."

Lorenzo slapped the coffee table, making everyone jump. "Stop wasting our time."

My mother lurched to her feet. "We're wasting *your* time? That's a joke. You forced your way into my house and now you're trying to get my daughter to admit things that aren't true." She grabbed my elbow and hauled me out of the chair and over to the door. She tried to yank it open, but it didn't budge. We were locked in this box, just like we had been in the patrol car. "If you want to talk to us again, I'll have my lawyer present. His name is Franklyn Flores."

Lorenzo slapped her notepad shut. "Your daughter is free to go, Ms. Gold. But we're holding you on charges of possession with intent." She muscled her way between Mom and the door and rapped on it. A guy opened it from the outside.

Before I realized what was happening, Lorenzo had ushered me out of the room. I managed to get just one last glimpse of my mother, whose eyes were wide with shock.

"Call Franklyn," she said, then the door clicked shut.

Lorenzo had already set off down the hallway, expecting me to follow. I didn't seem to have any other choice.

CHAPTER 7

Developing Unlikely Allies

Back in the waiting area, I called Franklyn, got his answering service, and left a desperate message, then plopped down between Anwar and his mother. I was in shock. My mom had just been arrested. Charlene wasn't here—she must still be in her interview, and she wasn't in any shape to be questioned right now. Red and Timbit were gone now. Their dad would make them pay for the inconvenience of being dragged down to the police station in the middle of the night, but it would happen later, when there were no witnesses. At least Red was big enough to fight back. Timbit, not so much.

Beside me, Amina was strangling the life out of her large black-leather purse. Impulsively, I leaned over to hug her. She stilled as I gently leaned my head on her bony shoulder. The fabric of her shirt was cool and silky. She even pressed her cheek against the top of my head for a moment. When I pulled away, she wouldn't look at me, but her face spasmed as if she was struggling to maintain control over powerful emotions. Her hands hadn't stopped squeezing the purse. My heart broke all over again.

"You okay?" Anwar asked me, keeping his eyes on his mother.

"They just arrested my mom and tried to get me to say a bunch of stuff about Trissa that isn't true."

He swore and closed his eyes for a moment. "I'm sorry, Michie."

"It's bad. Now I've got to call Franklyn and ask him to deal with the situation."

"He got her charges dropped the last time."

I nodded. "Hopefully he can do it again. Be careful in there. Answer the questions honestly, and don't let them mess with your head. We've got nothing to hide." I was highly conscious of Amina, who was pretending not to listen, and of the cameras recording us from all angles. "Charlene shouldn't be left alone right now, but I really need to get out of here."

"You shouldn't be alone either." Anwar's concern was plastered all over his face. "And Char's already gone. They put her in a taxi to get her shoulder fixed at the hospital."

"Oh. Well, at least they did that much after being the ones who hurt her." I glanced at the time on my phone. It was nine on a Saturday morning. No wonder Franklyn hadn't answered his work phone. He was probably awake, though. The idea of going home alone just to worry about Mom scared the crap out of me, but at least I could finish tidying up while Franklyn figured out how to help Mom. Not to mention trying to find out what happened to Trissa. "Don't worry about me, okay? Call me when you're back home."

Anwar relaxed a fraction and nodded.

I flashed what I hoped was a reassuring smile, then headed toward the exit, deliberately not looking over at the spot where Kelli D was sitting. I had no clue whether she'd been watching my exchange with Anwar. Didn't want to know.

The pouch-faced bulldog of a desk sergeant barked at me to sign out. His beady, mistrustful eyes made me feel guilty, even though I hadn't done anything. I took the pen he handed over and scrawled my name on his form.

Outside, I took out my phone and called Franklyn at home. It went through to voice mail as well, so I explained a second time what was going on. Then I checked that my phone had enough battery left and that the volume was on high. He'd call as soon as he got the messages.

Cold globs of rain splattered my face and head as I bent into the wind and ran for a bus stop around the corner, only to discover the shelter's roof was broken. Typical of autumn, the sun had risen only to reveal angry grey storm clouds. At least I was wearing a jacket, thanks to Mom, but this one wasn't waterproof. By the time the bus arrived, it was soaked through, and so were my shoes. I'd been splashed twice by cars that sped by too close to the sidewalk. I leapt up the steps, flashed my student pass at the driver, and hurried to grab a seat on top of a heating vent.

I ripped open a granola bar and devoured it while I searched for news about Trissa's disappearance online. Apparently, the police still hadn't reported it to the media. Or maybe I just didn't know where to look for that kind of news. This morning's biggest story was an over-turned furniture store truck on the twelve-lane freeway just east of the city—a bunch of sofas and recliners had caught fire and taken out six commuter vehicles during rush hour.

The second most important piece was on the Strangler, a feature that detailed similarities between the killings and the places where he'd kidnapped girls. I found a three-dimensional version of the image that had been hanging in our interview room. When I swiped right or left, it rotated from side to side to show the suspect's profile. I wondered if he'd had any cosmetic surgery done—a tuck here, a nip there to make himself look like a handsome Everyman. A female voiced droned over top of the image: "This vicious killer is someone's brother. Someone's son, husband, nephew, or landlord. He is suspected of murdering eight girls and will continue to commit atrocities until a good citizen like you stops him. You may know more than you realize. Click on the link below to reach an anonymous hotline and keep our girls safe." Why did they promise anonymity? There was no way the police wouldn't track who was accessing the website.

I pictured the Strangler himself tapping on the link to sending a false tip, just to throw the police off his scent. As I stared at the screen, an image of Trissa's face, blue and bloated, her eyes wide open and unmoving, filled my brain. I had to fight not to burst into tears. How could I just go home and sit around waiting? I had to do something. Find her. Bring her home.

The bus stopped, and Mr. Booger got on. Perfect. He sat across from me deliberately and tried to make eye contact. Weird. He'd never done that before, since I wasn't a hipster wearing a designer outfit, and I knew better than to meet his eyes. Eventually, he looked away, only to identify an extremely skinny woman with salon-blond hair who teetered in her high-heeled boots as the bus swayed. Her massive rose-gold earrings were shaped like hearts. They glinted every time she peered up at the transit map. The stops lit up as we moved along. Clearly, she didn't know the area very well.

I couldn't handle the thought of Mr. Booger eating a palmful of snot right now, so I did something impulsive. I spoke to him. "Hey, mister."

His eyes widened, bounced to my face, then immediately bounced away. He gulped, looking panicked. Maybe nobody had ever addressed him directly before. Was he going to run? There was nowhere to go until the next stop.

"We ride this route together all the time," I continued. "I normally get on at Beadle Street. Were you staring at me a second ago for some reason?"

He blinked hard and glanced at the rich woman again, but she moved toward the stairs, preparing to get off.

"Mister," I said again. "Sometimes I'm with another girl. You'd recognize her. She has curly red hair and wears bright colours. She's pretty loud. Talks to strangers. I'm not pissed off or anything, just want to ask you a question."

His eyes landed on mine again for the briefest moment, letting me know he was listening.

"Any chance you saw her yesterday?" I asked.

He shrugged.

The bus pulled up to the next stop, and the rich woman carefully descended the back stairs, holding on to the rail with two fingers as if she were afraid to catch something. Mr. Booger looked disappointed, but after the doors shut, his eyes shifted back to mine. He still didn't speak.

"Look, she's missing, and I'm worried about her. It might be life or death. The cops think it's the West End Strangler. So if you saw her, please tell me."

He fidgeted.

"You did, didn't you?" I guessed, forcing my voice to remain calm. I had a feeling he would bolt if I gave him the chance. "Do you remember what time that was?"

He cleared his phlegmy throat. "Early," he muttered. "First train."

"The subway? Huh. That would be just after five. Was she going east or west?"

"East. Had a big bag."

The one the police found behind Club Jelly? "A knapsack?"

He nodded.

"Did you see where she got off?"

"Nah. Kept riding after me. I went to Spadina."

Three stops after that was Yonge, just a few blocks from Club Jelly. "I think I might know where she was headed, thanks so much. Hey, is there any way you could get in touch with me if you see her again?"

To my surprise, he reached into his pocket, extracted a battered flip phone with a cracked screen, and held it out toward me. I entered my number into his contacts and sent myself a message that just said *hi*. A name—Salvatore Menzies—and a pixelated photo of his face that had clearly been taken a long time ago appeared on my screen. Huh. Mr. Booger had not only a phone but also a real name.

"Thanks, Salvatore," I said.

"Sal." He slipped the phone back into his pocket.

"I'm Michie."

Just at that moment, a well-groomed man in his thirties stepped between us and held on to the pole in front of Sal. I leaned to my left, confirmed that Mr. Booger had chosen a target, and quickly straightened again. I kept my gaze averted but could see his nose twitching out of the corner of my eye. He was preparing to sneeze on the guy's buttery suede jacket. Sure enough, less than a stop later, the explosion happened. The guy's body ricocheted backward—he'd been slimed— and he staggered toward the back of the bus. Sure enough, Sal was licking his palm clean. So gross. He winked at me and began to hum the refrain from the song "We Are the Champions."

Instead of continuing home, I got off at a junction and waited in the rain for a bus that would take me closer to Club Jelly. Tracing Trissa's last known steps seemed like the best way to feel like I was helping. Franklyn hadn't called back yet, so I needed to distract myself. If I just sat at home, I'd probably just have a panic attack.

As I rode, I searched for articles about Nadia's hit and run. I did this every few months, so I'd already read them all a hundred times, and it tortured me, but she was on my mind after seeing Amina so disturbed. A photo of Nadia's small angular face lit up my screen. She'd had the best smile. So unselfconscious, despite her huge crooked teeth. That was how I remembered her: Anwar's gangly, sweet little Mini-Me, scraggly dark-brown hair pulled back in a braid, wearing a pink turtleneck and a red corduroy jacket.

A flood of memories swept over me as I read: "Ten-year-old Nadia Ali was riding her bicycle on the street in front of the apartment building where she lived when a vehicle apparently jumped the curb and hit her. She died instantly. The driver fled the scene. The only eyewitness was building superintendent Yorge Milos, who didn't manage to capture a licence plate or a description of the person behind the wheel, though he noted the car was a grey sedan and thought the driver was a man."

There was a photo of Milos's benign, plump face—he'd always had a slightly shocked expression, as if daily life was too chaotic for him. After Nadia's death, he slipped into a profound depression, hid away in his basement apartment, stopped fixing anything in the building, and eventually refused to answer the door when tenants tried to find him. He hanged himself a year later. Anwar was convinced that Milos was actually the one who killed his sister—his old white work van disappeared around the same time she died—but he'd successfully shifted the blame away from himself, and the police hadn't pursued it.

I chose another article at random from a few days later and kept reading: "Nadia's tragic death inspired her community to create a shrine, where people leave stories and photos and gifts." There was an image of all of us—Anwar, Amina, me, Trissa, my mom, Charlene, Franklyn, Red and Timbit with their mother, and Anton—gathered together in the centre of a massive cluster of neighbours and friends. We all looked so much younger, even the adults. We'd shut down our street for a whole day for Nadia's memorial service. It was unbelievable that a person you loved could be here, totally alive, and the next minute be gone forever.

I couldn't let my mind go there with Trissa. It just wasn't something I could handle. Charlene would become a husk of a person, like Amina. No way. Then again, Nadia's death was unbelievable when it happened, and there was nothing any of us could do to reverse it.

The stop for Club Jelly was next. With a sigh, I tucked the phone into my bag and fought back a multi-layered sadness as I swung down through the folding doors and out onto the rainy streets. At some point, it had started pouring. After stepping in a sidewalk puddle, the tiny twinkle lights on my sneakers started shorting out. Sharp little zaps pricked the sides of my feet each time I took a step. Mom had warned me that getting knock-off wired shoes was a bad idea. I should have listened to her. My faux fur jacket, which was just as cheap as my shoes, was starting to leak streaks of lavender all over my jeggings.

I trudged on, determined, ignoring the tentacles of soaked hair plastered to my cheeks. At least my phone was safe—I'd spent good money on a waterproof case.

My phone rang. It was Franklyn. Relieved to hear from him, I ducked under a tree for refuge from the rain and answered. Just hearing his calm, deep voice was reassuring. He asked me what had happened and then waited until I paused for a breath before saying, "Believe me, they don't want the bad PR of assaulting a grieving mother. They'll drop the charges against your mother. Let me handle this." He promised to keep me updated and then disconnected.

The word he'd used, *grieving*, caused a stone to plummet to the bottom of my stomach. Trissa was still alive. I considered calling him back to tell him that, but I didn't, because I knew he was going to use it as leverage to get my mom out of jail. He cared for her. He'd do everything he could to get her out. Mom cared for him too. I think maybe she even loved him. He was the only man who'd ever lived with us, for a couple years, back when he'd first immigrated from Grenada and was working construction under the table to put himself through his degree equivalency.

At the time, he'd kept a shotgun hidden above the kitchen cupboard because he was worried people from back home would come after him here. I wondered whether he still had that gun. When I asked him why he had it, he told me in his soft-spoken way that back home he was a revolutionary, and he'd had to leave in a hurry or else he would be dead now. He explained that this time around, he was specializing in criminal defence law so he could stand up for accused criminals, who were usually poor and racialized people. He took his job very seriously and was respected across the city. If anyone could get Mom out of jail, it was Franklyn.

Shivering from the cold and damp, I headed up Club Jelly's front walkway. During the daytime, it could have been mistaken for a deserted building. There was no signage out front—everyone who mattered knew what it was—and the windows were covered with plywood painted to blend in with the red brick. The multicoloured lights that illuminated the exterior at night were turned off, and the enormous wooden gates were locked. This place woke up after the sun went down, when working stiffs loosened their ties and hiked up their skirts for dancing.

Everyone who kept what a local nightlife blog referred to as "the orgasmic Jelly-verse" running was already hard at work deep in the bowels of the club, tallying last night's sales, scrubbing out bathroom stalls, restocking the bar, training new servers, and strategizing about how to make it a bigger and better night than yesterday. Jellybean, the owner, lived in luxury suite in the VIP section and almost never left the premises. His minions went out and fetched whatever he needed.

He'd always been friendly enough whenever I ran into him with Trissa—she was one of his favourite dancers, and he treated her like a princess—but she'd told me that he didn't like surprises. He ran the place like he was the king and this was his fiefdom. Trissa told me he paid the police to leave him alone so he could deal with security issues internally. His bouncers were better equipped than a SWAT team. I didn't like the idea of getting on his radar any more than I already was, but if Trissa had come here this morning with her packed bag, she must have had a specific reason. And it was a safe bet the police would be showing up soon, most likely a detective Jellybean wasn't paying under the table. He would be in better mood if I caught him before that happened … and if he didn't already know Trissa was missing, he would appreciate the heads-up.

I forced myself to not blink as Club Jelly's retinal scanner took an image of my eye. Jellybean was paranoid enough to keep track of everyone who passed through the doors during off-hours. The only way to get inside was to check in through the machine. There was no doorbell and no phone number listed anywhere.

Jellybean gave me the serious creeps, in the same way the police did. While I was inside the club, he could do anything to me. I schooled my face to project innocence and worry—there was for sure a camera somewhere—and flattened my body against one of the doors to get out of the rain. The overhang was so small that droplets rolled down my hair and onto my neck.

To my surprise, Jellybean himself answered over the intercom. "What is it?"

"I'm looking for Trissa," I said. "Is she here?"

"No. Come back at midnight."

"She's missing. This was the last place she was seen. I'm her sister. I'm scared for her safety."

"Trissa doesn't have a sister."

"Chosen sister," I clarified, scanning the corners of the doorway for the camera—it must be so tiny it was almost invisible. "We grew up together, in the same house. Our moms are, like, BFFs. You've met me a few times."

He grunted to acknowledge he knew who I was. "She's not here, Michie."

"Please. I just want to ask a few questions. Maybe you can help me find her."

Silence, then, "Unlikely."

"Please let me in. The police think maybe the West End Strangler took her. I'm soaked and freezing out here …" I'd located a dime-sized speck of dark glass embedded in a natural whorl of wood near the upper-right corner of the doorway and held up my hands in a praying position to the camera. I was willing to bet it was infrared and recorded audio too. I wondered if Jellybean kept footage of everyone who entered the club, along with their retinal scans.

A series of clacking noises shot down between the wooden doors. Jellybean was opening the locks—he'd granted me access.

CHAPTER 8

Providing the Investigators with a Conclusion

I shoved the brass handles of Club Jelly's enormous wooden doors. To my surprise, the doors swung inward easily, and I stepped inside. It felt like I'd just passed through the gates of a castle. I paused for a moment and blinked to adjust to the dim interior light, then rested a hand on the wall to guide me past the coat check and up the ramp of the entry hall. Overlaid on the greyish darkness was my memory of reflective silver flooring, textured wallpaper with a pattern of bubbles on it, and jelly-bean-shaped light fixtures dangling from the ceiling—they were made of blown glass and lit with LEDs. The club was designed to be dazzling and to engage all the senses. They were turned off right now, but in the walls, there were machines that released bubbles.

At the top of the hall, I turned left to enter the Chill Zone, where I could see clearly again. Right now, bright fluorescent overhead lights were turned on, but when the club was open, the room would be kept dimmer than the main floor; it was a place to relax on couches shaped like marshmallows and candy, catch your breath, make out, or close your eyes and let the sexy music wash over you. The four walls were covered in velvet, which muffled noise; it reminded me eerily of a glammed-up padded cell in a psychiatric hospital. In one corner, there was a small bar where you could get a handful of free jelly beans and order simple drinks.

Up a short staircase was the Great Room, which was three storeys high and had silver linoleum flooring, huge chandeliers dripping with jelly-bean-shaped LEDs, and exposed brick walls covered in glittering art. In the corner near the bar were dozens of stainless-steel tables and stools. The vast, open dancing space took up most of the room. Against one wall was a stage where DJs spun music and took requests. Occasionally, Jellybean booked live performances, and each night just after midnight, the dancers did a showcase for the crowd in their sexy bird outfits that bordered on burlesque.

It was surreal to be here while it was empty and the only other people in the room were a bartender, restocking and checking the bottles that lined the glass shelves behind him, and a cleaning woman, aggressively mopping near a pit filled with electric-purple Jell-O where every night at eleven, girls in bikinis—and the occasional intoxicated guest—wrestled each other. Trissa had tried it a few times when she first started but hated getting all sticky.

I passed four giant cages on my left. Several times a night, Trissa and the other dancers got inside them, attached satin safety ropes to the belts built into their costumes, and were raised thirty feet in the air, where they did acrobatic dance routines. There were locked boxes attached to the wall down at floor level where people could leave tips and even messages for their favourite dancers. Trissa made good money, especially on Fridays and Saturdays, when the crowd was relaxed and feeling generous.

She swore to her mom that dancing didn't interfere with school. Trissa was one of the smartest people I knew, but teachers hadn't been kind to her growing up. She had ADHD and took medication for it but was never comfortable just sitting still and memorizing abstract knowledge, and Charlene wasn't the kind of parent who would lobby the school for special accommodations. My mother, on the other hand, had no problem marching into a classroom and demanding that my teacher ensure I succeed. She'd learned that kind of behaviour from her parents, who were university professors. They would have learned it from theirs.

In grade eight, she'd made an appointment with my principal to complain about my English teacher giving us a reading list of only dead white male writers. I'd heard her offer to bully people at Trissa's school when they did something stupid, but Charlene refused.

Beside the bar and beneath the VIP balcony was a wooden staircase. At night, people hung over the railing to scan the room. Beside it was a door marked with a sign that said "RESTRICTED ACCESS" in gold letters. Club Jelly's real VIPs hung out in the busy restricted area, where you could find dancers changing into their costumes; servers taking smoke breaks or eating sandwiches to fuel a few more hours of constant activity; candy girls refilling trays of free jelly beans, expensive energy shooters, and candy-flavoured vape juice; and scary-looking bouncers dressed in black who were on break from scanning the crowd for fights to break up and drunk people to haul off the dance floor.

Jellybean's luxurious suite was there too. He lived in and ruled this den of iniquity from his living space like a jolly Mafia don. His suite was hidden behind an unmarked door and only accessible through the restricted area of the club. I was really hoping he'd be in his office and not in his bedroom, lounging in his massive heart-shaped bed, which was where he was the last time Trissa had brought me back here.

The bartender glanced at me and nodded at the restricted door. I finger-waved awkwardly. Jellybean must have told him I'd be coming through. Or maybe conversations over the door intercom were broadcast throughout the club? Probably not. I considered stopping to ask the guy if he'd seen Trissa but decided it wasn't a good idea to keep the boss waiting.

The first part of the inner hallway was even more opulent than Club Jelly's other areas, but the glamour ended abruptly just a few steps past the stairwell that led up to the VIP balcony. Farther along, the doors were all locked, and there were no signs on any of them, but I knew from memory that I was passing the dancers' dressing rooms, a small kitchen stocked with bottled water and fruit, green rooms for the DJs and other talent, and some rooms with reinforced doors where the bouncers dragged out-of-bounds patrons to dry out and cool off.

I knocked on Jellybean's office near the end of the hallway. Not my lucky day—there was no answer. I continued on to the final door. It was ajar, and soft jazz filtered out.

"Hello?" I called, sticking my head and shoulders through the door.

At least he wasn't lounging in bed. Jellybean was sprawled on his "throne"—a massive beanbag chair covered in buttery purple suede—looking every bit the club queen in a maroon-satin housecoat tied over paisley lounge pants, a pink floral dress shirt, and a dusky-pink cravat. His bald scalp was so shiny it gleamed in the light of the Art Deco lamp on the table beside him. On his lap sat his enormous Persian cat, grey with light-grey eyes. It had tiny gold hoops in its ears—which was so upsetting—and wore a bow tie made from the same fabric as Jellybean's shirt.

"Come in, come in," he said, waving me forward.

My mouth was suddenly bone-dry. I fought the urge to run away and slipped into the room. Jellybean looked peaceful in repose, but he could move lightning fast, and he was strong. Once, I'd seen him cross the dance floor in seconds, grab a server by the throat, lift her, and slam her onto a table, flat on her back. For a moment, I'd thought he was going to kill her. Instead, he calmly emptied the cash from her pockets and then released her. She slid to the floor like she had no bones, clutched her throat, and gasped for air. He bent over and hissed something in her ear, then disappeared behind the restricted access door. Two bouncers materialized to scrape her up and drag her through the crowd to the exit. Later, Trissa told me the woman had been caught stealing from the bar till.

"Have a seat," Jellybean said. "How can I help?"

I chose a red suede beanbag, which was strategically smaller and shorter than his throne. "Nobody's seen Trissa since Thursday at midnight," I said. "The police and her mom are searching everywhere. I was, uh, hoping you might have heard from her?"

Jellybean hesitated. "She stopped by around closing."

"She doesn't normally work on Thursdays," I said, thinking aloud. Why had she woken up, left my room, and come here at two, only to be seen three hours later by Mr. Booger—Sal—riding the subway in this direction again?

"I have no idea why she came here other than to make a fool of herself."

"Trissa made a scene?"

Jellybean made a noise that was halfway between a laugh and a snort. "You might call it that. She got in one of the dance cages, hit the button to raise it, opened the door, and hung off it like it was a set of monkey bars."

That surprised me. "Why?"

"Who knows. Didn't attach the safety rope either," he added, shuddering. "Patrons were terrified she was going to fall or jump. They were traumatized. I was forced to refund their entrance fees and give them free drink tickets."

"Jump?" I echoed, way more concerned about Trissa's headspace than about Jellybean's patrons. There wouldn't have been many people here at closing time on a Thursday, because last call was an hour early. Besides, he wasn't hurting for money. He owned the building, charged an exorbitant cover, and his bartender watered down the ridiculously expensive drinks.

"She was out of her mind," Jellybean snarled.

"You mean she was high?"

"Oh yes. And dangling off the cage like a trapeze artist at the circus. If I hadn't lowered her immediately, who knows what … There would be no way for Club Jelly to come back from a suicide. I'd be finished."

"She didn't jump, though," I said. "So it's okay?"

He shook his head. "Security escorted her out. She never showed up for her shift last night. Ungrateful little girl. She was my star, Michelle, and she let me down. On a Friday! My second-biggest night of the week. I had to put an untrained dancer in her cage. Absolute nightmare."

Irritation flared through me. He didn't care at all about Trissa. Neither did his patrons. They only wanted to see hot dancers dressed in thongs, feathers, and pasties. Probably couldn't even tell them apart. Also, the three other more experienced dancers would have shown the newbie what to do. Trissa was more than just a way to make money.

The sparkly shadow on Jellybean's eyelids caught the light from the strategically placed disco ball as they fluttered. He sucked air through his teeth. "It will be difficult to replace her, but replace her I must. She betrayed the Club Jelly code. I can't allow that. Please tell her Jellybean has rescinded her VIP entry pass."

My jaw dropped. "You're firing her?" I took a deep breath and tried to calm myself down before I said the wrong thing. "What do you think was going on with her that night?"

"My dear, she was a natural in the cage, but a little too … wild."

"Well, it doesn't sound like her usual behaviour. Something must have happened. The cops found some of her stuff in the alley out back. I was hoping maybe you'd have some idea where she went next?"

"My bartender found the bag yesterday afternoon," he said, "and brought it down to the station. We have an arrangement with the police. They don't enter my club because it … upsets my clients, but I keep them in the loop whenever something happens."

"Like when a dancer threatens to jump from her cage?"

A flicker of anger crossed his face, but he sniffed and didn't respond.

I didn't trust Jellybean, but I believed his story about the bag. If his employees knew any more about what happened, they hadn't told him.

He liked to think he maintained absolute control over his Jelly-verse. Maybe he did.

All the fight left me. I started shivering from cold—my broken heart couldn't compensate for sitting around in wet clothes for this long—not to mention my underlying exhaustion now that all the adrenalin of being interrogated by the cops had left my body.

Maybe Trissa had just gotten too drunk and left her bag out back, I decided. If she was making so much money that losing two thousand didn't matter, she might be sleeping off her shame somewhere and afraid to face Jellybean after the scene she'd caused. She'd probably come looking for the bag eventually, but it wouldn't be there.

Could Jellybean be connected to her disappearance somehow? He'd been pissed, but would he have physically hurt her? I wasn't sure. As I sat there, I realized I'd been hoping Detective Lorenzo was right about Jellybean introducing Trissa to some famous rapper or artist who was keeping her busy at a fancy hotel. I'd been praying that once the fun was over, she'd come home and tell me all about it in excruciating detail.

That didn't make any sense now. It didn't sound like she'd been in a partying mood, plus if she had been, she'd definitely have messaged me to brag. She wouldn't have wanted Charlene to lose her mind with worry. She would never intentionally scare her family like that, not after Nadia's death.

Jellybean interrupted my spiral of thoughts. "I can't bear it another second. We must get you out of those soaking wet clothes. You look like a drowned purple rat." He stood up in one fluid movement, suddenly towering above me. I craned my neck to keep my eyes on his face.

As he headed for an ornate wooden wardrobe like the one the Narnia kids stepped through, I shook my head to clear the mental image from the news of a water-logged duffle bag being hauled out of the lake. One of the Strangler's victims. Suddenly, my knees started trembling, and the world began to fade. I leaned forward and waited for the dizziness to pass.

Jellybean was beside me in a flash, holding on to me so I didn't fall over.

"S-sorry," I mumbled. "I have a heart defect. It acts up when I'm under stress." I reached for my soggy canvas bag on the floor at my feet and rummaged around for my pills.

Jellybean spread a fluffy red cashmere throw over my lap, then placed a small silver bowl filled with his namesake candy on the table beside me. "Eat. Get your blood sugar up. I'll find you something dry to wear. Two shakes of a lamb's tail."

I mumbled my thanks and concentrated on getting a pill into my mouth with my shaking fingers. I chewed, swallowed, and grimaced at the sour taste. A handful of candy helped wash it down.

Behind me, Jellybean was pulling items out of the wardrobe and tossing them over his arm. I pictured myself riding transit home in a brightly coloured club outfit with sequins. At this point, I didn't care as long as it was dry. The beanbag chair was so comfortable, and the fuzzy blanket was warm. I took off my squelching sneakers, grabbed some more jelly beans, and tucked my feet up under me. As I waited for my medication to kick in, I focused on guessing the artificial flavours without looking at their colours. The first was green apple. The next one was grape. The third was fruity. I glanced. Red.

Jellybean lumbered over, carrying his pile of fabrics and some cute red ankle boots. He set them all on my lap with a flourish, then headed back to his throne.

Cautiously, I stood up—the sugar was already helping—and peered around for a place where I could change without him watching. Every corner of the room was visible. He noticed my consternation, smiled, and waved toward an elaborately painted Japanese screen on the far side of his enormous bed. I wanted to get out of these clothes badly enough that I could deal with him watching me through a semi-translucent sheet of rice paper. He wasn't into women, Trissa had told me. In fact, she didn't think he'd ever taken a lover. Maybe he was just private.

Everything he'd given me seemed brand new. And expensive. Behind the screen, I shook out thick white tights with scarlet bows in a row up the back, a red pleather skirt, several ultra-soft shirts that were meant to be layered on top of each other, a dusty-pink cardigan, and a slim-fitting red-leather jacket. As I tied up the dark-red boots, I was impressed that everything fit perfectly. He'd pegged my fashion sense and amped it up.

As I bent to pick up my wet clothes, a memory of Trissa flashed into my head. When we were ten, we'd tricked out our bicycle spokes with plastic gems the exact same shade of red as this jacket and added long red-and-silver handlebar streamers and two matching rainbow seat covers that sparkled when the sun came out. Trissa had a black mountain bike with metal pegs on the back wheel so she could do tricks. My ride was second-hand and orange. I'd attached a wire basket to the front and made pockets for my magnifying glass, notebook, pen, *Nancy Drew Sleuth Book*, and cheap binoculars.

Back then, I was completely obsessed with Nancy Drew. I had a used collection of them that were given to mom when she was a kid. I'd already devoured *Harriet the Spy* and the Enola Holmes series and decided I would be a private detective when I grew up. Trissa already knew she was going to be a dancer, so I figured I should have a calling, too. I went around inspecting "clues" and sneaking around to peer through people's windows. There were more old houses on our block back then. Over the years, they'd all been knocked down to build townhouses and condos.

We spent that entire summer on our bikes. Sometimes Anwar joined us, but his mother was more protective than ours, and he had to babysit Nadia. The more confident Trissa and I became, the farther from home we roamed. Our moms had no idea we made it all the way to High Park sometimes. It was far enough away to feel like we'd escaped their control. We'd zip around, doing wheelies and air jumps off the sidewalks, following suspicious-looking people, and tracking footprints until the sun started to set.

Our moms' only rule was that we had to be home before dinnertime. This one day, we were about to ride back when Trissa announced that she had to pee. The public bathroom was locked, so she told me watch her bike while she went into the nearby woods. Five minutes later, she shot out of the trees, snatched up her bike, and tore off, yelling at me to hurry.

It wasn't until we were out of the park and halfway home that she slowed down and told me what had happened. The zipper on her jeans had gotten stuck, and she was struggling to close it when a man materialized from the trees and offered to help her. She was naive enough to believe him, but instead of helping, he'd unzipped her fly all the way down and stuck his fingers inside her underwear. Trissa had freaked, bent down and grabbed a rock, and hit him in the forehead. Then she ran away.

"Did you kill him?" I asked, shocked.

She spat on the road. "I hope so." She noticed the look on my face and added, "Oh, come on. I didn't hit him that hard." Then she took off pedalling furiously.

I carried my wet clothes out from behind the screen and discovered that Jellybean was leaning forward and staring at the screen. So creepy. His fingers formed a temple under his double chin as if he'd been meditating while he watched me. I wondered just how much my silhouette had been visible, lit by the antique lamp on his bedside table. So creepy.

"Simply luscious," Jellybean announced—referring to the clothes, hopefully.

I flopped back down in the beanbag chair, grabbed my phone, and checked whether Franklyn had sent a message about my mom. Nope.

"I'll clean these and bring them back."

"Of course not. They're for you," Jellybean said, and licked his lips. "Now tell me more about what's going on."

"Nobody's seen Trissa since you kicked her out," I said abruptly.

He thumped his massive chest over his heart. "I can feel that Baby Girl is safe and that you don't need to worry. Jellybean has a sixth sense about this sort of thing."

I wanted to snap back that he couldn't possibly know that and didn't have the right to call Trissa his baby girl. He'd fired her. She wasn't his anything. Holding my temper only increased the knot of dread in my stomach. I fussed with the miniskirt, trying to make it cover more of my thighs, then gave up and spread the fuzzy blanket over my lap. I'd never learned how to keep my legs crossed, anyway. Manners were another thing my mom hadn't bothered to teach me. Anwar used to joke that Trissa and I were raised by wolves.

"Trissa's my sister. Of course I'm worried about her. You just told me she almost killed herself. She's always watched out for me. I need to do the same for her now, so—"

He clucked his tongue. "Your *sister* can handle herself."

"When we were kids, we used to ride our bikes up and down those steep hills in High Park. You know the ones?"

He nodded.

"I'd always cover my brakes—you know, to go slowly. Some of those turns are sharp. You can't see what's ahead. Trissa never did. She whipped down the hills like she was flying and didn't care what was around the corner. One time, she lost control. Her front tire hit a rock. She went right over the handlebars and skidded across the sidewalk face first. Blood everywhere. I went into shock or something. Like, I was always the sick one who needed saving, so I had no idea what to do for her. I didn't even ask if she was okay, just abandoned her and pedalled all the way home to get our mothers. They'd know what to do."

"Sounds fairly sensible for a child."

I shook my head. "Trissa never would have done that to me. She would have sat with me until I calmed down and helped me limp home."

Chin still resting on his fingers, Jellybean frowned contemplatively. "Well, I assume you returned?"

I snorted. "Oh yeah. Trissa's mom grabbed the keys to my mom's car, and we all drove back to the park. I can still see Charlene smoking two menthols at the same time while she sped through stoplights and traffic signs. You know the gate that says no driving in the park unless it's Sunday? Turns out it swings out of the way if you smash into it." I paused. "Trissa was walking along, leaning on her bicycle for support and ugly crying. She thought I'd just taken off." I paused. "We failed her. She's run away before, but this time is different. What if the Strangler got her? He took a girl just a few blocks from here."

Jellybean didn't respond. What could he have said? Maybe I was just telling him all of this so he'd see Trissa as more than some crazy party girl who danced for him. I couldn't say it to those detectives. I almost mentioned what Lorenzo said about Trissa making extra money with VIPs, but I stopped myself. It probably wasn't true and could get her in worse trouble with Jellybean.

My stomach rumbled audibly. I shoved another handful of candy into my mouth and chewed. The sugar made my saliva so thick I almost gagged. I swallowed, wishing I was at home. "Sorry for rambling. I kind of hoped she'd be here or that you might know something I don't."

He shook his shiny bald head. Glitter powder twinkled on his cheeks and the tip of his nose. "Sorry. When the other staff arrive, I will ask if anyone's seen her."

"Can I talk to the person who brought her bag to the police?"

He frowned. "Cal doesn't know anything."

"Wait, she's mentioned Cal. They're friends. He's not the bartender, is he?"

"No, that's Taytay. Cal handles the door." He pulled his phone out of one of the pockets of his satin robe. It was covered in an outrageously sparkly rhinestone case—at least I assumed they were rhinestones and not real diamonds. He dialled. No answer. He tried another number. Nothing. "Still sleeping."

I crammed my wet clothes into my shoulder bag and picked up my soggy shoes. "Maybe I can catch him out front later? I'll clean your clothes and bring them back tonight."

"Keep them." The expression on Jellybean's face told me he had no interest in seeing me again but wanted to keep up the nice guy performance. After a moment, he rolled his eyes. "Here, flash me your contact info and I'll send you an invite so you won't have to wait in line."

I held my phone next to his. An all-access pass that granted me entry to the club's restricted area appeared on my screen.

"It times out at midnight," he said, without looking up. He began texting.

It took me a moment to realize I'd been dismissed. I headed for the door.

"Have a sweet day," he mumbled.

Back in the main room, the cleaning woman was now wiping down one of the dancing cages, and Taytay was nowhere to be found. Trissa's cage had already been polished. It gleamed in its spot near the stage.

Why had she come to the club after leaving my place? What had happened to upset her? Falling from the ceiling probably wouldn't have killed her, but she would have broken some bones. And after Jellybean's militia had evicted her, where did she go? Somewhere with one of the other employees? Cal the doorman?

I was no closer to finding an explanation for why Trissa had skipped her shift the next night and wasn't responding to anyone's messages.

CHAPTER 9

Lock-Picking and Other Essential Skills

The leather jacket and booties kept my feet and torso dry, but my head and legs got wet as soon as I stepped through the back door that was steps away from Jellybean's suite. He used it as his personal entrance and, like usual, his black Land Rover was parked beside the battered green dumpster.

This was where Trissa's bag was found, I realized. It looked like any other narrow delivery alley in the downtown core. Several of the nearby buildings had garbage dumpsters identical to Club Jelly's. I wondered how the bartender had noticed anything back there. In the dark, it would have been hard to see.

As I headed to the bus stop, I checked again for messages. Nothing. My backup battery was almost dead. I wished for the thousandth time that I had the cash for a new phone. As I stood there glaring at it, a message came in from Anwar. His second in twenty-four hours, after we'd barely spoken for months. It seemed we were friends again.

Can I come by tonight?

Apparently, he wanted to go back to exactly how things were before Kelli D. That meant he'd show up around ten, after Amina took her sleeping pill and passed out. I sighed, knowing I wasn't being entirely fair. He must be almost as scared about Trissa as I was.

Company would be good, I replied. Maybe I'd be able to convince him to return to Club Jelly with me. *Use the bedroom window in case I'm sleeping*.

Sure thing.

The transit ride home took decades. When I entered our front door, I was blasted by a skunky smell coming from the upstairs apartment. Charlene had hotboxed the entire house.

Standing in my empty kitchen, I nearly broke down. I was exhausted and starving. The house was too quiet. Mom was still in jail. Franklyn always had her back, but I didn't know how long it would take him to work his magic and get her released. Then it hit me that Trissa might not be coming back *ever*, and I slid down to the floor and dropped my head in my hands. There was no good reason for her to go to the club at two in the morning, threaten to jump from her cage, ditch her bag in the alley, then get on the subway three hours later. What happened?

On the slim chance that Charlene had some news, I trudged up the staircase and found her slumped sideways on the burgundy-velvet sectional couch. Beside her ashtray was an open bottle of tequila and a bottle of Ativan. Her eyes were slightly ajar and glassy, but she was snoring. Her skin looked splotchy from crying, and her injured arm was in a sling against her chest. As I stood there, her eyes fluttered opened. She noticed me and sat upright with a jolt.

"How's your shoulder?" I asked. "Sorry if I scared you."

Charlene licked her dry lips and slumped back against the cushions. "The least of my worries. Heard from Trissa? Or Rachel?"

I shook my head sadly. My heart shattered.

"Bring her home, Michie," she slurred, and her eyelids closed. "Franklyn will get your mom out. Everything will be fine, right?"

Was she reassuring me or expressing hope? I had no idea how to bring Trissa home safely and I honestly didn't know that my mother would be okay. She was likely in serious trouble again. The last time she was charged, the courts had dragged her case out for over a year. But Charlene looked like shit and I seemed to be the only one capable of doing anything useful right now. That weighed on me. I'd have given anything to rewind forty-eight hours.

"Where have you looked for her?" I asked.

Charlene's eyes closed for a moment, then opened again. "Hospitals. Morgues."

"What made you run around the city in the middle of the night?"

She groaned. "Trissa does her own thing now, but she always calls to tell me when she's going to stay out overnight. I couldn't fall asleep because I hadn't heard from her since Thursday afternoon. A mother knows when her child is in trouble."

"Yeah. She loves you, Charlene, and she's still your baby girl." As soon as I said the words, I remembered Jellybean using them. Trissa wasn't his. She was ours. Family. I covered Charlene with a plaid throw blanket and stood up. "You should get some rest if you can. I promise I'll find her."

"Those cops are awful," she said, peering down at her arm.

"They are. But we can't let them convince us we don't know Trissa. She's not the girl—"

"Love you, sweetie," she said before I could finish. "With Franklyn on your mother's side, all will be well for her."

"I know." Charlene seemed to want to sleep more, so I headed downstairs to defrost some frozen spaghetti sauce and boil some noodles. I ate half and saved the rest for Anwar, since Amina probably wouldn't be cooking tonight. I showered and changed into comfortable sweats, warm socks, and a long-sleeved grey-cotton shirt onto which Anwar had silkscreened the city skyline in black. I felt better, but even more tired.

I plugged in my phone and my backup battery and curled up in bed to search online for news about Trissa. It looked like the police had issued a press release with her face on it, saying that she'd been missing since early Friday morning and was last seen at Club Jelly. They didn't include any other details but asked people to get in touch if they knew her whereabouts. A few news channels had picked it up, and one of them pointed out that Trissa fit the West End Strangler's victim profile: in her teens, pretty, athletic, and independent. Ugh.

For some reason, I clicked over to Kelli D's personal video feed again. She'd posted a monologue about how goddesses ought to be treated like goddesses, and she was banishing anyone from her life who treated her like a mere mortal. Whatever. At the very end, she mentioned that "one of her best friends" was missing, conjured up a few crocodile tears, and added a link to the press release about Trissa. Then the tears disappeared, and she brightened up as she told her viewers she'd be bringing on a special guest tomorrow to help her share some beauty tips fit for a goddess. Apparently, 2,329 people had already liked the video. Did they agree she was a goddess, or they were genuinely worried for Trissa?

I scanned through Kelli D's earlier videos and found one of her and Anwar from a couple weeks ago called "My Boyfriend Does My Makeup." He looked so cute, though he did a hideous job and seemed a little bored. She hadn't deleted it, though. Maybe she was holding out hope for a reconciliation. I didn't like that idea at all.

In my mind, I heard Trissa cackling and telling me I had totally been in love with Anwar forever and most definitely wanted him for myself. It was true. Admitting it to myself helped make the feeling that we'd done something bad to Kelli D disappear. So did the memory of how she and her friends had acted toward me at school.

Even though my life had gone to shit, I was actually worried about Anwar ditching me again. Pathetic. I tossed my phone on the bedside table, burrowed down, and shut my eyes. An image of Kelli D nestling into Anwar filled my brain, but it was better than body parts in a wet cargo bag. I wouldn't abandon Trissa this time. I'd find out what happened and tell her I was sorry for being a bad friend. In the future, I would pay attention to what was going on with her so that things like what Jellybean had told me wouldn't surprise me. I'd be a better sister.

*

I opened my eyes to find an orange sunbeam slicing the pillow beside my head. Sunset. It was a miracle that the sun actually managed to find its way into my room, given how close our house was to the one beside it. I slipped out of bed and headed upstairs to check on Charlene. She was now snoring on the sofa, and the TV was playing an advertorial for a giant fleece onesie that changed colour depending on the wearer's mood. A helmet-haired suburbanite was fake-arguing with her "husband" to demonstrate the angry red mode.

The police had searched Trissa's room for clues this morning, but they didn't know her hiding places like I did. If I took a look, I might find something they'd missed.

Her bedroom took up most of the third-floor attic. She was a human tornado and hadn't cleaned it in years, so it was impossible to know whether the cops had searched thoroughly. It didn't look worse than usual. Dirty clothes were piled on a chair, the bed, and the floor. I counted twelve pairs of high heels strewn around, including a red stiletto hanging from the old-fashioned crystal chandelier that had come with the house. It was missing a lot of the crystals, but it was still kind of cool.

The room smelled like jasmine oil. Trissa's scent. Swallowing a lump of pain that rose into my throat, I paused to watch the screen saver on her computer run in a continuous loop. She'd set it to never turn off. Clips of her favourite musicians and movie stars paraded past, interspersed with shots of her friends and family. There were some short videos of us as kids, pics of Charlene when she was young, one of Trissa's bio dad—whom I'd never met—and lots of Trissa dancing.

An image of her jumping off a dock into a lake was foregrounded by two pairs of brown legs stretched out on a flat rock. My breath caught in my chest. Those were Nadia's knobby knees and Anwar's hairy legs, taken the summer I turned twelve, at this cottage Charlene and Mom rented up north for a couple weeks every summer. Nadia must have been playing with Trissa's phone—she was always grabbing our phones so she could take pictures and play games. It would have been just a few months before she was killed. Amina had worked long hours back then, and she'd trusted the mothers enough to let them bring her kids along on vacation. That was the first time Nadia had ever been fishing or canoeing, or eaten alive by mosquitoes.

The screen saver switched to a selfie of Trissa rocking out at a recent concert. I tore my gaze away. In a giant homemade cage on Trissa's desk, her guinea pigs, Tink and Tonk, were just waking up for the night. They had a pretty good life in the homemade fortress it had taken us a week to build out of plywood, branches, driftwood, and recycled glass jars. I bent down to see what was going on with them and noticed their food bowl was empty.

"Nobody's fed you lately," I cooed, leaning over and opening the metal door on top of the cage.

Tink ran around, chittering excitedly.

Too bad I couldn't speak guinea pig, or I could have asked them whether Trissa had come up here the night she disappeared. I gave Tink a scratch on his fluffy white head, poured a generous serving of food into the bowl, checked the water bottle—still mostly full—and shut the cage again before heading over to the closet to riffle through Trissa's dresses and dance outfits. Next, I opened the desk drawers beneath the cage and searched through them. Nothing interesting, just a whole lot of half-used and dried-out makeup, some sewing supplies, hair ties, tangled cherry-red hair extensions, and scarlet Manic Panic dye.

Trissa kept one of the drawers locked, but the police had jimmied it open. They didn't know she kept the key on a tiny hook near the wall.

I bent down and peered around but couldn't see it, so I ran my fingers along the back of the desk. My fingers touched the key tucked into a far corner. I removed it from its hook and put it on the desk. It was useless now, of course, but it was comforting that I knew something they didn't. Inside the drawer was a shoebox filled with papers: her original birth certificate, a couple of old passports, napkins and scraps of paper with notes on them, lined sheets from school she'd scribbled song lyrics on, a love letter from one of her boyfriends, and fading ticket stubs for concerts.

Under the box was a pack of expired banana-flavoured condoms—gross—a stack of magazines, and a couple of diaries I'd given her for birthdays. I was pretty sure she'd never used them but decided to check just in case. The first one I picked out was almost a decade old. It had hearts and flowers on the cover and a flimsy lock that flapped open. A few pages had been used and a couple more ripped out. I scanned the entry dates, feeling guilty for snooping. Nothing recent. Rooting around at the bottom of the drawer to see if I'd missed anything, I came up with a handful of dust and a broken necklace.

I flopped down on the tangle of linens that had been pulled off Trissa's mattress and felt emotion burbling up inside me again. Where would she have gone in the middle of the night? She'd packed to go away but somehow lost her wallet and her bag of supplies. That meant she wasn't planning to take off to Mexico or anything. Besides, if she had been going on a beach vacay, she'd have rubbed my face in it.

It was unlikely I'd find anything in here that the police hadn't. I rolled onto my stomach and buried my head in a pillow, stretched out my hands, and touched the wall. When we were kids, this double bed had seemed massive. I remembered us lying sideways on it, toes pressed against the cool wall, heads flopping off the side. Trissa had gotten some glow-in-the-dark star stickers for her ninth birthday. We'd put them up on the ceiling by jumping on the bed. Now they'd faded to a pale yellow.

I sat upright. Another memory came to me, of Trissa hiding things she didn't want her mom to find deep in the stuffing of her mattress. She'd actually cut a hole under a seam and sewn in a strip of Velcro so it stayed closed and was practically invisible. I ran my fingers along the mattress's side and discovered a hole the width of my hand down near the foot of the bed, next to the wall. I poked a finger inside and felt something hard. I pulled it out. A brand-new phone. Apparently, the police hadn't figured on her ingenuity.

This wasn't the phone Trissa normally used. If she had that on her, the police would probably be able to ping the GPS, like on every cop show I'd ever seen. Why did she need a second phone? It looked expensive, but it wasn't a brand I recognized. When I tried to turn it on, it asked for thumbprint security. Hmm. Maybe Anwar would be able to crack it. He understood technology better than me. Even if we couldn't unlock the phone, Trissa didn't want the police to find it. I slipped it into my pocket and got back up.

The guinea pigs were chittering noisily now, as if they could tell something was wrong in their universe. Someone would have to take care of them. I disconnected the cage from its elaborate network of tunnels and rooms, put a giant bag of food on top, and was about to hoist it up when I remembered a section of *Girl's Guide* on how the best hiding places were right in plain sight. Bolstered by my discovery of the secret phone, I opened the little cage door and rooted under the thick layer of damp wood chips that lined the bottom. Tink and

Tonk got alarmed and ran to hide in their little burrow. These chips definitely needed to be changed, but there was something down there. A slim box.

I took it out and wiped it down with a dirty shirt. It was a diary, not a box. This one had a sturdy little padlock—Trissa had replaced the cheap one that would have come with it and drawn all over the covers with black markers to obscure whatever girly pattern was originally on there. The edges of the pages indicated it was well thumbed through. I would be able to get it open with a hammer.

I wedged the diary under the bag of food pellets, grabbed a half-empty bag of wood chips and another one of hay, and awkwardly managed to carry everything downstairs. As I passed the second floor, I listened for a moment but heard only light snores. Considering Charlene had been awake more than twenty-four hours, she'd probably be out until morning.

The only place in my room where I could put the cage was on top of my dresser. I cleared it off, shoving books and clothes onto the floor, and placed Tink and Tonk's home safely on top. A moment later, they poked their heads out of their burrow and looked around, unsure about this new, unfamiliar environment. Trissa gave them leftover veggies as a treat. Maybe that would calm them down? I got some chunks of rubbery cucumber and a carrot from the fridge and dropped them beside their food bowl. The chubby little rodents scampered over and stuffed their cheeks with cuke, and Tonk dragged the carrot back to the little wooden cave.

Trissa's mystery phone worked with my cheap multi-connector cord, so I plugged it in and took another look at the padlock on the diary. If I smashed it with a hammer and Trissa came home, she'd be

pissed. Whatever—she'd done worse to me. It was worth incurring
her wrath.

Then again, Chapter 21 of *Girl's Guide* explained in detail how to
pick various kinds of locks with a couple of rigged bobby pins. I'd
already sharpened and bent some according to the instructions but
hadn't managed to open anything yet. At school, I'd unsuccessfully tried
my locker (forgot my key), the cafeteria kitchen (got the munchies
after it closed), and the staff bathroom (so much cleaner), but now I
was motivated. One pin was shaped into a pick with a loop on the end,
and the other looked like a crooked lever.

It took me almost an hour and half a dozen video tutorials, but
eventually I got the lock open. A handful of tiny baggies like the ones
my mom used for grams of cannabis dropped into my lap. This wasn't a
diary at all, but a secret compartment book. I picked up a baggie with
ten grey tablets in it. They were shaped like tiny robots. Another one
had eight red phone booths that looked like the TARDIS from *Doctor
Who*. A third had seven yellow suns. There were so many different pills:
pink lips, white unicorns, purple hearts, and green dollar bills … This
was a Lucky Charms box of drugs.

Where had Trissa gotten them? Maybe the detectives were right
about her selling, but she didn't get these from my mom. What had she
gotten herself into? This stash must be worth a lot of money. No doubt
it was where the big money in her knapsack had come from. I wasn't
sure what kind of pills these were, but someone had to be looking for
them. And her. I tried googling the shapes, but the internet wasn't any
help. There was only one way to find out what they were.

Before I could convince myself otherwise, I popped a purple heart
into my mouth, swallowed it, sealed the baggie, put everything back

in the diary—even the phone fit in the compartment—and buried it under wood chips in the cage.

At first nothing happened. I got thirsty and drank some water.

When I returned to my room, the Pink Chicks poster on the wall above my bed was wiggling, like the band members were dancing holograms. Weird. I lay down.

*

Someone tapped on the window frame, a sharp *tak tak tak tak*. My eyes flew open. It was pitch-dark. Huh. I tried to sit upright, but the room spun, so I lay back down a moment before reaching over to turn on the lamp. Anwar was standing outside, as cute as ever and a little soggier than usual. He pointed at the window lock.

I scrambled over and turned the lock, then pulled the pane upward. "It's pouring."

"Yes. What took you so long?" he asked, already fitting his head and shoulders through the window. His wavy black hair was sleek with rain.

"Sorry, I think I was asleep." I yanked the curtains out of his way, stepped to one side, and wobbled. "Also, I'm having a little trouble with the floor. And, um, the ceiling."

"What are you talking about?" Anwar asked, sliding through the window and tumbling at my feet the way he had done hundreds of times when we were kids. Except he wasn't a child anymore. He stood up, and a droplet of water ran down his forehead into his eyebrow. I had an urge to lick it away.

"I've missed you," I blurted out.

He shook his head and moved a couple steps so the lamp lit him from behind. "It's only been a few hours."

"You're glowing," I confessed. "Like a firefly."

"Huh?"

"Never mind."

"I missed you too." He leaned over, like he was going to kiss me. I froze. Were we at that stage already?

At the last instant, he noticed something behind me and pulled back in surprise. I followed his gaze to my mirror and the lipstick heart with our initials in it. Why hadn't I cleaned it off? Because it might be my last interaction from Trissa. And because I was a dink.

Anwar tilted his head, processing what it meant, but didn't say anything, just reached into an inner jacket pocket and produced a half-eaten bag of lemon wafers. He slung the jacket over my desk chair, opened the package, and shoved a handful in his mouth. The smell of fake lemon assaulted my nose.

I gagged and threw myself onto the bed so I could bury my face in a pillow. "Get those out of here."

He laughed. "I thought you loved lemon cookies."

"Not tonight. Maybe it's the pill."

Anwar paused mid chew. "The what?"

"Searched Trissa's room when I got home and found a stash of pills in a fake book. Wanted to know what they were. Ecstasy, I think? Or GHB."

"How would you know?"

"I'm guessing based on how it feels."

He stuffed three cookies in his mouth and ignored me when I gave him the middle finger with one hand and pinched my nose with the other.

"This is all I've eaten since breakfast."

"There's spaghetti for you in the kitchen."

"Cool." Still chewing, he headed over to the guinea pig cage. Tink chittered and stood up on his hind feet, nose twitching excitedly. Anwar dropped a chunk of wafer inside. Tink shoved it into his cheek. Apparently, guinea pigs liked lemon cookies. They had no taste.

Anwar put down the cookies long enough to let Tink scurry up his arm and hide under his T-shirt sleeve, then he came over and lay down beside me. The mattress wiggled like a trampoline. Or a boat on the waves. A boat in a storm.

"What's going on with you?" he asked.

"Nothing good. My best friend is missing. My mom's in jail. And I'm obsessed with this cute guy I've known since kindergarten, but he has a perfect girlfriend."

"Wait, you're—are you talking about me?"

I blushed and reached for my phone so I wouldn't have to answer. Somehow, I'd missed a call from Franklyn. After listening to the message, I reported, "Okay, Franklyn says he's working to get the charges dropped. Apparently, Mom will be released tomorrow, and he'll pick her up."

"That's great."

I nodded and looked up to find Anwar only inches away. He was so beautiful. His stomach peeked out from under his shirt, which had hiked up a little, and a strip of dark hair disappeared below his belt. I put my fingertip just below his bellybutton. He hissed in a surprised breath but didn't stop me, so I traced the hair lower, lower. My entire world was dissolving and somehow all I could think about was—

Anwar swore and dropped Tink on the bed. "The little pig pissed on me!" He jumped to his feet, put Tink pig back in the cage, then yanked off his shirt. Beneath it, he was wearing a white cotton undershirt with a small yellow splotch on the shoulder. He removed that too, and my mouth went dry. Without asking, he spun around and rummaged in my dresser for something clean. He settled on a tomato-red shirt I used for PJs that had an image of Maggie and Hopey from the *Love and Rockets* comics. He'd introduced me to the series when we were fourteen; that summer we borrowed every single issue from the public library. The Hernandez brothers had inspired him become a professional illustrator.

"That shirt looks hot," I said, wishing I could stop staring.

Anwar kneeled on the bed and gently cupped my chin. "Michie, why would you take some random pill?"

"I needed to find out what it was." I gulped, trying to ignore the tingling in my cheek where he'd touched it. "What about Kelli D?"

He groaned. "We just talked on the phone for over an hour. She dumped me."

"That sucks."

He nibbled on a cookie thoughtfully. "I guess."

A whiff of foul lemon scent reached my nose, making me gag again. "Go eat the spaghetti, and throw those out while you're in there."

He grinned, grabbed the package of cookies, and left the room. When he returned five minutes later, he was patting his stomach contentedly and no longer carrying the cookies. He made an ostentatious chef's kiss gesture to indicate that the spaghetti was superb.

"Thank my mom when she gets out. I just boiled the noodles. So, okay, to fill you in, the police think Trissa's a sex worker and Jellybean's her pimp, but I'm not so sure. Jellybean told me she showed up at the club just before closing on Thursday night and hung off her cage up near the ceiling like she was going to kill herself. I think she's been selling drugs, but maybe not for him. How could I have been so oblivious? It's like I don't even know her." I closed my eyes and allowed my mattress to swallow me up like a giant marshmallow. I caught a faint whiff of Trissa's jasmine oil on my pillow. My heart ached. "I'm a terrible friend." I sniffled. "I'm also really thirsty."

"There's half a glass of water on your bedside table."

"Oh right." I sat up and took a gulp. "That's better. I need to go back to Club Jelly tonight so I can talk to people." The marshmallow bed sucked me in again. My eyelids drooped. "Why are you here? You've barely acknowledged my existence in months."

"That's not my fault! You never replied to my texts."

"Whoa. Because you were surgically attached to Kelli D."

He shook his head. "I wanted to talk to you before I hooked up with her, but you blew me off. Five times. Remember? I thought you weren't interested in me."

"I was ..." *Shy* was what I didn't say. Also, jealous and terrified he didn't like me that way and that I'd ruin our friendship. "Of course I blew you off. You only wanted my blessing to be with Kelli D."

"Why would I want your blessing, Michie? For such a smart girl, you're totally clueless. Just promise me that if your feelings about me have changed, you'll tell me. Okay?"

I couldn't speak.

Anwar sighed. "Okay. Let's figure out what you took. Where are the pills?"

"Under the wood chips in the guinea pig cage."

He gave me a funny look but got up and extracted the diary, opened it, and sifted through the baggies. "She's definitely selling—no other reason to have this much product. Which one did you take?"

"A heart."

"There could have been fentanyl in it!" he snapped.

"Why would she have opioids? Anyway, I'd know by now. Everything's just, uh, moving around, and it feels kinda nice. There's a weird light trail when I move my eyes quickly."

He sucked his teeth. "You're either going to have fun tonight or one of your panic attacks. Speed is really bad for your heart."

"It's not speed, either." I pointed at the second phone. "And that was hidden in her mattress. Why would she have a burner? Think we can unlock it?"

"I'll take a look. You rest for a couple more hours."

"Chapter 26 of *Girl's Guide* has a long section on hacking people's passwords," was the last thing I said before succumbing to another light and weird sleep. My dreamscape was vivid—I returned to the park where we'd used to bike, hoping to find Trissa, but I was seconds too late. She was gone. Taken into the woods. Then I saw Nadia happily riding her bike and ran to catch up with her, but couldn't …

CHAPTER 10

Preparing for Any Eventuality

I woke up sweating with my head on Anwar's thigh. He was drawing in his sketchbook, resting the bottom of it on his chest so he wouldn't jostle me. I looked around. Inanimate objects were still moving of their own volition but not as dramatically as before.

"How are you feeling?" he asked.

"What time is it?"

He glanced at Trissa's phone, which was next to him. "Just past eleven."

I leapt out of bed. "Why didn't you wake me?"

"You needed rest."

"But we need to get to the club." I hurried over to my closet and grabbed clothes. "Did you unlock the phone?"

"Nope, but I studied the section of *Girl's Guide* on making fake thumbprints using crazy glue and gel paint—"

"Art supplies."

"Right. I'll bring them over in the morning. I'll also need something with Trissa's prints on it. Those baggies might work, but they probably have other people's prints as well."

"Excellent. Right now, we've gotta move. Go make some hot chocolate?"

By the time Anwar returned with two huge mugs, I was dressed for the club. His eyes widened at the sight of my tiny black skirt and silver-mesh crop top that was transparent enough to show off my black bra underneath. I'd even managed to excavate my thigh-high silver platform boots from the bottom of the closet—Trissa had convinced me to buy them. I wasn't all that stable on high heels, though, so I decided to stay seated for now.

"You're skinnier than me," I said, nodding at a shirt on the bed. "That should fit."

"Wiry," Anwar corrected, then lifted his arm and flexed his guns. "Guys aren't skinny. I'm not wearing your clothes."

I raised an eyebrow and glanced pointedly at the *Love and Rockets* shirt he was wearing. "They'll turn you away."

He hesitated, then sighed dramatically. "Fine."

I laughed and took a sip of cocoa. "Get dressed."

"Bossy," he complained, but he picked up the ripped black sleeveless shirt that said "work it, girl" in silver bubble letters.

I pranced to the bathroom and put on some eyeliner and lip gloss. When I got back, Anwar was wearing the ridiculous shirt and hand-feeding Tonk a small chunk of cookie.

"I look like Zayn Malik," he whined.

"So? He's adorable. At least you get to wear sneakers."

Anwar burst out laughing. It took all my willpower not to grab him by the hair and pull his face against mine. He quickly sobered, as if he was having the same thought.

I shoved the packet of red pills into a small silver purse along with my phone, wallet, lip gloss, and heart medication. Maybe if I flashed the pills around, someone would claim them. It was a terrible idea, but it wasn't like I had many others.

Anwar's phone buzzed, startling us both. He removed it from his back pocket, glanced at the screen, and switched it to silent mode.

"Your mom?" I asked.

I deduced from his confused expression that it was Kelli D.

"Do you need to call her back?" I asked, when what I really wanted to know was whether he wanted to get back together with her.

As if he could read my thoughts, he reached for my hand and laced his fingers through mine. My light-pink skin contrasted with his brown skin. We'd never really held hands before, but they fit together. I needed this boy in my life.

"She just wants to pick up her stuff up from my place."

"Ahh." I gently removed my hand, drained the rest of my drink, clunked the empty mug down on the old chest of drawers, and led the way out to the lobby. I searched again for my favourite jacket but couldn't find it, so I put on the red-leather one Jellybean had given me.

It was still buttery smooth. No one would have guessed I'd worn it in a rainstorm earlier.

"There's a bus in six minutes," Anwar said, looking up from his phone. "Think you can run in those boots?"

I groaned.

*

The laser lights on Club Jelly's roof swooped across the sidewalk in an elaborate dance, then veered upward, slashed the windows of a darkened office building, and spiked the night sky. The club's external walls were awash in neon colors, turning the brick monolith into a rainbow of light. All the plywood-covered windows had projections on them: candy spilling endlessly downward, bubbles floating upward, and geometric shapes twisting through patterns. A slight trail of light swished across my view when I moved my eyes, but otherwise the effects of the pill were gone.

By the time we made it to the purple velvet carpet that led from the street, where cars waited for fares, up to the front door, I was already desperately wishing I'd worn my high-tops. People were streaming in and out of the club. They looked so much alike—the kind of people Sal would pick as targets if they were on the bus. Would Anwar and I be like them in a few years? I tried to picture myself working an entry-level job in one of the office towers, failed, and swore to myself that I wouldn't become one of the clones.

As I minced past the lineup, a reed-thin girl with a long blond ponytail staggered outside on needle-point heels with platform soles— definitely much harder to walk on than my boots—supported by an older business man with salt-and-pepper hair, expensive shoes, and a shark face. There was no way she could dance in those. She'd probably just swayed from side to side, looking sexy and helpless.

At the front doors, a bouncer with massive biceps, a slick pompadour, and a square jaw glowered at everyone as he checked ID. Was this Cal? I cut in front of three dude-bros high on pheromones and whatever else and ignored their complaints as I handed over my phone with the VIP entry coupon. The guy scanned it. I worried he was going to card me when he swung his gaze from my feet up to my face. Instead, his eyes bounced to Anwar, and he shook his head. "This pass is only for one."

"Call Jellybean," I insisted. "I'm sure it's fine."

"We're a package deal," said Anwar, looking irritated.

The bouncer grunted, "Fine. No drinks." He picked up a stamp and pressed it to the backs of our hands, then waved for us to move along. The stamp was a dark-red circle with a wineglass in the middle and a thick line through it. Whatever. It wasn't like we were here to get drunk.

"Hey, is your name Cal?" I asked.

He was already reaching for the IDs of the guys waiting behind us, but he paused and held up a hand to stop them. "Why?"

"I'm, uh, Trissa's sister. Michie. I mean, we just call each other sisters because we grew up together in the same house. Our moms are best friends." I was blathering nervously. "She's mentioned you. I just wondered if you've heard from her. No one has seen her since she left the club early Friday morning ..."

The expression on his face had changed subtly. It was softer. He cared about Trissa, I could tell, and he knew exactly who I was. She'd told him about me too.

"Did you see her here on Thursday night?" I asked.

He whistled a low note. "Everyone did."

"What do you mean?" asked Anwar.

Cal looked at him appraisingly and then jerked his chin at the group waiting behind us to back up a little. "That girl has a death wish. She climbed into her cage, raised it to the ceiling, swung off it like an orangutan. If she'd fallen, she would have broken every bone in her body."

A message appeared on my phone screen, interrupting my next question. Jellybean was summoning me and said Cal should join us instead of standing around making small talk. Was he somehow listening to our conversation? Cal had an earpiece in. Maybe Jellybean spied on his employees that way. Was he pissed that I was holding up the line? I didn't want Cal to get in trouble because of me.

Reluctantly, I tipped my screen to show him the message. "Jellybean wants you to come along, but it looks like you're busy here, and I know the way."

"Boss wants me to take over for you," said a tall, angular woman wearing a gold lamé bodysuit and strappy dark-gold sandals. She was surprisingly muscular, the kind of woman nobody would argue with, and she was already striding toward us, beckoning for the next people in line to move up and show their ID. To get here that fast, she must have been standing just inside the door, near the coat check.

Cal swept a strong hand toward the door. "After you."

I clutched Anwar's hand and used it to keep me steady as we hurried to keep pace with Cal's long legs. My feet were sore. Cal didn't even look back at us, just plowed through the crowd in the entry hall, parting guests like they were strands of hair.

Bubbles plumed out of tiny holes in the wall and tickled my nose. I let go of Anwar's hand and held it up in front of my face, worried I was going to sneeze. The bubbles were stunning. They reflected the light from thousands of tiny LEDs that made the silver floor and walls shine like gemstones. For a moment, the wild scene disoriented me. There was some kind of fruity perfume in the soap they used to make the bubbles. I grabbed the wall to keep myself from stumbling. In these boots, it would be too easy to sprain an ankle.

We headed through the Chill Zone. Once we reached the main dance floor, it would be too loud to speak, so I hurried to catch up to Cal.

"Was Trissa with anyone that night?"

"Nah. Wait. I think she called some guy to pick her up. She was probably pissed that I didn't stand up for her."

"What did he look like?"

He shrugged. "Brown hair. Kinda big, but not as big as me. Doesn't work here."

That could be anyone, I thought. Then we reached the main room, and speech became impossible. For such a big guy, Cal was really good at darting around writhing bodies.

Did Jellybean know that she'd left with someone? If so, why hadn't he told me earlier? He'd acted like a concerned papa, but if Trissa had actually threatened his business ... I shuddered to think what he might have done to her. The club would definitely have shut down for a few days if she'd jumped. A little frisson of anxiety rippled down my spine. Maybe Jellybean was calling me to his rooms because he didn't actually want me to question his staff?

I glanced upward at the girls in cages doing acrobatic moves. Their cage doors were all securely latched shut, and they were wearing the safety ropes that attached to their belts on brightly coloured outfits. My brain played scenes from a horror film in which Trissa lost her grip and smashed into the floor. My heart started racing.

I paused and scanned the crowd. Was I hoping to find a clue in a stranger's face? It wasn't like I could look into someone's eyes and suddenly identify the West End Strangler, but a club like this would be easy pickings. Everyone was drunk.

Sweat prickled my forehead and neck. This was ridiculous. If Trissa were here, she'd have laughed at me and probably called me a prude for not joining in the fun. Maybe she'd been a little feral, but not depressed. Not suicidal. I shook my head to try to clear it of the nonsensical situation.

For Jellybean to make his club so successful, he must be ruthless. Could he have done something to Trissa that morning? Made her run? Hurt her?

Artificial smoke billowed out of a machine, catching me by surprise. The chemical smoke went straight up my nose and down my throat to settle into my lungs. My head was already messed up. Now the building was starting to pulsate in time with the music.

I realized I couldn't see Anwar or Cal anywhere. I squeezed my eyes shut for a moment, focused on my breathing, and waited for my head to clear and my heart to slow down. I needed to get away from the fog, into the fresh air.

A topless guy covered in glowing body paint and wearing short shorts and long light-ropes wrapped around his arms and legs suddenly appeared in front of me. His face was flushed. He grabbed my hands and tried to make me dance. I shoved him away. He sneered and squeezed one of my breasts really hard. Pain jolted through me. I swore, but the music was so loud.

Just as suddenly as he'd appeared, he slipped back into the sea of bodies and disappeared. I looked down at my mesh shirt and realized he'd left a greasy makeup smear on my breast. A perfect set of fingerprints. Exactly what we needed from Trissa to get into her phone. This was the kind of thing that happened whenever I went clubbing—and why I avoided it.

Livid, I shoved my way to the VIP entrance. Anwar and Cal were waiting outside the door, scanning the crowd for me. I pointed at my chest and grimaced.

Anwar looked concerned. He leaned over and yelled into my ear, "What happened?"

"Some asshole groped me when the smoke machine went off," I hollered back.

He scanned the crowd, ready to go charging off.

"That's not why we're here," I said. And this was just one more thing girls had to deal with—stopping other guys from trying to defend their honour. I wanted to get out of here. Go home. Trissa wasn't here, I could feel it in my bones. This was her world. She could handle herself here, not me. I was fresh meat. To Jellybean, an interchangeable human doll he'd draped in designer clothes. Girls in this club were treated like playthings.

Before I could stop Anwar, he leaned toward Cal, presumably to tell him what happened. Cal spoke to the bouncer stationed outside the VIP door and pointed at my chest. Then he opened the door to the club's backrooms, and all four of us moved into the inner hallway, where it was quiet enough to talk.

"Tell us exactly what the guy looked like," said Cal.

The other bouncer nodded.

I frowned. "Um, tall. Very short hair. No shirt. Lots of glowing body paint and LED light-ropes around his arms and legs."

Cal lifted his wrist and spoke into a watch—so that was where the microphone was located—and repeated my description. His co-worker hurried back out to the dance floor. I had a horrible vision of Mr. Groper getting hauled outside and beaten to a pulp.

"What's gonna happen if you catch the guy?" I asked as we started walking down the hall.

"We'll ban him," said Cal. "*Persona non grata* at Club Jelly. Ladies need to feel safe, or they'll stop coming."

Well, at least Mr. Groper would understand how it felt to be intimidated. Hopefully that was all. No broken bones or loose teeth.

"I guess that means Trissa's not welcome either?" asked Anwar.

Cal looked concerned. "She's in Jellybean's inner circle. He might forgive her."

Remembering how Jellybean had suggested I should pass along his message if I found Trissa, I doubted it, but Cal knew his boss better than I did.

We passed a room where a couple dancers lounged on a loveseat with Taytay, the bartender who'd been here earlier, surrounded by a whole lot of half-empty drinks. Did they take a couple sips from each one and then abandon it? Maybe Taytay tried out new recipes on the staff or something. The faint scent of tobacco lingered in the air. I stepped inside, lifted a hand in greeting, and opened my mouth to say hello.

The venom in Taytay's eyes stopped me from saying anything. Plus, he mumbled something that sounded like "rat," jumped to his feet, and pushed past me. The girls he'd been drinking with deliberately turned their backs on us.

Wow. Was everyone so pissed at Trissa that they were taking it out on me? Why would Taytay think I was a rat? Something felt wrong here. This morning, Jellybean had been fine with me talking to his employees, but now I was being escorted directly to his office. Do not pass Go, do not collect one hundred dollars.

I lunged for Anwar's hand and tugged it, trying to get him to stop walking. I didn't want to speak out loud, but I tried to communicate some of my fear.

His eyebrows furrowed in questioning.

"We should leave," I whispered.

"But—"

Cal twisted around. "Come on."

Anwar started forward again. Cal led us to Jellybean's office instead of his personal suite, rapped on the door frame, and waited. It seemed weirdly formal, given that Jellybean had literally summoned us.

"Enter," came Jellybean's command.

Cal indicated for us to go inside. As soon as we were in the office, he turned and left, closing the door behind him without so much as a goodbye. We were now in Jellybean's office with the man himself and four members of his security team I'd never seen before.

Jellybean was standing behind his massive antique walnut desk. He'd changed into a monochrome white outfit that brought out the angry flush of his cheeks and somehow minimized the roundness of his body. The bouncers flanked him, two on each side. Their body shapes ranged from tiger muscles like Cal's to tank-like. Jellybean's forehead was covered in beads of sweat, but the starched pale-pink handkerchief in his breast pocket remained untouched. The expression on his face made Taytay's glare feel like a cozy hug.

Without a single word, he charged across the room, grabbed a fistful of my hair, and yanked my head back so I was forced to stare up into his eyes. "Little bitch, how dare you call the cops on me!"

"Wha—" I stammered.

Jellybean backhanded me across the face. Pain exploded in my jaw.

Anwar lunged to help me, but Jellybean swatted him away with his free hand like he was a baby bird, and two bouncers grabbed him before he could even regain his footing. I couldn't turn to see, but I heard Anwar being hit. He smacked into something. A bookshelf maybe, or the door.

The angle Jellybean was holding me at made it difficult to keep my boots on the ground. One foot skidded out, and I would have fallen if his fist weren't so deeply entwined in my hair. It hurt like hell. I wailed.

"I invited you into my home and you betrayed me!" he bellowed.

"N-no I didn't!"

He shook my head, and I caught a glimpse of Anwar. The two bouncers were holding his arms behind his back. He looked dazed.

Jellybean tightened his grip on my hair even more, causing pain to rip through my skull. What I saw in his eyes made my blood freeze. If I'd thought Anton looked dead inside, now I knew better. Jellybean was the law in his club. He could do anything to us right now. He would enjoy it too, and none of his employees would try to stop him.

He wrenched my head back farther, then shoved me down onto my knees. "The police showed up half an hour after you left and searched the whole place. My arrangement with them is over, do you understand that? You've ruined everything."

"B-but I said nothing to them." It was hard to speak with my neck twisted. "I haven't talked to them since this morning, and they were the ones who told me Trissa was dealing and sleeping with VIPs. I said there was no way."

"You have the nerve to come back here." He snorted and shook his head in disbelief. "They searched my private rooms. My sanctuary! Charged one of my security team with possession with intent to distribute and delayed the club's opening on my most profitable night of the week. I think you owe me that profit. How should I get the money from you?"

He shook me one more time, then released me. Blood rushed back to my scalp, and I fell down on my butt. He bent over and shoved his shiny red face in mine. "You're not worth it. Just get out of my sight. I don't want to see you or Trissa ever again." Then he straightened up, turned on his heel, and stalked out of the office. From the hall, he called out, "Take out the garbage."

The bouncers looked gleeful. I managed to catch Anwar's eyes for an instant before two men grabbed my arms and legs. As I was swept off my feet, I heard a thud, then a crack.

"Stop hitting him!" I screamed.

One of the bouncers said, "Stop squirming," and kneed me in the ribs.

I went limp. If they carried us past patrons, I could scream for help. But they were going the other way, toward the back exit. The alleyway. We passed the door to Jellybean's bedroom, which was wide open. I could see that his beanbag chairs had been slashed, and gleaming bowls of candy were upended on the floor. Bright clothing and bedding lay crumpled on the floor.

"None of this is my fault!" I yelled at nobody in particular.

When we got to the metal fire door, the man holding my legs shoved it open with his hip, and they hauled me into the alley behind the club. Other than Jellybean's car and the dumpster, there was nothing else around. No one.

The bouncers started swinging me from side to side, like a really heavy skipping rope, until they got some lift. When I was high in the air, they released me. My elbow smashed against the side of the dumpster as I tumbled inside. My shoulder hit the far wall. I landed on something squishy that smelled bad.

A moment later, Anwar fell in beside me with a thud. His knee jabbed into my thigh, and his head hit the metal wall. He didn't move.

I heard Jellybean's security team heading back inside, laughing to each other about barely getting their hands dirty. They'd fulfilled their orders. To them, we were nothing but trash to be removed from the club. Like the boss had asked.

CHAPTER 11

Cultivating True Accomplices

My heart pounded erratically, and my ribs, elbow, and thigh throbbed. When I sucked in a deep breath, I gagged at the hideous stench inside the dumpster. My left hand was resting on something wet—a rotting lemon rind from the bar's garbage. Disgusting. I tried to wipe it on some cardboard and struggled to sit up. Anwar lay nearby, face down in a plastic bag.

"Shit!" I clawed my way toward him, across oozing plastic bags and empty bottles of cleaning supplies. My knee went down on something sharp that tore through my stockings and sliced my knee open. For some reason, seeing blood made my other aches soar to life even more intensely. My shoulders ached, and my scalp stung.

As soon as I reached Anwar, I grabbed his shoulder and heaved him over onto his back. "Please be alive. Please …"

Confusion flitted across his face. He looked a little dazed, but he pushed himself up, then groaned, fell back down, and grabbed his ribs. Impulsively, I titled his face toward mine and kissed him. My puffy lip got in the way, but it made him stop grimacing.

He grinned crookedly. "If I pretend to be dead, will you do that again?"

"Shut it."

There was a smear of blood on his bottom lip, and his eye was swollen. I cleaned his mouth with my top and somehow found myself kissing him again, harder this time, ignoring the pain in my lip. What was going on with me? We needed to get out of here.

"What the hell happened?" he asked, sounding a little breathless.

"Not sure. Jellybean blames me for the police ransacking his club, but they were the ones telling me things I didn't know. Must've come here after questioning everyone today." I lurched to my feet and searched for a steady foothold so I could stagger over the side. "Talking to Trissa's co-workers was my only hope for a lead. They won't answer questions now."

Anwar tried again to stand up and clutched his ribs. "Maybe the cops searched the club because they learned something new. You could call and ask?"

"The less I hear from those assholes, the better. But we should get out of this garbage heap before that bartender comes out and tosses more on top of us. He'd probably enjoy that." Bracing myself on the solid steel wall, I reached down with one hand. "Let me help you stand. Try not to use your abs because your ribs might be cracked."

"Just bruised," he said confidently. "It feels exactly like that time I got injured sparring in judo. This kid gave me a flying kick to the chest, and I went down like a pancake." He lifted his arms but kept his torso stiff.

I dug my heels into a wet box that crumpled and sagged but allowed me to gain a stable enough footing to heave Anwar upward. He teetered for a second, then gripped the dumpster's side, panting from the pain.

"Think you can climb?" I asked.

He whimpered. "Do I have any other option?"

I clambered over the side and slid to the pavement, noting that my very impractical silver boots were now smeared with at least three unknown substances. I made a silent vow to never wear high heels again—it was much more sensible to stick to shoes I could run in. The expensive leather jacket was also probably ruined, not that I'd ever want to wear it again. It would remind me of Jellybean … Oh, who was I kidding? It was too pretty to throw out, if it could be cleaned.

With a lot of help and groaning, Anwar maneuvered himself up onto the edge of the dumpster and tumbled into my arms. We were like a couple of PIs in some silly detective story with the genders reversed, except this was our real lives. If this were a movie, then by the ending, Trissa and my mom would be safe at home, and Charlene's arm would be miraculously healed. And we'd all look great.

Anwar leaned against me for a few seconds. Our bodies fit together like pieces of a puzzle, and beneath the putrid odour of garbage, I could smell his hair pomade.

"This is so weird," I mumbled.

"Yes. But, uh, which part of this are you talking about?"

"Me and you," I admitted.

"That I want to be making out with someone who's covered in trash?"

I nodded in agreement. "And, well, Trissa's missing, you were melded with Kelli D until forty-eight hours ago, we've been friends forever, and you're obviously injured."

"I'm fine," he insisted hoarsely. "Come on, Michie, you have to know I've always wanted you."

I made an odd noise, somewhere between a squeak and a moan. "How could I have known that?"

"Everybody else knew. Trissa definitely did."

The words she'd said about how I should be thanking her returned to me and made me sad. I hadn't appreciated her.

I began to walk toward the quiet street behind the club, not wanting to risk seeing Cal out front. He'd seemed like a genuine human being, but he must have realized what was going to happen after he left us with Jellybean. A wave of hopelessness hit me when I glanced sideways at Anwar, who was moving like a robot whose joints needed to be oiled, and I had to stomp down my feelings. If I kept poking around, things might get even worse.

My purse was still miraculously around my neck. I took out my phone. It wasn't broken. I used a ride share app to call us a car, then helped Anwar to the end of the alley, propped him against a wall, and watched the tiny car on my screen edge closer to us. The fact that we had to listen to the muffled sound of bass thumping inside the club was like rubbing our faces in dirt.

"We should get you to urgent care," I said. "You hit your head."

"No way. I'm fine." Anwar felt the same way about doctors as I did about cops because of the way his mother had been treated during her breakdown, so I didn't waste energy trying to convince him.

"I'm sorry for dragging you into this—"

"Michie," he interrupted, "I want to find Trissa almost as much as you do."

I made a guilty face, acknowledging he was right. "Still, it's my fault Jellybean was furious."

"Because he thinks you snitched to the cops, when in fact they told you Trissa was dealing in the club and you denied it?"

I nodded. "Yeah. I really want to ask Cal more questions. He might know why Trissa was so worked up." I hesitated, then whispered, "Do you think she wanted to die?"

Anwar opened his mouth to respond, but our car pulled up before he could speak. We slid awkwardly into the back seat, and Anwar squeezed my hand comfortingly.

The driver made a face and opened the windows, but didn't ask any questions. That earned him a huge tip. My address was already plugged into his GPS, so he started rolling, muttering in Arabic into his wireless earbuds. We drove through downtown streets that were deserted, except for the occasional person stumbling along or sleeping under an overhang in case the rain started up.

"Want to stay over?" I asked Anwar.

He shook his head. "I need to check on my mother and take a hot shower, but I'll come over as soon as I wake up." He leaned against me so he could root in his pants pocket and pull out a couple rumpled bills. He tried to hand them to me and whispered, "Make sure to give the driver a tip. He's gonna have to disinfect his car after we get out."

I snickered. "Keep your money." I pushed his hand back. "The app is connected to my bank account, so I've already paid."

"Fine, but admit you didn't drag me out tonight," he insisted.

"I admit it," I lied.

He nodded and leaned back against the vinyl seat, closing his eyes. Every time we hit a small bump in the road or turned a corner sharply, he hissed in pain.

The drive home took ten minutes. When we pulled up in front of Anwar's place, I thanked the man, got out, and headed around to the curb so I could lever Anwar onto his feet. He was focused on not moving his core muscles, but his eyes lifted to meet mine. He looked exhausted, and I remembered that I had taken a nap, but he hadn't.

"If you came over," I said, grinning, "I'd even let you sleep."

He tucked a stray clump of my hair behind my ear and wrinkled his nose exaggeratedly. "You stink."

I laughed. "Can't smell it. I think my nose has adjusted."

"I really do need to check on my mother," said, and trudged up the walk to his building. After he'd unlocked the door and disappeared through the lobby, I turned and headed up the street, past the driveway where Nadia was killed, to my big old house. An image of Kelli D whipping her shoe at me came to mind, followed by Trissa saying that the girl didn't deserve my pity. God, I actually wanted Anwar in my bed tonight, despite everything. I couldn't help it if my hormones overrode common sense. I mean, we could have showered first. Together. Ugh, why was life so complicated?

In my room, I stripped off all my clothes, put them in a plastic bag and tied it shut, took my second steaming-hot shower of the day, slathered a topical antibiotic on my knee gash, pulled on fuzzy pyjamas with a blue whale screen-printed by Anwar on the pants, checked Tink and Tonk's food supply and water bottle, then collapsed into bed. I'd just pulled the covers up to my chin and started to breathe deeply when my phone rang. Only someone who desperately needed me would be calling at this hour. I snatched it off the table. "Mmph?"

"It's Cal, from the club," said a deep booming voice. "I heard what they did to you, and I'm so sorry."

How had he gotten my number? Oh, it would have been on my ID, which he'd scanned tonight. I had no doubt Jellybean's system kept track of every single patron. I plumped up my Jem pillow so I was partially upright and rubbed my bleary eyes. "Right. I'm sure you had no idea."

"Look, taking out the garbage is Jellybean's way of handling people he's angry at, but I had no idea he was going to do that. My buddy said he blames you for the police search this afternoon."

"Was your buddy one of the guys who tossed us in the dumpster?" I asked sarcastically. "I'd never rat someone out. Not even an evil person like Jellybean."

He didn't reply. "Yeah. He's pissed at me too, for telling you what happened that night with Trissa, but screw him. He's not going to fire me. And you and I need to talk."

"We *are* talking."

"Not on this phone. He pays for it."

I was hungry for information about Trissa, but I wouldn't survive a rematch with one of Jellybean's bouncers. "Why should I trust you?"

"Jellybean pays my salary, but he doesn't own me. That's why I'm stationed at the door instead of another place. He knows I'm good with following rules but a wuss about violence. I'll be at your place in fifteen minutes."

He hung up before I could ask how he knew where I lived. Right, my ID. Or maybe he'd been here before and knew Trissa better than I realized.

My knee and shoulder complained when I swung my legs out of bed and pulled on a massive sweater long enough to be a dress. I took two acetaminophens, made another mug of hot chocolate, shoved my feet into rubber boots, and headed out to the front porch. Heavy droplets of water rolled off the eaves and trees, forming puddles in our muddy yard.

I'd blocked out being slapped by Jellybean until my swollen lip touched the hot ceramic. Ouch. Sipping carefully from the other side of my mouth, I'd almost finished my drink by the time Cal's black Jeep jumped the curb out front. He killed the engine but left the headlamps on. I headed down to the sidewalk and stood in the bright light, swaying from tiredness. Either the rain was actually forming a rainbow as it passed through the beams, or I was still feeling residual effects from that pill I'd taken.

Cal was still wearing his black shirt with its logo of a pile of jelly beans, but he'd pulled on a black-silk bomber jacket over it. I'd forgotten how tall he was. I craned my neck to look at his face and, for some reason, that made me even crankier than I already was.

He ran his fingers through his damp brown hair. The unconscious action made him seem more vulnerable. He was genuinely worried. "I ... I think it might be my fault Trissa's missing."

"Why?"

Cal swallowed hard. "Trissa trusted me, and I liked her. She's fun. I kept an eye on her. Drove her home after her shifts because she told me someone was stalking her."

"What? Who?"

"No idea." He rubbed his face. "Look, I'm not sure if she was just saying that or there really was some guy hanging around, making her uncomfortable."

I nodded. Trissa wouldn't have been above lying to get free rides home.

"I just ... Trissa started taking pills to help her dance all night and—"

"What kind of pills?" I demanded.

"MDMA, I think. The dancers pop them at the beginning of their shifts." His eyes bounced away from me as if he couldn't stand to see my reaction, and he sighed heavily. "Jellybean knows but looks the other way. A couple months ago, she started providing it to the other girls. Some guys on the security team got them from her as well. I don't touch any of that stuff." He sniffed righteously. "My body's a temple. Anyway, I asked her where she was getting it, and she just laughed and told me it was a gift, so she was sharing the wealth. I warned her to be careful, but she complained about how hard it was to shake her ass all night long. I get it. I mean, the bar goes through a lot of energy drinks. Jellybean has a rule against dealing in his club, though, and I've seen what he does to people who break that rule."

My stomach turned. It wasn't difficult to imagine what Jellybean would have done to her if he'd found out. But Trissa wasn't high when we hung out together—except for when she smoked a little cannabis. I frowned, trying to reconcile what he was saying with the girl I knew.

Admittedly, I'd only gone to the club when she was dancing a couple of times in the summer.

"On Thursday, I caught her selling in the ladies' bathroom and threatened to tell Jellybean. I wouldn't have, because, well, you know. I wanted to scare her though. She was putting everyone at risk. If she sold to an undercover cop, they'd have shut down the club."

"So the cops were right about her dealing?" I asked, and as soon as I said the words, I knew they were probably true. Suddenly, I flashed back to the piles of new clothing and makeup in her room. I'd assumed it was all thrift store and BuyMart stuff, like mine, but I wasn't savvy about labels and brands, thanks to my mother being anti-everything big money, so I didn't really know how much clothes cost. Maybe that was where most of Trissa's money had gone?

"I'm pretty sure it was a new side hustle," said Cal. "Maybe someone was pressuring her to make money?"

My heart started racing. "Someone at the club?"

"I don't think so." Absentmindedly, he wiped a raindrop off the tip of his nose. "When I shut down her, uh, transaction, she burst into tears and begged me not to tell Jellybean. Said she was being forced to sell and even offered to give me a cut of her profits. I got the feeling the club job meant a lot to her, but that she'd be in serious trouble if she couldn't bring in regular money. I pretended to be a hard-ass and left. Next thing I knew, she was hanging from that cage. I seriously thought she'd jump. And now she's disappeared. It's been eating me up." He hung his head miserably. "I can't live with myself if Trissa's been hurt because of me."

His feelings seemed genuine, so I tried to reassure him. "This isn't your fault, Cal. It sounds like she was in trouble. Was the guy she left with there while she was in the cage?"

"Not sure. I was focused on her, not the crowd."

"I need to find him. Maybe he's her supplier. Or the stalker?"

Cal nodded. "Normally, I could check the security cam footage from that morning, but Jellybean cleared the system and limited employee access after the cops showed up."

"He's paranoid," I said, knowing that was an understatement.

Cal nodded and made me promise to keep him updated, then got back in his truck and roared off, leaving only the sound of his powerful engine.

I headed inside and texted Anwar what I'd just learned. Now we definitely needed to access Trissa's second phone. Hopefully he'd fallen asleep as soon as he got home and wouldn't get the note until morning. As I switched my phone to silent, I noticed an email from my bank had come in, telling me my account was in overdraft and I needed to make a payment immediately. Since there was almost a thousand dollars in there from my summer job running programs for kids at the community centre, I almost wrote it off as spam. I'd never received an email like that before, though, so I opened my banking app and discovered that paying for the ride home had triggered the email. Over the past few days, there'd been several withdrawals from machines that cleaned me out. What the hell? On top of everything, I'd been scammed somehow.

Thinking about it only made my head ache. I was exhausted and overwhelmed with worry and couldn't deal with this now. I promised myself I'd deal with it later.

CHAPTER 12

Planting Clues for Misdirection

I smelled coffee and heard a mug plunk down on my bedside table. Mom said good morning and perched on the edge of my mattress. She started to rub my back over the comforter.

My eyes flew open. I sprang into a sitting position, grabbed her, and hugged her so hard she begged me to let go so she could breathe. "You're home!"

Her response was to wrap her arms around me, pull me against her again, and rock me gently from side to side, like I was a baby. She hummed a few lines of Ella Fitzgerald's "Summertime," which is what she sang when I was sick or sad. My grandma used to sing it to her when she was little. Tears sprung to my eyes. I wished we could stay like this forever. It was safe here.

"Franklyn was a rock star," she told me. "You should have seen him. He convinced the cops to release me this morning, without a bail hearing, and offered to be my surety. That means he's going to live here again for a few months. I hope you're okay with that? He's in the kitchen now, making breakfast."

I had absolutely no problem with Franklyn being around more. In fact, I wished he and Mom would get back together permanently. He had a calming effect on her and refused to let her do stupid things, like sell her medicinal cannabis. "What's a surety?"

"He, uh, has to make sure I follow the bail restrictions and accompany me when I leave the house. I'm on house arrest until my court appearance next month, which means being squeaky clean. Franklyn's hopeful he can get the charges dropped altogether, though. I mean, it doesn't look good arresting the auntie of a girl who's gone missing."

Her curly brown hair was in a high ponytail that bobbed around— she was still an eighties girl at heart—and she'd made an effort by putting on mascara and eyeliner. She tugged on a lock of hair, one of her nervous habits. "I guess in the meantime I'm stuck at home and need to be more like my daughter. Straight edge."

I flashed back to swallowing that unidentified pill, and a tiny pang of guilt prickled in my gut, followed quickly by a small stab of irritation. Most teenage daughters didn't need to be role models for their mothers. It was supposed to be the other way around. She loved me and kept a roof over my head, and we were all going through a lot, but my best friend was missing and I couldn't fall apart even around my mother, because she was in a worse situation than me. Story of my life.

I pulled away and took a sip of coffee, concentrated on how good it smelled and tasted, and eventually said, "Thank god Franklyn's around to deal with legal issues."

"Tell me about it. The po-po were only holding me because they hoped I could give them information about Charlene and Trissa's home situation. Bullshit. That woman detective threatened me with jail time if I didn't tell her what happened."

"You mean they wanted you to lie and say Trissa ran away from home?"

She made a sour face. "Yep. They've already decided she's not really in trouble. All cops are bastards—isn't that what kids say these days?"

I nodded. The thought of the police not even searching for Trissa was so infuriating that tears stung my eyes for the second time in ten minutes. I couldn't handle this drama right now. "Ma, do you ... think Trissa is ..." My mouth wouldn't form the word *dead*.

"Oh, sweetie." Mom squeezed her eyes shut for a second, like she was praying. "I hope Trissa's safe and comes home to us soon. I don't know what's going on or where she might be, but I do know Charlene raised her to be tough and to think for herself."

"Who cares if she's tough!" I cried. "She's exactly the Strangler's type. And his last victim disappeared from right by Club Jelly. That girl was the same age as Trissa and had—"

Mom hugged me again, stopping me from going too far down that path. "I know you're scared. Me too. But Trissa isn't Nadia, okay?"

I sniffled and nestled into her arms. She already smelled like weed, which meant she'd been home long enough to smoke. "What time is it?"

"After ten. You must have been exhausted, honey. You didn't even hear us come in. I wanted to let you sleep, but I just heard from—" She froze and tipped my face toward the light coming in my window. "Is that a fat lip?"

Making up a story that wouldn't scare her involved more brain power than I currently had, so I just told the truth. "Anwar and I went to Trissa's club because I thought somebody might know what happened to her, but the police had just searched the place, and the owner took out his frustration on us."

"He hit you?" She leapt to her feet and put her hands on her hips. "That asshole! Who does he think he is? I'm going to kill him!"

"Ma, chill out. He's the size of a tank, and you can't leave the house without your surety. Trust me, Franklyn's not going to let you anywhere near that club. Jellybean pays a bunch of buff men on steroids to be his private security force."

"What kind of name is Jellybean?" she scoffed. "Doesn't sound all that scary with a name like that."

I ignored her. "I'm okay, all right? It doesn't even hurt." I poked my lip to show her but didn't get up from under the covers. No way was I going to let her see my knee and my shoulder. Or the shape Anwar was in. I'd have to meet him at the park around the corner instead of letting him come here. Everything Cal had told me last night came rushing back into my brain. I felt like I would explode if I didn't talk about it all with someone, but it couldn't be Mom. She didn't need another reason to get in trouble with the police.

"We'll talk more about this later," she said. "All I've eaten since yesterday is two stale processed-cheese sandwiches and sugary grape juice."

I shuddered at the thought of my mother languishing in a cell like the ones I'd see on TV shows, getting fed cheese sandwiches through the bars. Oh hell, at least it was better than a dumpster. "I'm just glad you're home. I—I couldn't handle losing you and Trissa right now." To my surprise, tears filled my eyes again, and this time they spilled down my cheeks.

"I'm not going anywhere," she said, and patted my hair.

When I eventually rubbed my eyes and looked up, Franklyn was standing behind her, looking concerned. His tight black curls were shot through with grey and he was wearing a suit. "Rachel won't be giving them any reason to haul her back in there. Believe you me. I'll keep an eye on your mother from now on."

"That's right," piped up Mom, with false cheeriness. "Those detectives will get so bored of how squeaky clean I am, they'll have to do their actual jobs and find Trissa."

Franklyn's expression tightened. "Arresting you and hurting Charlene is symptomatic of all that's wrong with the police force in this city. It's one of the reasons white men like the West End Strangler have been able to get away their ugly deeds."

Mom nodded vehemently. I recognized the look on her face—she was gearing up for a lecture. "We train the police to be paramilitary forces who treat people as if they're guilty until proven innocent—especially the poor, people of colour, and those of us who deal with disabling health issues."

She was right about all of it. Back when Nadia was killed, the first homicide detectives who'd shown up had assumed Amina couldn't speak any English and made openly racist comments about Arabs within earshot. Even if I hadn't been raised by my mother and Charlene, seeing the way the police treated people in this area would have made me distrust them.

"They know I have too much to lose, Michie," Mom continued, "so I will play by their rules. Jump when they tell me to jump. I should be out there hunting for Trissa, but instead I'm going to be stuck at home twiddling my thumbs for the next two months."

"I'll come over right after work," promised Franklyn. All of us knew he worked twelve-hour days running the local Community Legal Aid Centre. "Now, both of you should come eat the breakfast I made," he said firmly. "The eggs are getting cold."

Mom stood up. "And can we talk about Anwar? You're friends again."

"How do you know?" So awkward.

"I have my sources. Doesn't he have a girlfriend?"

"They broke up."

She grinned. "Ha! I knew it. I saw how close you two were sitting at the station."

I scowled at her. "I'm allowed to be friends with guys. You're supposed to be a badass feminist."

She gave me a look that said I couldn't distract her. "The two of you have always been very close, and you've been through so much together. Tragedy has a way of showing you what matters. You know, I've always wished I was there for Amina the way you were for Anwar, but she shut me out after Nadia died. We used to be almost as close as I am with Char."

"I know that." I reached for the mug of coffee on my bedside table and took another sip. The warmth cleared my head a little. I couldn't get out of bed until she left, but as long as there was something in my mouth, she couldn't expect me to speak. Plus, my head was now filled with memories of Amina and Anwar hanging out with the four of us.

"I think it's probably too late to save that friendship." Mom sighed and rubbed her face.

"You could invite her over. It's not like you have anything else to do for the next month."

"True." She headed for the bedroom door. "Oh, I almost forgot what I wanted to say earlier. Put some concealer on that bruise. Those detectives are on their way over. I have no idea why, but I figured you'd want to be dressed."

"What I want is to never see them again. Get rid of your mushrooms! And the extra pot plants in the basement."

"Franklyn flushed the shrooms down the toilet as soon as we got home. The plants are a bigger job—that's what I'm doing for the rest of the day."

As soon as Mom was gone, I tossed off my comforter. I needed to do something about Trissa's drugs, which were still in the guinea pig cage. I pulled on skinny jeans, fluffy rainbow socks, and a black off-the-shoulder shirt with lacing up the sides. Maybe I should tell Mom and Franklyn about Trissa's second phone and the fake diary filled with drugs. But if I did and Trissa came home, she'd be in so much trouble. No. Flushing them and pretending I knew nothing was the best option at this point.

Before heading to the kitchen for a refill of coffee and some food, I checked my phone and discovered that Anwar was already awake. He said he'd meet me at eleven in the park. In order to work his hacker magic, he needed me to find something that had only Trissa's fingerprints on it. No problem. He finished his message with a heart emoji. It gave me a little thrill.

I pulled a heavy shirt with strawberries all over it over my outfit. It was September, after all, and I liked the way the berries matched my lip gloss. Then I shoved Trissa's pills into my canvas bag and hurried to the bathroom to flush them. Our sewage system was getting a lot of action this morning.

*

With my stomach full and way too much caffeine in my bloodstream, I filled a Thermos with hot chocolate, used the leftover eggs to make a quick breakfast sandwich for Anwar, added it to my satchel along with my phone and Trissa's burner, and dropped the bag on the ground outside my bedroom window. I wanted to be ready to flee in case the detectives arrived while I was upstairs. I dropped two small chunks of cantaloupe into the guinea pig cage along with a handful of pellets and headed upstairs.

Franklyn was in Charlene and Trissa's kitchen, boiling water for tea. Mom must have gone to bed for a while. Charlene was slumped over the dining room table, using her good arm to toss back shots from a bottle of alcohol—not the same one she'd had last night. She looked even worse than the last time I'd seen her—her face was chalky, and there were big dark circles under her eyes—but at least she'd changed her clothes.

"I'm going to tidy up Trissa's room a little more," I told them. "I wanted to say thanks for everything, Franklyn. What you did for my mom …" My voice cracked. "I'm worried about her."

"Of course, Michelle," he said in his lilting Grenadian accent, his voice warm and comforting. "Your mother means the world to me. As do you. I was in court yesterday, or I would have gotten your message sooner. I only wish I could have been here when the police arrived so we could have avoided the whole mess."

Another wave of emotion swept over me like a tidal wave. My chest ached, and I felt dizzy. My eyes leaked. I blinked furiously, trying to keep it all from bubbling out.

He reached out to give me a hug, and I launched myself into his arms. After Mom and Charlene, Franklyn gave the best hugs in the world. He always smelled like the lemon cough candies he was always crunching. Ugh. The gross cookies Anwar was eating last night had ruined that artificial lemon smell for me. I took a couple steps back to get out of smell range.

"Charlene's right on the edge," I said. "We need to watch out for her and Mom."

"Understood."

I nodded gratefully. There was no need to explain anything else. Franklyn knew what it meant to fall apart. When he came to Canada a decade ago, he'd left everything behind, discovered the law degree he'd worked so hard to get was useless, and had to start his life over. We became his first Canadian family by accident when he rented a room from my mom on the recommendation of a mutual friend. I don't remember much—I was only six—but Mom had a photo of him from that first day, carrying his suitcase, a leather briefcase, and wearing his only suit. She still kept it on her dresser.

Slowly their relationship changed from landlady and tenant to lovers. It was weird at first, because Mom never brought men home. I mean, she didn't really trust them. Even had a T-shirt that said, "A woman needs a man like a fish needs a bicycle." Our house had only included women and girls up until the point Franklyn moved in.

Gradually, they spent more and more time together. They argued about everything from politics to what to make for dinner to Mom's cannabis use. He was just as radical as her about everything except intoxicants. Things hadn't always gone smoothly between them, but even when he and Mom were "off," he still showed up for holidays and birthdays. They were each other's preferred sparring partners.

I knew Franklyn loved Mom. She was the one who didn't want to compromise—the reason their relationship ran hot and cold. I rested my hand on top of his briefly, then grabbed a rag and a bottle of cleaning solution and ran up the stairs to Trissa's room, wondering whether his staying here for a couple months would switch their relationship "on" again. He was good for both of us.

Trissa's room was still a disaster. I'd already known that but had hoped that somehow it wouldn't look as bad as it had yesterday. I unstuck a half-eaten green lollipop from her wooden dresser and stuck it in my mouth. The sour apple flavour might help me focus. Cleaning up when I had no idea if she was even alive was beyond depressing.

No. I'd know if she were dead, I told myself firmly. I'd feel it in my heart. My bones. We were connected. Sisters. Closer than sisters. Chosen sisters.

Maybe she'd left her bag in the alley on purpose, to make it look like she'd disappeared? No, that didn't make any sense. She'd never have just ditched two thousand dollars, her phone, and her passport. I tamped down rising terror. For my own sanity and that of people I loved, I needed to find answers to all my questions.

Making the bed was a manageable first thing to do, and it gave me a place to fold clothing. I shook out a tiny tank dress that probably barely covered Trissa's ass and took a photo of the label: IcePink XXXtra.

There were empty hangers in the closet, so I hung it up along with a handful of fancy tank tops and shirts. I folded three pairs of hot pants and a couple miniskirts and shoved them in a drawer. Their labels all said things like Pretty Little Thing and Glama. If it didn't say Prada or Gucci, I was clueless. But I snapped photos and looked up the brands online. Some of them were outrageously expensive. That pink sweater with rhinestones she'd been wearing on Thursday evening cost several hundred. I tossed it on a pile of dirty laundry. The fact that it was up here meant that she did stop by after I'd fallen asleep.

Trissa had a wardrobe filled with pricey clothes that she didn't care about. Anwar usually registered changes like that in other people, but he'd been so busy with Kelli D the past few months that perhaps he hadn't been paying attention to Trissa. I sent him a text asking if he'd noticed anything different about her clothes lately and when she'd started buying expensive stuff. He didn't reply right away.

I shot off a similar note to Anton. He was always bragging about how much his clothes cost. A couple weeks ago, he'd shown off a navy-blue four-hundred-dollar hoodie that, to my eye, looked no better than one I'd picked up for $5.99 at BuyMart. Anton wrote me back right away to say that Trissa's bling had started appearing a few months ago. He figured she had more cash because she was dancing.

Once I got all her clothes hung up and put away, I poked around in the overflowing waste bin. Most of it was wrappers for chips and candy, clothing store bags, tags from clothes, and packaging for makeup.

Her computer's screen saver photos were still cycling. I paused to watch a series taken at the cabin on Lake Simcoe that our moms used to rent every summer. There was a great one of me jumping off the end of the dock into the lake. Then Nadia, her hair in two lumpy pigtails, holding a baby snapping turtle she'd found half-hidden in the reeds along the shoreline. Mom and Charlene in the cabin kitchen, making dinner. All of us feasting on corn and burgers at a picnic table. Anwar was there too. He looked so young. The only one missing was Amina. She'd probably had to work, which meant it was Nadia's last summer alive.

The series ended. An image of Anton in the park around the corner popped up. He was leaning on Timbit's shoulder and seemed to be whispering something in the younger boy's ear while he stared right at the photographer with his heavy-lidded expression. His size made Timbit appear even smaller than he actually was. Meanwhile, Timbit was looking off to one side, as if he were confused by whatever Anton was saying. What had Anton been saying to Timbit, I wondered?

I shut off Trissa's computer. It hurt me to look at these photos. Nadia was gone, and Trissa might be gone too. There was no one here to watch the screen saver anyway.

Cal's description of the guy who'd been at the club with Trissa on Thursday night actually sounded like Anton, I realized. He'd put on weight recently, so he could be described as "kinda big." Of course, so could lots of other people. I was pretty sure I'd never seen Trissa with any other men of that body type, though there were several working at the club. Anton and Trissa were in touch fairly often, though. I went on social media and peered closely at some pictures of him. Brown hair, menacing. He might be the one who'd picked her up.

I downloaded a picture of Anton and sent it to Cal, asking whether this was the guy Trissa had left with. Cal was probably still asleep at this hour. If Mom hadn't woken me up, I'd still have been passed out. I considered calling Cal because I really wanted to know, but there was a small chance he was already at work with Jellybean, so I decided to wait for a response. Then I remembered I had contact info for Mr. Salvatore Booger, so I texted him to ask whether Trissa had been with anyone on the subway.

I tossed my phone onto Trissa's dressing table and swept empty makeup packaging into the recycling bin on the floor. The table was littered with new eyeshadow palettes, tubes of cream, and bottles of serum. How could I not have realized she'd been spending more money recently? I sighed and started to snap the lids eyeliner pencils and lipstick tubes back on.

It was hard not to compare this assortment with my own minimal collection of BuyMart's in-house brand, which was probably made from toxic chemicals that would give me cancer. Using my phone calculator, I added up a rough estimate of how much all this stuff cost. There was nearly five hundred dollars' worth of cosmetics on the table, all of it either still unopened or used only once. I dabbed a little concealer on my bruised face, but it was the wrong colour, so I tried to wipe it off.

Using a pair of eyebrow tweezers, I picked up a tube of neon-blue mascara that looked like it had just been removed from the slim cardboard box next to it. I slid it back into the box and slipped the box into my pocket. This container would have only her fingerprints on it, right? Unless an employee had packaged it by hand. Uncertain, I also pocketed a barely used tube of lip gloss. Trissa probably wouldn't have shared it with anyone. Other than me, of course. And I hadn't been up here recently.

Downstairs, the doorbell played out "Rudolph," which meant the police had arrived. I quickly searched through Trissa's garbage again to make sure I hadn't missed anything and noticed a glossy flyer that looked like it had been torn off a pole. It was a casting call for female dancers to audition for a new reality show in Hollywood. The audition date was this week, and it promised great pay and a chance to make it big.

When Trissa was younger, she dreamt of being on *Dancing with the Stars* or in a Broadway musical. Maybe she wanted to get out of the club scene. I folded up the flyer, slid it in my pocket, and tied a knot in the bin liner. The room looked much better than when I'd gotten here, but it wasn't clean by anyone's standards.

The detectives were coming up to the second floor as I descended. I smiled as innocently as possible, plastering my face with the expression that worked on my homeroom teacher whenever I was late, and flattened myself against the wall so they could squeeze past.

Lorenzo frowned suspiciously. "What happened to your face?"

"I tripped," I said, cursing inwardly. "Clumsy me."

The lines on Lorenzo's forehead deepened. She peered at the bag in my hand. "What've you got there?"

I glanced down at the bin liner in my hand. "Trissa's garbage. I just cleaned up her room."

Her eyes narrowed. "That's an active crime scene."

"Why?"

She stuck out her hand. "Hand it over."

I relinquished the bag and held up my hands as if to say *don't shoot*. As far as I knew, there was nothing relevant in there, and there was no way she'd be suspicious about what I was doing with a couple tubes of makeup.

She blocked the stairs and pawed through the garbage. Ew. After a moment, she shoved the bag back at me. "We might have more questions for you. Don't go anywhere."

"I won't," I promised, even though there was no way in hell I was going to sit around waiting around for them to get bored and intimidate me or haul me back down to the station.

Salvatore replied to tell me Trissa was alone on the subway, which meant he didn't have any more information.

I pawed through the pile of jackets in the lobby—my waterproof teal one was definitely not here—grabbed Mom's black leather jacket, which she said reminded her of Cyndi Lauper, shoved my arms into the sleeves, and zipped it up. Then I hurried into my bedroom, shut the door behind me, and followed my satchel out the busted window screen.

Making Sense of the Nonsensical

The small park around the corner was deserted, not a huge surprise on a rainy day at this time of year. Anwar was the only person in sight. He was slumped against a wall of the small wooden playhouse—the only sheltered spot—drawing in his sketchbook. I winced at the sight of his blackened eye as I clambered up the rope ladder. Somehow, the bruise made him look even hotter than usual.

"With that jacket and your bruised face, you're a badass," he said, as I climbed up to join him. The look he gave me made heat rise from low in my abdomen to my cheeks.

"Right?" I said. "Tell that to my mom, though."

He winced. "Is she okay?"

I shrugged. "She will be. How's Amina?"

He whistled a low note, as if to say *not good*. "Her psychiatrist left a message on my phone telling me to keep the home as calm and non-stressful as possible."

That didn't sound like appropriate advice, considering Anwar was not responsible for his mother's mental health, but I knew he'd do anything to make sure she didn't backslide. Both of us sometimes had to act like the parents. Maybe that was why we understood each other so well. I crouched down and ran a finger over his black eye. "Speaking of bruises ... does this hurt?"

He snorted. "Only when somebody pokes it."

"Sorry," I said, laughing, and plunked myself down cross-legged on the cold wooden floor. If I wanted to stop picturing him naked in my bed, I'd have to focus on something else. Like the large grey spider industriously spinning a web in a corner of the playhouse roof.

"What do the cops want this time?" he asked.

"Dunno. Probably still trying to pin Trissa's disappearance on Charlene."

Anwar huffed angrily, then surprised me by reaching over, wincing at the pain in his ribs, and gently cupping my cheek. He turned my face so I was looking at him, and the heat in my cheeks and abdomen became a bonfire. I moved forward to brush my lips over his, careful to avoid the spot where my mouth was swollen. He sucked in a breath and deepened the kiss.

If my swollen lip hurt, I didn't notice. Instead, I found myself straddling his legs and exploring his mouth with my tongue. He tasted so good. My hands moved through his hair. His arms were around me. He rubbed my arms, my back, my ass. God, he smelled amazing. I felt drunk on his scent. I reached between us for his zipper, but he pulled my hand away, laced his fingers through mine, and stopped me from trying to rub him.

"Too fast," he whispered.

I groaned and breathed into his ear, "I want you so much."

"I want you too." His voice was thick with lust, but he didn't let go of my hand. "You have no idea how long I've waited for this—for you to give me a chance—but we can't do this. Not in a playground where anyone could walk past."

"Who cares where we do it," I said.

"Me," he responded. "You've been my best friend for a decade. We can't fuck this up by rushing. We need to talk about what's going on between us, and our first time should happen somewhere where we can go slow."

I didn't want this to stop, and I didn't care where we had sex, but I wasn't even sure whether he and Kelli D were definitely finished, and if we did this and then he went back to her, we could never return to just being friends. Disappointed, I removed myself from his lap.

I noticed his knapsack was open on the other side of him. Sticking out of the pocket was an old pill bottle with a couple of white tablets at the bottom. I scooped up the bottle to read the label. Codeine. These were left over from when he'd broken his wrist a couple summers ago. "If you're in that much pain, we can crack Trissa's phone later. You should see a doctor."

"Not going to happen, but I do know something what would make my ribs feel better." He looked almost shy as he patted the spot right next to him.

I hesitated, uncertain I would be able to concentrate on anything other than sex, but when he slung an arm around my shoulder and pulled me to his side, I allowed it. Electricity pulsed through my body, until the image of perfect Kelli D pressed up against him like this in the empty condo came to mind. I reluctantly pulled myself away enough to sit up straight, admitting to myself that we had been moving too fast.

"So, have you heard from Kelli D again?" I asked, hoping the question was coming across as more casual than I felt.

He scowled. "Not unless you count a text telling me to watch her latest video."

My eyebrows shot up and I stifled a giggle as I removed the Thermos of hot chocolate and the breakfast sandwich from my bag. "The one about cheaters?"

"No. She posted a new one this morning." He gratefully accepted the sandwich and immediately took a huge bite. After he'd chewed and swallowed, he added, "Check it out so you can see exactly how much she's suffering right now."

Against my better judgment, I pulled up her channel on my phone and hit Play on the latest video. Red was getting his makeup done and staring at Kelli D's chest like the sun shone from inside her bra. "What? She's with Red!"

Mouth full of sandwich, Anwar nodded in agreement.

"That green eyeshadow really doesn't go with his orange hair."

Anwar mumbled something that sounded like "truth."

I peered at him and raised an eyebrow. "You, on the other hand, looked hot in her makeup. And, yes, I did watch that video with Trissa."

"Thanks, I think?" He picked up the Thermos, opened the lid, and smelled the hot cocoa. A blissful expression spread across his face as he filled the small plastic lid that doubled as a mug. "Anyway, as you can see, she's not exactly mourning the loss of our relationship. It took her exactly two days to find a replacement."

"She might be doing this to make you jealous," I suggested. "How do you feel about the Red development?"

"Fine," was all he said.

"She's way hotter than me."

"No, she isn't. Besides, there's no other girl I'd like to play detective—and other things—with." He wiggled his eyebrows. "We fit, Michie. It's always been that way." His gaze dropped to my mouth, and he raised one eyebrow meaningfully.

I brought my face within inches of his, licked a breadcrumb off his top lip, then pretended to chew it exaggeratedly.

He cracked up.

"You know, my mother told me this morning that she wishes she made more of an effort to stay close to Amina."

Anwar smiled sadly. "I doubt it would have worked."

"I suggested she reach out and invite your mom over to hang out or something."

"I'm not sure she'll accept, but it might cheer her up if she does." He brushed some more crumbs off his jeans. "I've missed you, Michie. This isn't the time to get all mushy, but it's such a relief to be with someone who doesn't expect me to pretend everything's normal at home."

"Same."

We used to sleep beside each other without thinking twice, but this kind of closeness was different. Everything had changed when Trissa dared us to kiss. I stared at his nose—prominent and straight. Same full lips as ever. Same brown skin and wavy black hair. How would he react if I leaned over and kissed him again? He'd probably kiss me back. These thoughts led me to wishing Trissa was around so I could talk to her about what was going on with him.

"How are you planning to unlock the phone?" I asked, wrenching my thoughts back to safer territory.

"Magic. Well, science magic." He had to remove his arm from my shoulders to get a bunch of materials from his backpack: latex gloves, transparent Scotch tape, a tube of rubber cement, a sheet of cloudy plastic Mylar, and a paintbrush with soft bristles. He lined up the items in a row on the ground, being super careful not to jolt his ribs. The last items he removed were a container of baby powder, a white plate, and pair of sharp nail scissors.

"You learned all this from *Girl's Guide*?" I asked.

"I also looked it up on the internet."

I carefully used the bottom of my shirt to remove the box of bright-blue mascara from my pocket, followed by the tube of lip gloss. "I'm hoping one of these will work. They're brand new, and I don't think anyone other than Trissa's touched them. I used a pair of tweezers to slide the mascara back into its original box."

He grinned. "Still think you're Harriet the Spy, huh?"

"I have to admit, when I was in Trissa's room I was thinking about Chapter 14: Planting Clues for Misdirection: 'A criminal mistress-mind knows how to transform a crime scene into a story that will feed police an easy resolution and lead investigators anywhere other than toward her.'"

Anwar pulled on the latex gloves, balanced the plate on his thigh, removed the mascara from its package, and gently blew some fine talcum powder onto the dark tube. He held it up and slowly rotated it. Satisfied it was completely coated, he put it aside and squeezed a bunch of rubber cement onto his sheet of Mylar, spreading it in a fine layer. He counted to sixty and rolled the tube across the glue so the powder was now stuck to the layer of rubber cement.

"We have to wait a couple more minutes for the glue to dry so I can peel it off."

"Cool!" I exclaimed. If I'd had any doubt that this was the boy for me, it disappeared while I watched him act like a true detective.

He helped himself to more hot chocolate before peeling the dried rubber cement off the Mylar and identifying what looked like complete fingerprints. He cut out fingertip-sized ovals, licked his thumb, pressed it to the back of one of the glue prints, and held it against the phone's fingerprint scanner. Nothing happened. I tried using a second print on my thumb, then I tried a third one. At which point the phone locked us out for sixty seconds.

"Maybe Lacey Milan's advice isn't always correct," I admitted.

He sighed. "I'm not sure what's wrong. This worked before."

"You've broken into Trissa's phone in the past?"

"No, Red's. He kept bragging about all the girls he was flirting with on BlitzChat, so I unlocked his phone, deleted all the data on his fitness app, and sent the girls he was texting a photo of some carrot-coloured fuzz. Every single one of them immediately blocked him."

My eyes widened. "Ouch. I'm pretty sure the girls didn't appreciate getting a—"

"Oh, no. I wouldn't do that." He rubbed his hands and cackled gleefully. "It was actually a close-up of golden retriever fur. You know Larry, the dog who lives in the apartment next to us? Anyway, Red never figured out who burned him."

Once the phone allowed us to try again, I decided to give good old-fashioned guesswork a shot and entered a few variations of Trissa's name changed to numbers, then her birthday, Charlene's name and birthday, even our home address. The phone kept temporarily freezing me out after every third entry. Super annoying. I tried variations of the club's name and the names of friends. Nothing worked. I was about to give up when I thought of the guinea pigs. I tried *tinktonk*—nope. Then I entered their names with the vowels converted into numbers: *t1nkt0nk*. Finally, the phone clicked open to display the generic home screen preloaded by the manufacturer.

I hooted and waved the phone in Anwar's face. "Check this out!"

"Not bad, Watson," he admitted.

"We both know I'm the Sherlock Holmes in this situation."

"As if."

For some reason, now that Trissa's mysterious second phone was open, I didn't want to poke around. She'd kept it locked and hidden for a reason, and I hated myself for invading her privacy. Then again, Lacey Milan would definitely have advised me to keep going. I needed to find my friend. And if our roles were reversed, I was positive Trissa would have had no problem doing the same thing. She used to unlock my tablet to play games and use up all my premium coins. She also read my diary and then picked fights with me over things I'd never told her. One time, I wrote about how irritating it was that she'd gone full-on diva as soon as we got into high school, especially when boys were around. She was pissed, but I refused to apologize since it served her right. She still didn't talk to me for weeks and never apologized either.

Anwar had clearly noticed my hesitation. He was peering intently at me and I had the eerie feeling he knew what was going through my head.

"I don't know if I can do this," I confessed.

He nodded. "Okay, then I will. There could be information on the phone about who she was with when she left the club. What if she sold pills to the wrong person or—"

"You're right, I know you're right." I picked up the phone. Since it had turned off, I had to unlock it again. I took a deep breath, and opened the single folder on the home screen. It contained videos that were all an hour long and created three times a week—Monday, Wednesday, and Thursday, from one to two in the afternoon—over the past two months. So that answered the question of when she'd started skipping school. She wouldn't have been able to record long videos like that in class.

I showed Anwar and started up the most recent video, dated Thursday, the last day we'd both seen her. It began with a close-up of her face. Seeing her very much alive, wearing the same pink sweater she'd had on at the condo, took my breath away and made my heart thump.

She was in her bedroom, making sure the camera was angled properly to catch her bed. Satisfied, she got back up, sat down seductively, and addressed the viewer. "You paid for fun, but are you sure you're ready for this?" She tugged one shoulder of her sweater down to expose her bra—the one she'd been wearing at the condo—then slid onto her hands and knees, arched her back like a cat, and pushed her ass up, slowly hiking her skirt up to show off the same G-string she'd flashed me that night.

Anwar tapped the screen to pause the video. "I'm not sure I want to watch this. She's like a sister or ... a cousin."

"We need to know what's going on," I said, but I tilted the phone away from him before playing a random video from a few weeks earlier. Same set-up, different outfit. I dragged the scrubber to the middle and was rewarded with a full-frontal shot. I jumped to the last minute and found her faking the mother of all orgasms, her bed littered with sex toys. "So she was working as a cam girl. Between dancing at night and recording these videos, she can't have been going to school very often."

"Didn't you head out together every morning?"

"She stopped meeting me a few months ago. Right around when she started making these videos."

"I'm going to text Timbit to see if he's seen her at lunch lately," Anwar said, taking out his own phone.

A memory of my mom and Charlene dressed up to go to the annual SlutWalk march came to mind. They went together every year, always in their sluttiest outfits—tight miniskirts and bras—carrying home-made placards that said "slutty and proud" and "no clothes doesn't equal consent." On their reverse side, the signs read, "end rape culture." This summer, Trissa and I went with them. She wrote "sex workers have rights" across her stomach with black marker and added a statistic about violence against them beneath the words. I never would have guessed that she was talking about herself.

Anwar's phone buzzed. "Timbit hasn't seen her at school for a few months," he reported. "They used to hang out at lunch and sometimes ride the bus home together, but not recently."

Curious, I checked her settings and found she didn't have a data plan, which meant she only used this phone on Wi-Fi or with a pay-as-you-go card. Her browser history revealed she'd only accessed three sites, but she'd done that a lot. Like dozens of times, on some days. One of the sites was an anonymous hub for uploading videos, the second was some kind of generic email server, and the third was an airline. None of the password guesses I'd tried earlier worked for these sites.

The only other way she'd used the phone was to respond to a few dozen text messages from numbers with no saved contact information. None of the numbers were familiar, so I tilted the screen back toward Anwar. "Recognize any of these?"

He scrolled through, then shook his head. "Nope. I think they're orders. She's giving them prices and amounts and times to meet up in the bathroom."

"Looks like business picked up recently." Here in my hand was definitive evidence that she'd been selling pills at the club. Fear for Trissa made my scalp prickle. "The police were right after all. They just got some of the details wrong. Maybe the person supplying her was responsible for her disappearance?"

Anwar's face was greyish. He was scared too. "Or maybe someone else wanted her out of the way so they could take over the job?"

In Lacey Milan's introduction to *Girls' Guide*, she wrote about how she'd gotten started in her life of crime by taking over her dead husband's car parts resale company and paying some boys to strip cars and bring her cheap parts. Lacey communicated with them via a burner phone.

"I'm going to call one of these numbers," I said.

"Maybe try the latest," suggested Anwar, pointing at the top number. "They messaged today and obviously didn't get a reply."

I tapped on it and hit Call. My heart skipped a beat when a young woman picked up before the second ring. "Hello?"

"Uh, hey. I'm calling about your order. Who am I talking to?"

She paused. "Why do you need my name?"

Shit. She sounded suspicious. "Are you still looking for four unicorns?"

"Yes."

"Meet me in the ladies' at eleven-thirty. Third stall will be shut, but not locked. I'll wear a pink miniskirt. I've got curly red hair."

"I know what you look like. I've bought from you before. That bartender introduced us."

"Taytay, right. Bring cash." I hung up before she could ask how much money it would be because I had no clue what to tell her.

"You're a natural," teased Anwar.

I pinched his arm. "That didn't give us much information."

"I mean, we know she was meeting customers in the club's bathroom and that someone named Lily is becoming a regular. We also found out that the bartender who has a hate-on for you was referring people to her. He might have been getting a cut." He scanned the older messages, then stopped suddenly, pulled out his own phone, and compared a number. "This is Anton's cell."

The thread had only two messages, dated five days ago: "Bought my ticket. One-way. United 7651 to LAX."

"LAX is the code for Los Angeles airport." I used my own phone to look up that flight number and discovered that it left later this evening. I couldn't imagine a version of my life where Trissa wasn't here, but it seemed as if she'd been planning to take off to LA. Why hadn't she confided in me about her plans? I remembered the paper advertising for dancers I'd found in her bedroom wastebasket. I took it out of my pocket and handed it to him. "I think she was planning to audition for this dance competition or reality show thing. I found the flyer in her room. But why was she telling Anton about the ticket?"

He unfolded the sheet and read it. "Maybe he was going too."

"A trip would explain why she needed to make so much money, and why she packed a bag, but why would she abandon it in the alley behind the club?"

"No clue," he said.

We sat there for a couple minutes, processing what we'd just discovered. He shifted closer and rested a hand on my thigh. Warmth seeped through my pants in a reassuring way. The rest of my body was cold.

"The message said the ticket was one-way," I muttered.

"I guess she was really optimistic about that audition."

"I guess." Trissa was resourceful, I told myself. She'd do fine in LA. More than fine. She'd love it. I'd never been there, but I imagined the place was all beaches and convertibles and movie stars drinking green juice and eating salads.

"Maybe she's still planning to catch the flight," I suggested. "How could she—" I stopped. "Wait. The police told me Trissa's passport was in the bag they found outside the club. I found her birth certificate in her room. She can't leave the country without ID."

"Um, she might be able to use a driver's licence or her health card."

My phone rang, startling both of us. It was Cal calling back about the photo of Anton I'd sent. I put the call on speaker so Anwar could hear.

"Who is that guy in the picture?" Cal demanded, not bothering to say hello.

"Someone from the neighbourhood. A friend of Trissa's."

"That's the guy who picked her up. I got a bad vibe from him."

"He's a variety of slime mould," I said, warming up a little to Cal. He seemed like a decent enough person, despite his job. At least he seemed to have a conscience. "Cal, did you know Trissa was making videos?"

"What kind of videos?"

"Web porn—that kind."

He hesitated. "Okay, shit. I shouldn't be telling you this, but Jellybean connects some of his girls with this company that pays well. They're Eastern European, I think. It's all done remotely. The girls get extra cash, and Jellybean gets a kickback."

"But she's only sixteen!"

He didn't respond.

"You think it might be connected to her disappearance?" I asked, once I'd calmed down enough to speak.

"Doubt it. It's anonymous. People all over the world watch those videos. Some of them message the girls and ask to meet privately, but unless Trissa told someone where she lives and they flew all the way here from who knows where—Poland and shit—it's unlikely. I think it's pretty safe. If you're looking for a desperate stalker, I'd say it was more likely to be someone who saw her dancing and followed her. That's why I drove her home."

"Okay, but you didn't that night because she left with Anton?"

He hesitated, then sighed. "Nah. After the stunt she pulled, Jellybean threw her out. And he threatened to fire me if I went after her."

My opinion of Cal dropped. "You mean the guys who tossed us in the dumpster did the same to her and you didn't check if she was okay?"

I could hear from his voice that he was ashamed of the way he'd acted. Or not acted. He sighed heavily. "Look, the way I heard it, a couple guys just dragged her into the alley and locked the door so she couldn't get back inside. They wouldn't tell me the details because they know Trissa and I are friends, but I don't think they hurt her. I only know that that guy picked her up because I was out front when he showed up in a car, jumped out, and ran down the alley. I figured he was taking her home."

I was too upset to thank him, so I just hung up and turned to Anwar. "We need to talk to Anton. You up for that?"

"Not really," he said, putting his stuff back into his backpack. "But someone needs to keep you from picking a fight with a guy twice your size."

CHAPTER 14

Cutting Your Losses

I'd never been to Anton's apartment and had less than zero interest in going there now, but I needed to know what he'd done to Trissa after picking her up at the club. His place was just down the street from the empty condo where we hung out, in a formerly glorious brick mansion built around the 1900s, which was the same era as our house. Judging by the number of mailboxes out front, this old house had been chopped up into tiny apartments and single rooms to maximize the landlord's rental income.

"His uncle owns it," Anwar murmured, bypassing the front door and leading us up a side path. He kicked the greyish frame of a frosted window that was partially below ground level. There were weeds growing in the window well. A little farther along, a peeling wooden door had black plastic rat traps on either side. The traps were so grimy that I was pretty sure they'd been sitting there for months. I wondered if anyone ever emptied them.

The window opened a crack, and Anton hollered out at us. "What?"

"It's me," said Anwar, and after an instant without a response, added, "Anwar. Michie's with me."

"Come back later."

Anwar shook his head in irritation but kept his voice even. "We need to ask you some questions about Trissa."

"Shit." There was heavy stomping on the other side of the door, then it swung open, and Anton scowled out at us. He was on one of the top steps of a narrow staircase that led downward. His hair was messy, there was thick black stubble on his chin, and he was wearing a tight black T-shirt with a beer logo on it and drawstring Raptors shorts that he'd hastily pulled on. Without saying a word, he turned and descended the stairs.

Anwar followed, so I did too.

The apartment was one big room lit by cheap fluorescent ceiling bulbs. The walls were beige, and Anton hadn't decorated at all. To the left of the stairs was a messy kitchen area with mismatched chairs, a chipped plywood table, an old electric stove, and a green fridge. The sink and counters were covered in takeout containers, pizza boxes, and empty bottles and cans. The living room area was to the right. It consisted of a grungy pink La-Z-Boy armchair and a red-velvet love-seat with blue flowers that had probably been dragged in off the street. The furniture faced a wall-mounted flat screen hooked up to a gaming system. The remaining space consisted of a bathroom door—through which I could see a disgusting toilet and sink—and the bedroom area, which was just a double mattress on the floor.

Timbit was sitting on Anton's rumpled bed, leaning against the wall and hugging his knees. He looked so young when he waved a greeting.

"Hiya Timbit," said Anwar, as if it was no surprise to see him here.

Timbit giggled oddly.

"Are you high?" I asked him.

"High on life, Karen," Timbit quipped, then stretched out his skinny legs, wiggling his knobby knees. For some reason, he was wearing shorts too, and blindingly white tube socks. An unzipped blue-and-red sleeping bag, the only bedding other than a single pillow, slipped off the mattress near his feet. He ignored it. Beside the mattress was a black duffle bag gaping open to reveal perfectly folded clothes. I was willing to bet that Anton's mom still did his laundry. Ugh. Reason number 479 why the feminist movement was still necessary.

Anton grabbed a cold beer from the fridge without offering one to anyone else, flopped down on the La-Z-Boy, and lifted the dirty footrest. He turned on the TV with a remote and put his can in a cupholder on the armrest.

Anwar headed to the loveseat, but when he sat down, its springs groaned, and a cloud of dust billowed up from the cushions. As he fought back a sneeze—which would definitely hurt his ribs—I opted to pull over a kitchen chair and found myself facing the open bathroom door. From this angle, I could see a beige shower curtain, some dirty towels on the floor, and a pile of clothes that Anton would be expecting his mom to deal with.

"Do you both live here?" I asked.

Anton snorted in response. He reached into his pocket for rolling papers and his stash and rolled a joint, then lit it.

"I'm hungry," whined Timbit, suddenly looking miserable. "Let's order pizza."

Anton inhaled slowly and deeply and blew smoke rings into the air.

Something clicked. This wasn't where Anton lived, it was where he met people who wanted to buy drugs off him. He probably went home for dinner and to sleep. That didn't explain why Timbit was hanging out here, but I believed him when he said he was sober. Considering how cannabis affected him, he didn't smoke often, and I doubted he did any other stuff.

Anwar was watching me carefully, maybe expecting me to freak out or waiting for me to nod for him to start talking. Had he known before today that Anton was a dealer? Irritation flared up in me. This was a relevant fact to our search for Trissa. Anwar should have told me that Anton was her supplier. Maybe that explained why she always arranged for Anton to join our group—she used our hangouts as an opportunity to pick up more product from him.

I jutted my chin toward the duffle bag. "Going on a trip?"

"Not anymore," Anton hissed.

Timbit sat up straight, looking shocked. "What trip?"

"You were planning to go with Trissa," I said.

"Los Angeles is really nice this time of year," piped up Anwar at the same time.

"Everyone shut the fuck up," snapped Anton, though his eyes darted toward Timbit and he stubbed out his joint in an ashtray hidden in the La-Z-Boy's armrest.

"You're horrible," I blurted out, unable to stop myself.

Anton made a face and clapped a hand over his heart like I'd wounded him.

"What did you do to Trissa?" I demanded.

"Nothing. If I knew where that bitch was, I wouldn't be wasting my time here with you three. She stole from me. She's probably taking a holiday in the sun, blowing movie stars and popping free pills."

"She could be dead," I snapped angrily.

He sucked on his teeth to imply that was what she deserved.

"You forced her to sell for you at the club. You're the one who—"

"Forced?" he echoed, shaking his head.

"He lost two thousand dollars because of her," said Timbit.

Before I realized what was going on, Anton lunged across the room at the younger boy. Timbit went flying backward into the dirty mattress and didn't even struggle when Anton started to pound him, hitting his stomach, thighs, face. Without a thought, Anwar hurled himself on top of Anton, trying to pull him off Timbit, but Anton was enraged and flung an elbow behind him. It smashed into Anwar's chest, sending him reeling and gasping for air.

"Your ribs!" I yelled, running over before Anton could go after him again. I put my arms under Anwar's shoulders and dragged him onto his feet. If his lung was punctured or something, I'd have no idea what to do. "You could die if he breaks something."

I helped him over to the chair I'd sitting been on. His eyes closed, and he concentrated on taking shallow breaths that moved his ribs as little as possible. His face was twisted in pain.

At least my screaming had seemed to stop Anton from beating on Timbit. I felt sick as I watched the boy crawl across the floor.

"What's your problem?" I spat at Anton. "You don't care about anyone other than yourself."

"You're all pathetic," said Anton. He got up, kicked Timbit, shook his shorts straight, stomped into the bathroom, grabbed his pile of clothes, and shoved it into his duffle bag on top of the clean stuff. He tossed the strap over his shoulder. "I'm out of here."

Then he took off, banging the door shut behind him. Anwar looked at me with wide eyes. He was holding his ribs but seemed okay. A strangled sound slipped out of my mouth—a mixture of worry and relief—as I went over to hug him. "I just—just couldn't survive something happening to you too."

Anwar buried his face in my stomach and put his arms around my waist. I stood there, cursing the fact that my body immediately responded to his closeness again. Now wasn't the time. How was I supposed to find Trissa?

Timbit was sitting cross-legged on the floor beside the mattress with his face in his hands. When he sniffled loudly, I reluctantly moved away from Anwar and went over to check on him. When Timbit noticed me, he sobbed and threw himself face down. I crouched down and rubbed his back.

"You okay?"

"Leave me alone."

"What's going on between you two?" I asked.

"He's my only friend. My—my boyfriend. You've ruined everything."

"Anton isn't your boyfriend, Timbit. He was planning to run off with Trissa. He's not capable of human emotions like the rest of us. And you have other friends, like me and Anwar."

Timbit wailed. "He promised I could move in with him because my dad is a homophobic prick."

"Anton is way worse," I said.

Timbit opened his mouth to disagree, but his eyes bounced toward Anwar, who was now nodding in agreement. "I'm such a loser."

"You aren't," I said softly.

Timbit's eyes swung from Anwar to me. I peered at Anwar, who was grinning crookedly, but looked away before the familiar feeling of wanting to drag him into bed rose up inside me. I had been so terrified of losing him that I pushed him away. That would end now. When this was over, I was going to tell him exactly how I felt.

Timbit rested his head on my shoulder, and I brushed a dark-red curl off his sweaty forehead. He'd never seemed younger than he did right now.

"The next time you fall for someone," I mumbled, "make sure he's not a golem."

Timbit's turned to peer at me, his face scrunched up in confusion.

"They're these Jewish monsters shaped from mud. They have no souls."

He wiped his nose with the back of his hand and giggled. "Can't promise."

*

Now that Anton had left, the basement apartment no longer felt toxic—just depressing. I didn't want to go home in case the detectives were still around, and if they'd already left and Franklyn had gone to work, my mom and Charlene would likely be getting high and drunk. One after another, the people I loved were either falling apart or disappearing: Trissa was gone, Mom was on house arrest, Charlene's shoulder was dislocated and it seemed like she wouldn't be sobering up anytime soon, Anwar had been tossed in a dumpster and hit by Anton. Even Timbit's life seemed to have imploded.

I also couldn't shake the feeling that I'd missed something important that would explain what had happened to Trissa. To distract myself from my growing helplessness, I focused on three fist-sized holes in the drywall. It looked like Anton had punched through the wall, likely in a rage. Hopefully Timbit hadn't been around. Anton was the closest thing to evil that I'd ever known. He deliberately used people who would put up with his bullying. And I'd been oblivious to what was happening to Trissa. Had he threatened her? I hated the idea that she'd considered running away with him. So messed up.

As much as it hurt to think about Trissa moving to Cali, if she'd planned to do it alone, she would have broken away from assholes like Anton and Jellybean. Why would she have asked Anton to come with her but not confided in me?

I knew why. My heart defect. When I was young, before I could speak for myself, my mother had sworn to protect me from stress and anything that could make me sicker. Doctors convinced her it was the only way I'd survive past my fifth birthday. She was like some kind of storybook knight on a crusade to make sure everyone who knew me kept me safe. Before I even came home from the hospital, Charlene had probably had it drilled into her head that I needed to avoid stress and not overexert myself. And she'd made sure Trissa was careful around me too. Growing up, I knew I was treated different, but didn't realize how much they walked on eggshells around me. It didn't help that after Nadia's death, the psychiatrist informed my mother that I had dissociative disorder. Another thing for Mom to worry about.

Mom had relaxed a little eventually because my heart seemed to keep on ticking, but after the new diagnosis, she shifted back into hyperdrive. That meant indulging my obsessions so long as I was quiet and calm. Memorizing a book from the bargain bin at BuyMart—even if it was about getting away with murder—was exactly how she wanted me to pass my time. Making up stories about imaginary friends and dreaming about being a fearless detective were the ways I coped with spending so much time unwell, lying around in bed or sitting around while other kids had phys. ed. and ran around playing tag.

"Remember that summer I was convinced a unicorn lived in my shed?" I asked Anwar. "I named him Gremlin and was convinced that one day he'd carry me off to an alternate world where my heart would be healthy."

He nodded and flashed me his sweet, crooked grin. "You read that fantasy series about goblins and unicorns and centaurs about ten times in two months. It was all you ever talked about. If I wanted to hang out, I had to look for you on that old tree stump in your backyard."

I gave a half laugh. "Everyone needs a happy place."

"You were too old to have invisible friends," he said. "But you insisted on keeping a packed bag in the shed, hoping that a unicorn would whisk you off on an adventure."

"We all lost it after Nadia … after she …" I couldn't make myself finish the sentence.

Anwar nodded, shut his eyes, and muttered something under his breath. A prayer.

Timbit had recovered enough to pipe up. "Yo, you were a nutcase, Michie. And your mom scared me and Red so bad when we moved into the neighbourhood. She showed up at our place with cookies, but it was obvious she just came over to lecture us about not stressing you out too much. I was only eight, but I still remember her saying you could literally die if you ran too fast playing tag."

"Rachel's a vigilante," agreed Anwar. "She means well. I never told you she forced me to take her to the principal's office at the beginning of grade nine so she could warn the woman to keep an eye out for you. I even heard her say that your teachers had better be nice to you or they'd have to deal with her. My mom never would have gotten away with half of what Rachel did. A Muslim woman in a racist country? No way. Ma immediately assumes people won't give her the benefit of the doubt."

"She's going to have to let me handle things from now on," I said. "It's my body, my life. I hate that people shelter me and treat me like I'm breakable. I think that's why"— my voice suddenly sounded high and thin—"Trissa didn't talk to me about what was going on. She thought she had to baby me or my heart would just give up. Just stop pushing blood through my veins."

From now on, I'd keep my eyes open, I vowed. My head was going to be firmly planted in real life, not in delusions brought on by reading *Girl's Guide to Murder* and hiding from difficult things. I might never be a genius girl detective and the twenty-first century's response to Sherlock Holmes. I had a heart defect and asthma, after all. Lacey Milan's book had no advice for sixteen-year-olds who needed to take control of their lives and stop letting other people protect them. And, by turning the tables and trying to keep Trissa safe, I'd pushed my own self so far outside my comfort zone that I was practically in an alternate dimension.

The worst part about realizing all of this was that I couldn't tell Trissa. She'd always been there for me because no matter what I said or did, she still loved me. We might not be biologically related, but we were family. She shook things up just enough to keep my life exciting, told me I was a narcissist when I needed to hear it, convinced me to take safe risks like kissing Anwar during Truth or Dare, and believed that I was stronger than I knew.

Except I hadn't reciprocated. I wasn't there for her. She'd stopped telling me her secrets. When had I started to lose her? The day I abandoned her after she wiped out on her bike? When she'd stopped coming to school every day and I hadn't noticed?

Timbit snorted wetly and wiped his nose on the back of his hand for the second time.

"That's gross, guy," said Anwar. "Go blow your nose properly."

Timbit laughed impishly but stood up on his socked feet, padded to the bathroom, and shut the door. When he came back out, his cheeks were all pink like he'd scrubbed his face, and his hair was wet. His shirt was straightened, although the collar was weirdly stretched out where Anton twisted it. He shook his head a little, sending water droplets flying. "Okay, so, other than Trissa, I win the award for most messed-up life of anyone in our group, am I right?"

"Pretty sure we're all tied," replied Anwar.

"Were you selling for Anton?" I asked.

His brow furrowed. "I was fucking him."

I ignored that comment. "That's not what I asked. Where did you sell? Did you give him a cut of the sales?"

Timbit sighed. "I paid him up front. I was saving up for my own place. It was easy cash. I only sold at school, to a select few people. Anton told me that even if I got caught, my records would be sealed when I turn eighteen, so it wasn't that big a deal."

"Did he mention that you'd be expelled?" asked Anwar.

"Or that your father would kill you?" I added.

Timbit shuddered. "My dad is a bully. I'm never living with him again."

My phone rang just then, making me jump. It was Mom calling. I knew I had to talk to her, but not now. I switched the phone to silent and put it away.

"Call her back," said Anwar. "Rachel has enough to worry about right now with Trissa and Charlene."

He sounded so serious. I knew he was speaking from experience. Only in his case, Amina didn't really check up on him. She couldn't. After his sister's death, she'd just ghosted the entire world and left him without a parent, without anyone. I was really lucky, in comparison. I went over, hugged him, and kissed his cheek.

He turned to looked at me with a curious expression, though his eyes ended up focusing on my lips. I moved away. We weren't going to do anything in front of poor Timbit right now.

"I will talk to her," I promised. "Soon. Hey Timbit, if you need a place to crash, you can always stay at my place. It's crowded because my mother's boyfriend just moved in to be her surety, but they'd be cool with it under the circumstances. Our couch is pretty comfortable."

Timbit's face lit up a fraction. "Seriously?" He mimed puffing on a joint.

"I'm not offering you free cannabis," I snapped. "My mom had to destroy all her extra plants after the cops searched the house. But the couch is a safe place to stay, if you need to be away from your dad. Anton's not allowed over, though."

He nodded. "Thanks. Your mom's cool. When my dad loses his temper, my mom leaves the room and pretends nothing's happening."

"She's scared," I guessed. "There's no more room in our lives for people who make us afraid. At least not for me. From now on, I want to really live." I stood up and slung my bag over my shoulder. "Starting with going to the airport to see who shows for that flight."

"I'm coming," Anwar said immediately, wincing in pain as he got to his feet. "Already feel a lot better."

I tried not to roll my eyes. "Okay. Well, Timbit, just let me know. My mom would want you to be safe."

He nodded.

"He isn't cracking a joke or clowning around, so that means he's taking your offer seriously," said Anwar, climbing the stairs in a robotic fashion.

"Ice those ribs tonight," said Timbit, lying down on the mattress and putting his hands behind his head. He stared up at the ceiling.

Before following Anwar outside, I turned back to Timbit and asked, "Did Trissa have a falling out with Anton, do you know?"

He nodded. "They showed up early in the morning on Friday, around three. Thought I was asleep. She was worked up, and Anton was livid. Punched holes in the wall. When she took off. I, uh, helped him de-stress."

Wasn't hard to figure out what he meant. "Where did she go?"

"Home?"

"No, she didn't. Did Anton know she was working as a cam girl?"

Timbit snorted. "Of course. Everyone did. He watched her on the big screen." He nodded at the massive TV. "Didn't do much for me, but she's, like, super popular. Thousands of viewers every week." He rubbed his thumb and forefinger together, letting me know she made lots of money off it.

"Has she uploaded any videos since she went missing?" I asked.

"Anton hasn't streamed anything."

"Right." I hurried up the stairs. It was hard to believe that Anton had sat here with who knew how many people, watching Trissa fake orgasms. I flung open the door, trying to keep a growing panic attack at bay. Anwar noticed I was upset and rested a hand on my shoulder. After a minute, I was ready to start walking to the bus stop.

"I thought Anton was Trissa's friend with benefits," I said. "Never guessed he was sleeping with Timbit."

"He might have been screwing around with both of them." Anwar tried to throw up his hands, but a stab of pain made him quickly lower them again. "It's none of our business."

"That power dynamic just feels really wrong," I said.

My mom told me this really upsetting story the first time I snuck out of the house late at night through my bedroom window, about how when she was younger, she and Charlene were part of this anti-racist action group in New York that was infiltrated by police officers to get plans for their protests and to cause problems. A few months before she got renovicted, an undercover cop entered her apartment when she was drunk and alone and raped her. She never reported it because he had friends on the sexual assault team, but it was another reason she and Charlene had moved to Toronto. It was a fresh start, away from the NYPD.

"Trissa kept so much from me," I muttered.

Anwar was busy staring at the ground to avoid puddles, but he glanced over at me. "She looks up to you, Michie. She was probably worried you'd judge her."

I rolled my eyes. "Please. No she doesn't."

"Michie, it's true. You're one of the best people I know. You're honest, caring, live by your own rules, and know your mind. You're ... solid."

"That's sexy," I said, pretending to be annoyed. "Like a fire door? Like not a gas or a liquid, but a—"

Anwar cracked up. "As in you know exactly who you are. You're not fake. I can trust you. You're you."

I scowled. "Great."

"It was a compliment," he protested, then shot me a sly sideways glance and reached for my hand. "You're also smoking hot."

"That's better," I said, laughing.

We stopped walking. I grabbed his belt, right there on the sidewalk, and pulled him closer. I slid my hands beneath his shirt and moved them slowly up his smooth, warm stomach. He didn't pull away when my fingers moved up to his chest. I couldn't stop myself from kissing him. I wanted to make sure we got to the airport early enough to see if Trissa showed up, but if we missed this bus, there'd be another one in a few minutes.

CHAPTER 15

Building a New Life in Hiding

The subway to the airport was quiet; we were the only ones in the entire car. When I tried to sit down beside Anwar, he surprised me by pulling me onto his lap. My brain went blank and wouldn't focus on anything except the way he was nuzzling my neck, lightly rubbing my inner wrist, and kissing my mouth, face, hands. I wished that we weren't on public transit.

We stopped our PDA long enough to switch to the driverless train that would take us to the brand-new international terminal. This one was half-full, so we gave people a free show they didn't particularly want as we held onto a metal pole and swayed back and forth.

Kissing him made me feel like I was dreaming. When we paused for a second, I whispered, "I can barely believe that this—is this all my imagination?"

He lightly kissed the tip of my nose. "No. And I feel the same way."

"Because I'm solid?" I teased.

"Because you do it for me. Even here in the airport connector train. And I trust you more than anyone in the world. And I think I've always loved you."

My heart thumped hard, and my mouth went dry. "You what?"

"Come on, Michie. Think about it. After Nadia died, you were the only one I could stand being around. I couldn't sleep without you beside me."

"We were just kids."

He shook his head. "We were twelve going on twenty. Anyway, when I'm feeling like shit and my life sucks, I picture your smile and feel better. I close my eyes and hear your voice. Just knowing you're in this world cheers me up."

"You ignored me for months after you started hanging out with Kelli D!"

"Only because I thought you didn't want me the same way," he confessed. "I was trying to move on."

"I want you," I insisted. "Ask Trissa. I drove her crazy ..." It sank in that he couldn't ask Trissa. Might never be able to ask her anything again. My mood plummeted. I moved away from him and pulled out my phone to check for messages. Nothing. "Where is Trissa?"

He tilted his head and peered at me. "Have you thought about the possibility that maybe she doesn't want to be found? Or that maybe something terrible really has happened? Do you think the police might be right about the Strangler?"

"Stop it!" I yelped. "I just can't think that way."

"Trissa's the closest thing you have to a sister, Michie, but you're really different people."

"I'm going to find her," I said, gritting my teeth, "and bring her home."

The crooked grin made an appearance. "If anyone can, it's you. When you start moving forward, everyone around you flows in your direction. You're unstoppable."

I might never become a real private investigator or a criminal mastermind, but if Anwar believed in my ability to find Trissa, then I could too. I moved closer to him again and tucked my forehead under his chin, breathing in his smell. Warm breath ruffled my messy bun. I wanted to stay curled into him forever.

"I'm pretty sure I fell in love with you," he whispered, "the day you shoved me down the slide in the playground."

*

We found the airline check-in area and stationed ourselves on a bench that was partially hidden behind a wall, but also had a clear view of the entrance to security. It was almost three hours until the flight departed, so there was already a lineup. Anwar went off to find us some coffee drinks, and I kept an eye out for Trissa.

A couple with four small children push two loaded carts up to the check-in counter. As they heaved giant suitcases onto the conveyor belt, one of the boys deliberately tripped the youngest sibling, who fell over and started to wail at the top of her lungs. The father snapped at the oldest kid to help the toddler up.

I was squinting at my reflection in a sliding glass door, futilely trying to fix my messy bun, when Anwar came up and startled me by tugging on a lock of my hair and making the whole thing come apart. The look on his face told me how much he liked seeing my hair down, so I put the elastic in my pocket and glanced at the cardboard tray in his other hand. It contained two huge Mocha Frozers with extra whipped topping and rainbow sprinkles.

"My favourite," I squealed gleefully, and grabbed one.

"How could I forget," he teased, and sat down beside me.

Against my better judgment, I went back to Kelli D's video with Red and watched the rest. Two seconds after I'd stopped it, she started kissing him, smearing an obscene amount of his bright-orange lipstick all over their mouths and chins. When they finally pulled apart, there was a gross popping sound. Nauseating. Kelli D blew the viewer a kiss, and Red tugged her back, presumably onto a bed or the floor, and then there was a cut.

When Kelli D reappeared onscreen, her face was washed and Red nowhere in sight. She shared a list of "ten ways to know he's a lying liar." These included him staring at his friend the "feminist slut with no conscience" all the time, swearing that the slut was just a friend, and not caring about things that mattered to you, such as helping make your #selfcare video channel more successful.

I found myself mildly amused by her insults. For one thing, I didn't care that she thought I was a slut. For another, her comments let me know that she'd been jealous of me while they were dating. I found it hard to believe one of the PPs thought I was competition for a guy's attention. This made me wonder whether I was as much of an outcast as I thought.

Beneath the video, there were several comments from viewers telling Kelli D she was a queen and deserved better than a lying liar. One girl piped up that Red was smoking hot and she'd steal him if Kelli D wasn't careful. I noticed a couple of hilarious posts calling the video nonsense. I considered posting a response under the username Feminist Slut, but shoved my phone away before I could do something I regretted.

We sat back down and sipped our drinks, watching a small line form behind the family. The kids were now playing tag around the check-in counter, getting in everyone's way, and the dad was yelling at the attendant about the extra luggage fees being highway robbery. The mom stood there silently, staring at nothing.

"Poor woman," I said to Anwar.

"She definitely wants the floor to swallow her whole."

I caught his eye and said, "You realize I have a terrible track record with relationships."

He shrugged. "You have a great one with friends."

"Well, I only have two." Had two, I thought miserably, then considered whether Vee now counted as a friend.

A small fleet of attendants materialized and began to set up their check-in counters. The woman still helping the family looked so relieved I thought she might cry.

More and more travellers arrived. Anwar and I watched vigilantly for the next hour and took alternating bathroom breaks, but there was no sign of Trissa. Five minutes before the check-in deadline, Anton ran up with his lumpy black cargo bag over one shoulder, tried to check-in at a kiosk, realized the time, and hurried to the nearest counter. He slapped down his passport, and the attendant shook his head in reprimand but printed his ticket, then waved frantically for him to run to security.

"Huh," said Anwar. "That's a surprise. I was positive he'd bail on the trip without Trissa."

"Let's hope the border guards catch him with a bunch of drugs in his suitcase."

"Wishful thinking."

The final attendant closed down their terminal and disappeared to wherever they went when they weren't needed here. I sighed, picked up my canvas bag, and offered Anwar a hand standing up. He accepted the hand but stood without any help.

"It was a long shot," he said.

I nodded and anxiously chewed my lip as we dodged people and their luggage. "Trissa's been missing for three days. I feel like we're spinning our wheels in mud."

"Yeah." He paused, pouted for a second, then his face lit up. "We need shawarma pizza!"

*

An hour later, I was still distracted by worry when we entered the Lebanese pizza parlour where we used to eat whenever our moms gave us money to buy dinner. The familiar smells temporarily distracted me: tomato sauce, yeasty dough, melted cheese, and meat. Despite the situation, my mouth started to water. I was starving. Anwar didn't know I hadn't been back here since he hooked up with Kelli D because it was our place. Well, ours and Trissa's.

"Get whatever you want," he offered, squinting at the specials. "It's on me."

"Only a fool would turn down free pizza."

We ordered cheesy slices piled with lamb and drizzled with tahini and vinegary hot sauce. Ali, the manager, had enormous round cheeks and a jolly demeanour. He chided us about not coming by all summer, and I realized Anwar hadn't been here with Kelli D either. Maybe he hadn't felt right bringing someone else. Or maybe Kelli D avoided carbs.

As we carried our trays to a faux-wood laminated table, I thanked Anwar for the food. "It's a good thing you offered to pay, because I'm missing my bank card, and something's wrong with my account." I showed him the email telling me I was in overdraft. "I swear there was almost a thousand in there last week."

"You better figure this out," he said, shovelling a full quarter of his slice into his mouth. Grease dribbled down his chin. "Could be fraud. The bank will reverse the charges."

"That would be good. I've been a little distracted. I only discovered the money was missing last night." I reached over to wipe his chin using my napkin, giggling at his embarrassment.

"Thanks." He took another messy bite and chewed. After swallowing, he said, "Happened to my mother last year. The charges were all big purchases from stores. They maxed out her credit card in five minutes."

I groaned. "With the luck I'm having these days, they'll tell me it's my fault. Accuse me of stealing my own money or something."

We finished our pizza, said goodbye to Ali, and hurried to my bank branch, arriving just minutes before it closed. The teller took a look at the account and showed me the three suspicious cash withdrawals.

They weren't taken out from official banks, she said, but machines owned by individual shopkeepers. It crossed my mind that Trissa might have taken the card because she couldn't go back for her own wallet and money.

"Can you tell where the machines were located?" I asked, hoping they were clustered in a particular neighbourhood, and that would give me a clue to her whereabouts.

"Not unless that information is included in the machine's name. Hmm." She pointed at the screen. "This one here, for two hundred and forty, has the name of a town."

"Orillia 24 Hour Exotic Convenience?" I asked, surprised. "I've been to Orillia. It's a few hours north."

She gave a small shrug. "Maybe the thief left Toronto."

As the teller got me a new card, set it up, and asked me to change my password, I thought this through. Trissa couldn't drive and had nowhere to go up north, so it probably wasn't her. But when would anyone else have had the opportunity to steal from me? My canvas satchel was almost always slung over my shoulder. At least the transactions would be reversed once the bank investigated and determined what had happened. It could take two days, though. Two days with no money of my own.

At home, I was surprised to find the house dark, upstairs and down. From the sidewalk, it looked like no one was home, but that couldn't be the case. I'd actually expected Mom to be livid that I took off this morning and didn't check in all day, since it was almost seven.

Before going up the walk, I paused and awkwardly glanced up at Anwar. "The detectives should be gone by now, and it looks like Mom's catching up on sleep. Want to, um, come in?"

He nodded, watching me closely, trying to figure out how I felt about this. "You sure?"

"One hundred percent," I said, and pulled him up to the door. "I don't want to be alone. I mean, sex isn't a huge deal for me. Uh …"

"I get it, Michie," he said.

I knew he understood what I was trying to say, which was that sex was fun, but it would only be a deepening of what was between us. It was clear we were already past the point of being able to return to just friends. I hadn't been raised to think I should wait until marriage or anything—my mom had never married anyone and said that society's obsession with female chastity was a way of objectifying and policing our bodies. She was more concerned about me being safe.

He took my hand and began to lazily play with my fingers, then raised them to his mouth to kiss my fingertips, sending electricity up my arm. The harsh porch light cast shadows under his eyebrows and cheekbones. He licked his lips. His mouth was so perfect. I already wanted him. This boy would always live in my heart. It really didn't matter if we had sex.

I fumbled awkwardly with the lock behind my back, and the door swung open. We tumbled into the lobby, trying not to laugh out loud as I tossed mom's leather jacket on a hook and peeled off his heavy overshirt. We kicked off our shoes before opening the door to my apartment. Mom's door was shut, but she'd left the bathroom light on—we used it as a night light—which meant she was most likely sleeping again. Considering she probably hadn't slept at all in the police station, it made sense.

In my bedroom, I closed the door and flipped the small latch hook. It wasn't strong enough to keep anyone out, but it would stop my mother from accidentally bursting in.

I turned around to find Anwar standing right behind me. He gently tucked a strand of hair behind my ear and whispered, "You're beautiful."

"That's just what I was thinking about you," I murmured.

"Maybe I'm dreaming," he said, kissing a trail up my neck to my ear. "I've wanted you for so long." He sat down on the bed and patted the spot beside him.

I swallowed hard and straddled his lap instead. Wanting to feel his skin, I tugged the bottom of his shirt up and over his head, then pushed him down on his back. I lightly ran my fingertips over his shoulders, his chest, his stomach. There was enough light to see how dark the bruise on his ribs was. "Does it hurt?"

"Yes," he said hoarsely. "But don't stop."

Heady with power, I planted soft kisses around the edge of his bruised skin. Inhaling that amazing smell—his smell—made me hotter. I planted wet kisses around his belly button, then moved down. His smell filled my head, made me feel high. We'd gone swimming together at the cabin and at public pools, but this was completely different.

"Michie," he moaned, "I need you."

His skin was so hot. He pulled the neck of my T-shirt down so he could touch my breasts, then rolled us over so that he was on top of me, resting on an elbow. He began to lick and suck my nipples, filling my body with fire. He reached around to unhook my bra, and I fought a momentary urge to cover myself up. His hands gripped my hips, and he moved down to pull off my leggings and underwear. What if he decided I wasn't as hot as when I was wearing clothes? What if he decided this was all a big mistake? What if—

When he began to remove the rest of his own clothes, all my fears disappeared. His cheeks were streaked dark pink, and his hazel eyes glinted. He lay back down next to me and slid a hand between my legs.

"You're wet," he said, as he found my clit. I clasped his hand and showed him how to touch me. Just so. He made a noise somewhere between anticipation and frustration, then bent over and kissed my belly, then my abdomen, and then lower. And for the first time in three days, I stopped thinking about anything other than how good I felt.

*

Hours later, I woke up, completely relaxed. The house was still quiet, except for the sound of Anwar breathing rhythmically next to me. He hadn't snuck out the window while I slept. Would Amina be okay with this? I didn't care. Happiness shot through me, and I was tempted to wake him up so we could go all over again. It took some effort, but I convinced my raging hormones to leave him alone.

Needing a glass of water, I rolled out from under the comforter, picked up my phone to see what time it was, and discovered it was only nine-thirty. I'd been asleep for less than two hours. I carried my leggings and T-shirt into the hall, put them on, and padded into the kitchen. I filled a big glass and drank the entire thing before checking the voice mail my mother had left when she'd called me earlier.

"Sweetie," she said. "I didn't want to tell you this in a text." My heart started to beat hard and fast. What was wrong? "I'm at the hospital with Charlene. She fainted, so I brought her to emergency. Franklyn came with us. The doctors are running some tests and want to keep her overnight for observation. Don't worry too much, okay? She's doing better, and we'll have more answers soon. Char's in good hands. Oh, and if you call back and I don't answer, it's because I have to turn off my phone. Apparently it interferes with the machines. I love you, okay? Charlene is okay."

I was already shoving my feet into shoes before the message ended. I barely remembered to pull on a jacket before running out of the house. If I'd had even twenty dollars in my account, I could have ordered a car, but at least my student transit pass was good for the entire month. It was torture sitting on a bus, though it gave me time to message Anwar and let him know why I'd left without saying goodbye.

To take my mind off looking up all the things that could be wrong with Charlene, I obsessively checked all my inboxes for other messages I might have missed. Nothing. While I sat there, my phone lit up with a new text from Vee.

I've been living under a rock, they wrote. *Just heard your friend is missing. Trissa's the girl who lives in your house, right? She's always posting embarrassing things on your socials. Hit me up to let me know how you're doing. Worried about you.*

I'm okay, I replied. *But I'm on the way to the hospital. Trissa's mom collapsed or something. If I told you everything terrible that's happened in the last couple days, my message would be an essay.*

What's wrong with Trissa's mom? they wrote back.

Heart trouble? Not sure. On my way to find out.

They paused for a moment before responding, *Maybe Anwar can provide some comfort in your time of need.* They finished the message with a smiley face, a heart, an eggplant, and a question mark.

Already on it, I wrote. *Err, on him. Err, until a few minutes ago when I took off while he was passed out on my bed.*

Srsly, Michie! I was just making a joke, but whoa!!!!! Hey, if your mom is staying at the hospital tonight, I could come hang out, so you're not alone?

Having Vee in my corner was no small thing. I'd always kept school people far away from my Parkdale friends. They were oil and water. Vee was different, though. I could see them fitting in with our group. They already liked Anwar. I had no idea whether he'd still be at my place by the time I got back. *That'd be great,* I wrote.

Perfect. Let me know when you're on the way home. Oh. Check out Kelli D's latest video if you want a distraction. I've already posted three anonymous comments.

She and Red deserve each other, I messaged. *Fake tears. Ugh.*

I told Vee I'd message later and got off the bus. I ran the last two blocks to the hospital entrance, pushed through the revolving glass doors, and stopped. I'd never visited anyone on my own before. Mom hadn't told me where to find her and Charlene. As I was considering how to proceed, I noticed an owl-eyed older man sitting behind an information desk and blinking in my direction. There was a computer in front of him.

"How can I help?" he asked cheerily.

"I need to find someone. She came in through Emergency, but I'm not sure if she's still there."

"Visiting hours ended at nine, young lady."

"I just want to make sure she's okay."

"Hmm. Let's see … name?"

"Charlene Taylor."

"A family member?"

"She's my aunt," I said, knowing it was stretching the truth a little and hoping he wouldn't ask for ID next.

He just nodded and picked at his keyboard with a single index finger, then squinted at the monitor. "Ms. Taylor has been transferred to the fourth floor." He pointed down a hallway. "Take the elevator down there and check with the nurses' station. They might let you say hello to your aunt, if she's awake."

I catapulted away from his desk, calling a thank you over my shoulder, and flew down the hall. My heart hadn't stopped skipping erratically since I listened to Mom's voice mail. The elevator doors clanged open right when I arrived, and I slipped in alongside an elegant Asian couple with a stroller. I smashed the fourth-floor button and tried to concentrate on breathing exercises as we travelled upward.

There was no one at the info desk, so I peeked into rooms until I found Mom and Franklyn nodding off in vinyl armchairs with their feet propped up on Charlene's hospital bed. Charlene was drowsy but awake, lying beneath a blanket and wearing a light-green hospital gown. There were wires going from her chest to a heart machine, and she had an IV line in her arm. Hearing the beeps of the cardiac monitor brought on a wave of terrible memories. I'd been in the hospital way too many times as a kid.

I stepped up to her bed and fumbled in my bag for a heart pill. Charlene waited for me to take it before squeezing my hand. The expression on her face was haunting.

"Lovey," she whispered, "I'm glad to see you."

"I just got the message," I explained, trying to ignore the painful lump of emotion inside my throat.

She gave me a sad smile. "Rachel just closed her eyes. We'll let her rest for a while, hmm?"

I nodded. If I tried to speak again, I'd burst into tears.

She patted my hand. "I'm fine, lovey. No need to worry about me. The doctor gave me something to help me sleep, but it seems to have affected everyone around me instead. The only thing wrong with me is a broken heart. Stress, the doctors said. I need to rest for a couple days, but I'll be back at Zumba class as soon as my baby girl comes home."

"You need to slow down on the whisky," I managed to croak.

When I perched on the edge of her bed, it made a loud clanking noise, and Mom jolted awake. She blinked as if she couldn't quite believe her eyes. "Michie?"

The lump in my throat turned into a fully formed sob. "I just heard your message and came down. I can't handle anything else …"

Franklyn stirred and sat up. "Hello there."

"Everybody shh," said Mom. "Other patients are trying to sleep."

I swiped at my eyes. They wouldn't stop leaking.

"You know, Michie," murmured Franklyn, "Charlene has a nurse who looks a little like you did that time Trissa shaved the sides of your head. The top was long and floppy …"

"And the colour," Charlene added with a small smile.

"Don't remind me of my Justin Bieber phase," I pleaded.

"The Biebs never had green hair," piped up Mom. "When your bangs were wet, they looked like algae."

"Blond suits you better," said Charlene. "But never be ashamed of standing out, Michie."

"Thanks, I think?" I pretended to glare at Mom and Franklyn. Their teasing had stopped my tears, which was the intended result. "At least someone appreciates my sense of style."

"Those were good days," said Charlene. "We went up to that cabin together. Remember how much my baby girl loved being in nature? She spent the summers swimming and running around."

"Why did we stop going?" I asked.

"It was expensive," explained Mom, "and things changed for you kids. You got older and wanted to hang out with your friends in the city. It just didn't feel right without Anwar and his sister, and Amina kept him close after Nadia died." She realized we were all in danger of being swept back into tragedy and abruptly changed the subject. "You'll meet Charlene's nurse any minute and see how adorable he is."

I sighed. "I'm just glad you were there when Charlene fainted."

"Me too," agreed Mom. "It was frightening."

"I stood up too quickly and couldn't catch my breath," said Charlene, waving away our concern.

"Your mother was amazing, Michie," said Franklyn. "Rachel knew exactly what to do. She caught Charlene and kept her head from hitting the floor. It was incredible." He leaned sideways and kissed Mom's cheek.

Mom's lips squeezed together like she had to stop herself from denying her incredibleness. She blushed a little, then rested her head on his shoulder. I'd inherited my tendency to turn bright red from her.

She knew exactly what to do because she'd been through so many scares when I was young. She'd even taken a CPR course and learned to stayed calm, call for an ambulance, monitor my heart rate, and explain to the paramedics what was going on. Since getting me on the right medicines, though she hadn't needed it as much, she continued to take refresher CPR courses every few years.

I really hated hospitals—the beep of machines, the smell of bleach, the generic art on the walls. So many doctors had studied my condition that I became a famous case: the girl whose defective heart just kept on ticking long after it should have given up the ghost. Eventually, they declared me a medical marvel and told us I'd outgrown the worst of my symptoms. My heart had partially healed itself. Would Charlene's too?

"Still no news about Trissa?" I asked, then immediately regretted it. I already knew the answer.

Charlene shook her head glumly. "The police have their theories, but they've got it all wrong."

"Michie," said Mom, looking at me intently, "we all hope Trissa's okay, but we might need to prepare ourselves for the worst."

"My daughter wouldn't forget to reclaim her phone, passport, and money," added Charlene. "It seems she was packed to run away. One way or another, I was probably going to lose her that night." The heart machine started to beep angrily.

I wished desperately that I could take my question back.

A man popped his head into the room. He was in his midtwenties with a poufy lime-green wave of hair on the top of his head and very short blond sides. "Well hello again, to the loveliest lady on my ward! Let's see what's going on." He pressed a couple buttons to make the machine stop beeping. "I figured you'd be asleep by now." Just then, he noticed me and did a double take. "You weren't here a few minutes ago!"

I shook my head, agreeing with him.

"This is my daughter, Michie," said Mom. "For a few weeks when she was twelve, she had the exact same hair colour and cut as you."

"It wasn't a great look on me," I murmured. "But you can pull it off. Super cute."

He flipped his bangs with a sassy flourish. "Thanks for noticing. I'm sorry, though, it's after visiting hours and this young lady"—he indicated Charlene—"shouldn't be getting herself more worked up."

Mom handed me her wallet. "She just came to make sure we were okay and to get me some dinner. Can you run down and bring back some hot tea for me and Franklyn?"

"Sure," I said, sliding the wallet into my pocket.

"I take my tea with double cream," said Charlene, "and a maple cruller."

The nurse wagged a finger and *tsk-tsk*ed. "I'm sorry, my dear, but you aren't allowed anything unless the doctor clears it." He inflated the blood pressure cuff on her arm. "If you're desperate, I'll get you a cup of ice chips."

Charlene grunted, making it clear how much she didn't want ice chips.

I saluted the four of them and hurried off to the food court. It was in the basement and oddly busy for late on a Sunday night. The Hawaiian-themed decor hadn't changed since I was little. Such a bizarre choice for an inner-city hospital in Toronto. Visitors and staff wearing their hospital badges ate panini and sushi at colourful tables decorated with tropical flowers, beneath plastic palm trees and murals showing sunny beach scenes.

Nestled beneath a string of pink patio lanterns was a bank machine. I popped Mom's card in and checked the balance to make sure she had a little cushion, then withdrew two hundred and fifty dollars. My allowance for five weeks, I rationalized.

Then I got three grilled cheeses for myself, mom, and Franklyn, stopped for tea and cookies, and carried it all upstairs. Mom immediately ripped open her sandwich and began to devour it. Franklyn took small dainty bites, as if he was beyond mortal issues like hunger. Charlene grumbled that the smell made her even hungrier.

"I'm sorry, but Mom needs to eat something," I said firmly.

Charlene crossed her arms. "Well then, she should at least give me a bite."

"Forget it," said Mom around a mouthful of sandwich. "When you get out of here, I'll make you a pot roast dinner with baked potatoes. All the fixings."

"Gravy?" asked Char, still peering longingly at mom's sandwich.

"Uh-huh."

Charlene sighed and deliberately averted her eyes. "Remember that roadside bakery on the highway where we bought delicious cherry pies to bring with us to the cabin? You kids always ate half of it before we even got there, then had terrible stomach aches."

"Nadia ate a huge piece, then went swimming and got a cramp," Mom said.

"She'd never been in a lake, only pools," Charlene reminisced. "Trissa told her that leeches would suck out all her blood but salt killed them, so she carried a saltshaker down to the dock every single day and positioned it right on the edge, where she could reach it from the water."

Mom smiled. "Mosquitoes absolutely loved that girl, poor thing. She was so itchy she slathered herself from head to toe in calamine lotion so her whole body was that pink colour."

"We never had to worry about you kids up there," said Charlene. "Even my baby girl put down her struggles for a while. She was so sensitive."

"They call it forest bathing," I told her. "It's scientifically proven that nature has a calming effect on people."

"We should have kept going," said Charlene.

"Maybe we can rent that place again?" I suggested. "Make some new memories. Once Trissa's back home."

Charlene groaned and slumped against her pillows.

"You should go home, Michie," said Mom, crunching her sandwich wrapper into a ball and handing it to me so I could throw it away. "You'll never make it to school in the morning if you don't."

"We'll keep an eye on Charlene," Franklyn reassured me.

It was a terrible time to bring up the fact that Timbit needed a place to crash for a while, but I'd promised him. When Mom didn't even hesitate before agreeing that it was no problem at all, a wave of love and pride swept over me. She might not be a traditional mom, but she was pretty wonderful. "You're the best."

"Love you," Mom responded automatically.

"Here's a kiss from me," said Charlene, blowing me one.

I pretended to catch it and throw it back to her.

"Try not to worry," said Mom.

I nodded, knowing that would be impossible, and headed back to the bus stop. It was almost eleven, and traffic had died down, so getting home only took twenty minutes. I messaged Vee, asking whether they were serious about the offer of staying over tonight, and they replied immediately, asking for my address. They'd leave right away.

CHAPTER 16

Celebrating Successful Crimes

Anwar wasn't in my bed anymore, which was a little disappointing, but he'd used black eyeliner to draw a heart on the mirror around the lipstick initials Trissa had scrawled. That made me grin in a goofy way.

I was glad Vee was on their way over, since I really didn't want to spend another night here alone. I tidied up my room a little and fired off a message to Timbit, telling him my mother was happy for him to crash here until he found a more permanent place. He showed up ten minutes later with a bulging garbage bag over his shoulder, looking like he'd barely stopped crying since we left him at Anton's earlier. There was hardly enough time to fill him in on what had happened to

Charlene and show him the small closet in the living room where he could store his stuff before the doorbell rang again.

"Try to keep things tidy," I told him. "Like, do what I say, not what I do, okay? Ha ha. There are clean towels in the bathroom closet, and any food in the kitchen is fair game. Consider this your home."

"Can you let your mom know I really appreciate this?" Timbit asked. "I was still at Anton's when you messaged. That wasn't good for my mental health."

Before heading to answer the door, I told him about Anton getting on the plane. Timbit took it better than I expected. In fact, he mimed dusting off his hands—dusting that boy out of his life—and stood up straighter.

As soon as I opened the door, Vee burst in with their characteristic energy and thrust a huge grocery bag filled with snacks at me. They immediately introduced themselves to Timbit. While I went to make some microwave popcorn, the two of them made themselves comfortable on the couch, as if they'd already known each other for years.

We streamed episodes of the original *Wonder Woman* with Lynda Carter and ate popcorn, ice cream bars, and three kinds of chips. I almost felt normal for a while. Almost.

Then Vee asked me if I had any news about Trissa, and it sent me into another spiral. I didn't want to talk about how little progress the police had made. To my surprise, Timbit took pity on me and distracted Vee by rattling on about how badly Anton had treated him. Vee let him talk for way longer than I would have, then announced that he needed to find a new man who was hotter and hornier. I fell asleep while Vee was going through all of their social media accounts, looking for cute guys to set Timbit up with.

*

I woke up with a stiff neck from sleeping on the floor. The photos on Trissa's screen saver, the ones from the cabin, filled my head. Now that Nadia and Trissa were gone, I kept thinking about us all of together, and it made me want to cry again. Both of them felt like ghosts haunting me. If only it were possible to rewind four years and get a do-over on that final summer. We could stop Nadia from being killed. I could make different choices and be a better friend to Trissa so she didn't have to deal with everything alone.

I stifled an urge to scream. I was carrying so much pain and pent-up energy inside me that needed to come out, but there was nowhere to put it. Not knowing what had happened to Trissa was almost as bad as finding out she was dead. I needed some answers but had no way of getting them.

Vee was already banging around in the kitchen. Timbit was still curled up on the couch, looking sweet and innocent as he slept. I searched my soul and was surprised that I no longer found him annoying, just young and misguided.

Less than a week ago, my life looked so different. Trissa had been pretty much my only friend, since Anwar was spending all his time with Kelli D. I'd dismissed Timbit and had no clue that I might get along with Vee enough to hang outside class. It was wrong to be grateful for the way my life had changed since Trissa disappeared, but these were good developments.

I shuffled into the kitchen to find Vee looking through cupboards. "Hey sleepyhead," they said brightly. "I found the coffee filters, but not the actual caffeine."

"Sorry for being a terrible host your first time over," I said, taking out a can of ground beans from above the stove. I handed it to them.

They measured coffee into a filter and got the percolator brewing. "Considering everything you're going through, I didn't expect you to entertain me. I came over to take your mind off everything."

"It helped," I admitted. "Thank you."

"Anytime." They pointed at the clock on the microwave. "I hate to bring this up, but if you don't take a shower and eat something quickly, we'll be late for first period."

Timbit entered the room, rubbing his eyes. His auburn curls were flattened on one side and perky on the other. "Do I smell coffee?"

"Good morning, Tim," Vee chirped, nodding toward the half-full pot.

"Yes!" he exclaimed and did a fist pump in the air.

"Nobody calls him Tim," I said automatically.

"My parents do," Timbit corrected me. "Honestly, I hate being called Timbit."

My jaw dropped. "Why didn't you say anything?"

He shrugged. "No one asked. My brother calls me that to bug me. The rest of you picked it up from him."

"Okay well, I'll call you Tim from now on," I promised, dropping two slices of slightly stale sourdough into the toaster. Vee was already setting the table. "You should probably just leave before me. I'm not sure I can sit through classes."

"Michie," Vee said firmly, "now is not the time for you to go all depressed loner. I'm staying with you."

Did all of my friends think they knew what I needed? "You sound like Trissa."

"I look forward to meeting her." Too impatient to wait for the brewing to finish, they pulled out the coffee pot and filled three mugs, then plunked them down on the table. When the toaster popped, they hopped up, handed me the warm slices, and put some more in the machine.

I slathered my toast with butter and jam, letting Tim and Vee's conversation fade out. There was no way I was going to school today. An idea had taken shape in my mind about where Trissa might have gone, and I wanted to check it out. The police interrogation at the station seemed like a really long time ago. I wished I could call those detectives and get a report, but I doubted they had much to say, and they would never report their progress to a sixteen-year-old girl anyway.

Vee and Tim rushed me out the door after breakfast, still chattering like BFFs. Uncertain how Vee would react, I walked them to the bus stop and waited until it had arrived before informing them I that wasn't coming. Before Vee could argue, I walked away. As the bus pulled onto the road, I caught a glimpse of Vee and Tim staring at me pointedly through a window. I was pretty sure Vee was swearing.

It was a chicken move, but it had to be done. I sent them both an apologetic text, then switched my phone to airplane mode and put it in my shoulder bag.

At home, I removed all the school supplies from my knapsack and replaced them with a change of underwear, a T-shirt, a thick sweater, six cheese and tomato sandwiches, a package of chocolate chip cookies, and filled my Thermos with hot chocolate. I crammed in *Girl's Guide to Murder*, my phone charger and backup battery, some noise-cancelling headphones, Trissa's second phone, and a bottle of water. After stuffing a handful of romaine lettuce leaves into the guinea pig cage and filling their food bowls to overflowing, I wrote a note to my mother saying I'd be home tonight or tomorrow morning and she shouldn't worry and left it on the kitchen table.

*

The downtown commuter bus terminal was surprisingly busy for a Monday morning. I'd assumed that on weekdays, people only came into the city early in the mornings, but the rows of orange plastic chairs were filled with people. There were teenagers heading back to the suburbs after partying all weekend, university students on their way to the handful of campuses in surrounding cities, and even business people working on laptops or speaking into Bluetooth headsets. Nearly a million people travelled between Toronto and the satellite communities for work each day, but for some reason, I'd figured most of them drove or took the express trains.

I used some of Mom's cash to buy a return ticket to cottage country and lined up to wait with a small crowd of people getting on the same bus. Judging by the way they smelled, half of them had come here straight here from bars. The guy in front of me was sipping from a bottle that said ginger ale but smelled strongly of rum.

I drafted a text to Anwar, explaining that I was going to see if Trissa was at the cottage up north but that he shouldn't tell the mothers where I was because I had no idea whether she'd be there. And if she was, she might have a good reason for not wanting to be found. He was probably in homeroom right now, wondering where I was. At the last second, I decided to hold off and send the text once I was safely out of the city. He would definitely try to stop me from going alone, and I was determined to do this by myself.

If Trissa wasn't there, I would be devastated, but maybe I could find some kind of peace in saying goodbye to the lake and woods that had made us all happy.

*

Once I was settled in my own double seat on the bus, I clapped on my koala bear headphones, put on some music, turned sideways and put my feet up, arranged my jacket over my legs like a blanket, and slumped against the window. The driver released the air brakes and lurched forward into the city streets. Before we'd reached the suburbs, it was pouring outside, and I fell asleep.

I woke up an hour later and sent the texts to Anwar and Mom. I knew it would be a bad idea to read the three he'd already written to me and the one from Vee, so I ate one of my sandwiches, poured some hot chocolate into my tiny Thermos cup, and concentrated on taking small sips without spilling it all over myself when the bus bounced around. My stomach was unsettled. It'd been a long time since I'd gotten car sick. Knowing the battery on my phone and the backup wouldn't last too long, I plugged them both into the jack on the back of the seat in front of me. Once my phone was fully charged, I unplugged and connected Trissa's phone. I needed to do this alone, but I didn't need to be foolish about it and unable to call for help.

How much money would someone need to move to LA? More than two thousand dollars. She'd have to pay for a deposit on an apartment, rent, and food until she found a job and started to get regular cheques. Maybe she'd been planning to find a club to dance at?

After passing Orillia, I got bored, opened social media, and discovered that Vee had just tagged me in a post. They weren't angry I'd ditched them. They'd shared an article saying the police had received an anonymous tip and arrested a thirty-year-old man they suspected of being the West End Strangler. Apparently, they had evidence but couldn't release it yet. I did a quick search and discovered that dozens of TV stations and news sites were reporting on the arrest. Relief spread through my body. Please, please let the murders stop.

I decided to do some reading about cam girls. I wasn't sure if the articles were credible, but I found several that said the men who owned these websites were the only ones who really profited. Trissa would have made a couple hundred per upload, unless she had viewers who were big tippers. Timbit had said she had a lot of regulars and that she could make videos from anywhere, as long as she had a phone. Maybe she'd planned to keep recording new ones in LA? But she'd left this phone at home and abandoned the other one behind Club Jelly.

The gross feeling in my stomach worsened as the bus travelled through the cute little towns north of Lake Simcoe. I couldn't stop thinking about how horribly I'd failed Trissa. Not just me. Everyone in her life: Charlene, my mom, our friends, Cal at Club Jelly. We'd all missed how hard her life had become. It was easier to close our eyes and imagine everything was fine than to think about how she was spending her time and where she was getting her money.

Despite everything, she still managed to make our lives so much more exciting. She gave me the confidence to deal with life. Well, sometimes it felt like she shoved me off cliffs, yelling, "You can do this, Michie!" That wasn't always the best way to treat a friend, but I kind of understood. I'd continued to act like she was frozen in time, a girl who played doctor and hide-and-seek who wanted everyone to fall in love with her and got jealous when Anwar liked me more. Our lives got so twisted when Nadia died.

I stared out the window at the changing landscape. It was cold and grey up here, which echoed the way I felt inside. The leaves were almost gone from the trees. Forests and farmland and cloudy sky stretched out on all sides. I burrowed into my seat and pulled my jacket up to my neck. Guilt and dread settled around me like a second skin. I couldn't go backward and fix things, but I might be able to love Trissa better in the future.

My phone beeped. Anwar again. This time, I glanced at the screen. *I wish you'd let me come with you.*

I've dragged you into too much already, I replied.

We're together now. You don't have to be the lone detective anymore.

He was right. I'd gotten used to not sharing my thoughts or real feelings with anyone. When he finally gave up on waiting and got together with Kelli D, I'd assumed it was because he didn't like me back, but that wasn't the case. He deserved to know what was going on in my head. When I got home, I'd start opening up more. But I was already feeling crappy enough, so I sent him a line filled with hearts and crying emojis, switched my phone back to airplane mode, tucked my extra sweater behind my neck, and slept some more.

Each time the bus pulled to a stop, I jolted awake to check where we were. The next time I turned my phone on, a whole bunch of messages came through from several people, including several from Mom that progressively more upset. She wanted me to know that Charlene was doing better and wouldn't need heart surgery. The school robo-called to inform her that I'd skipped class. She found my note and wanted to know where the hell I was. I wished I hadn't read her texts and felt awful.

I agonized over my response and ultimately wrote, *I'm really sorry for making you worry, but I can't tell you where I am. I'm okay. I need to check something. I'll probably be back late tonight. Tomorrow at the latest.*

The driver called out Westernville Station. I gathered up my stuff and moved to the front before we stopped. The only person who got off at the same time was a teen girl whose parents were waiting for her in an old wood-panelled station wagon. She glanced curiously at me as she passed by but didn't say anything. I was relieved. Small talk felt like too much pressure right now.

The sun would be setting soon. The darkening sky was smeared with bright-orange down near the horizon, under the black rain clouds. It was cold, and it didn't help that fat droplets of sleet pelted everything. The station was just a single room with linoleum flooring and cement walls that smelled like wet dog and burnt coffee. The ticket booth was locked, but there was a courtesy phone connected to a cab company on the wall.

I called for a taxi, put on the heavy sweater in my bag, and zipped up my jacket, then looked over a local map for the only street whose name I remembered. It was almost half an hour away from town. This would be an expensive ride. I really hoped I'd have enough left over to get back the same way if Trissa wasn't in the cabin.

The driver drove up and lowered his window to wave at me. I told him where we were going. He informed me that he'd have to let me off on the closest paved road, because they didn't grate the dirt roads in the fall and winter. It wasn't like I had a choice in the matter, so I nodded and asked for a flat rate. It would leave me just enough for a return fare.

He tried to make small talk a few times, but I replied with grunts, so he lapsed into silence, sipping from a takeout coffee that was probably the only thing keeping him going. I tried to catch glimpses of familiar landmarks. There weren't many. We'd always come here in midsummer, so everything would have looked different. Also, I normally read in the car and wasn't paying attention to the landscape. Eventually, I recognized a distinctive farm and general store where the mothers had bought milk and bread. A couple minutes later, we pulled over to the side of the road. The driver put the car in park and twisted around to look at me. "Can't go any farther. Those rocks would trash up my underside."

I glanced at the sagging wet trees, mud puddles, and fallen leaves. "We're pretty far away from where I'm going."

He shrugged. "Rules are rules."

I fished out a wad of bills and handed them over, then slid out of the back seat with my bags. The car sped off as soon as soon I shut the door, tires spinning on loose rocks and mud that splattered across the paved road.

I set off toward the cabin. I'd hiked parts of this road, picking berries and exploring. It was eerie to be here in autumn. All the cottages were closed down for the winter. There were no speedboats roaring on the lake. The normally tidy dirt road had deep wheel ruts on it and large rocks poking out of the gravel here and there—Mom called those tire busters. There were some giant potholes filled with dirty water. Not wanting to twist an ankle, I stuck to the space between the ruts.

My hood muffled the sound of rain, rustling leaves, and creaky tree branches, but it was still spooky. The longer I walked, the wetter my legs got. It felt like hours before I turned down a smaller dirt road that led past a cluster of cabins on the small lake. The one we'd rented wasn't much farther, only about a dozen properties away. I'd convinced myself she'd be there, but this felt like a ghost town. Some of the places were even boarded up with plywood to dissuade thieves and local teenagers who drove out here to party after the summer residents left.

Up ahead, I spotted the old tire swing we used to play on. It hung from a massive oak tree in front of the cabin. It looked like someone had recently replaced the thick ropes holding it up, but there were a lot of small trees and bushes that didn't used to be here. They completely hid the cabin from view. I sped up as I crossed the leaf-strewn lawn, hoping I'd stumble over the path to the door.

When the cabin came into view, my heart sunk. The lights were out—not too surprising at this time of year, since the electricity would be off—and the window shutters were closed tight. There were no footprints in the driveway or out back, and no smoke coming from the chimney. I circled around to the lake, thinking maybe Trissa wanted to stay hidden from the road, but the huge picture window was also shuttered. I couldn't see inside.

I knocked on the back door. There was no response, so I banged harder, went around to the front, and tried again. I'd brought some bobby pins to try to pick the lock, but it was pretty sophisticated, and my wet fingers kept slipping. The sun had gone down by now, so I wedged my phone under my chin with the flashlight aimed at the door.

Eventually, it swung open. I slipped off my boots on a mat and hung my jacket on a wooden rack, then went inside to look around. As I suspected, the electricity and heat didn't work, so it was just as cold inside as it was outside. Room by room, I swept my phone light around and opened all the closets. Trissa was not in the cabin.

In fact, no one had been here for months. The couple who'd rented it to us were old, even back then. Maybe they weren't able to visit anymore. I sank down on the sofa. It smelled strongly of mildew and dust, but I pulled a quilt around me and allowed the tears to fall.

I'd been so sure I would find her. Now I was stuck in a cold, wet cabin, in soggy clothes. and I'd have to stay here alone. How could I have thought that finding her would be this easy? I was just a sixteen-year-old girl, not a criminal mastermind or a genius detective. Why would she have come all the way up here when there were lots of places to hide in the city? Not even someone running for her life would have chosen to be here right now.

There was no way I'd be able to find my way back to the paved road tonight, so I drank some hot chocolate and ate another sandwich. I would have to spend the night here and hike back when the sun came up. I turned off my phone flashlight. The worst thing would be having no way to call a taxi.

Eventually the rain slowed. Through the window, the moon reflected off the calm, misty lake. It was beautifully eerie. Memories flooded my brain: canoeing through a grove of bulrushes with Trissa, Anwar, and Nadia; catching frogs and fireflies; roasting marshmallows over the barbecue; playing endless games of Monopoly; floating on the lake on air mattresses with our hands linked so we'd stay connected; crawling into Trissa's bed after the mothers told us ghost stories and drank rum late into the night around the fire.

Now was not the time to give up, I told myself sternly. I'd gotten this wrong, but I would keep searching. If Trissa was out there, she needed to know that we hadn't given up on her. She was loved and had to come home, or the rest of us might not survive.

*

It took a long time, but I finally warmed up a little, improving my mood just enough to shake off my failure and pull myself together. I changed into my dry shirt and socks—something I should have done right away—checked that the door wouldn't lock behind me if I went for a walk, shrugged on my still-damp jacket that was supposed to be waterproof, and headed down to the beach. I wanted to trail my fingers in the water. As I stood on a rocky outcrop, breathing in the familiar smells of lake and nature, good memories hovered around the edges of my mind.

I picked up a flat rock and skipped it across the surface. It bounced twice before sinking. My rock-skipping skills were clearly rusty. The summer before Nadia died, the four of us kids had had an epic competition that lasted for weeks. The winner wouldn't have to do any chores on our last week here. Of course, Trissa won every single time, until Anwar got the hang of it. He was not only single-minded but naturally athletic. But he always let his little sister win, just to see her jump around gleefully.

Amina had taken the bus up for a few days, using some of her limited time off to be with her children. She couldn't swim and didn't appreciate being in the trees like Mom and Charlene, so she spent most of her time on the deck sipping sweet iced tea with mint, reading novels, or cooking food. She'd seemed content, though.

I wandered down the beach. The memories were so strong that it felt like we'd been here a couple months ago, as opposed to four years. There was a small bay up ahead, I remembered, and a dock that extended over the water. I scrambled to take a seat on it, like I had hundreds of times before, and noticed a partially washed-out footprint in the smooth sand. A little farther up the beach, there was another one.

They had to be recent, or else the rain and wind would have erased them. Someone had traipsed back and forth on the beach within the past few hours. I found a relatively clear print in some wet sand and compared it to my own. It looked about the same size as my foot. Hope sparked inside me. Trissa and I wore each other's shoes all the time.

They seemed to be going farther down the way I was already walking, but these cottages were deserted, so I continued to followed the tracks until they cut up across rocks and grass into the woods. I lost the trail and cursed my weak tracking abilities. Carolyn Keene and Lacey Milan both shared tips for following footprints, but they didn't mention what to do if they went into a forest and it was nighttime.

There were some more secluded cabins up ahead, I remembered. They were away from the lake, surrounded by trees. One of them was so remote that the hippies who owned it had to carry in their supplies on foot. They'd bragged about how it was an eco-house made from logs that had fallen on their property, and it had a living roof where they grew vegetables in the summer. I decided to use some of my precious phone battery—I turned on the flashlight and made my way through the bushes and trees.

I smelled smoke. That meant a fire was burning in one of the cabins. Sure enough, I could see a trickle of smoke drifting up above the treetops ahead. When I got closer, I could see that a flickering light illuminated the window beside the door. Somebody was inside.

I turned off the flashlight and crept up the back steps to peer into the bay window.

It was Trissa!

CHAPTER 17

Choosing Your Next Victim

I stood outside, looking in through the cabin window at Trissa, who was sitting in a rocking chair before the smouldering fire. My heart began to pound hard. I swayed a little, feeling dizzy. I couldn't believe I'd found her and she was alive. The West End Strangler hadn't taken her. Anton and Jellybean had no clue she was here.

I wanted to burst in and tell her how much she'd scared the mothers, demand that she come home, but I knew that would be the worst thing I could do. She might run off. So instead, I headed back to our old cabin, collected my bag and wet clothes, locked the door behind me, and returned to where she was staying.

When I rapped on the window, Trissa bolted to her feet and desperately looked around for somewhere to hide. She must think it was the police or the cabin's owners come to haul her away. When she turned, I could see dried mascara running down her cheeks and a bruise on one cheek. Was hers from Jellybean's bouncers too?

"It's Michie," I called out.

Her body relaxed a fraction, but she didn't look happy that I was here. She came over to unlock the door and let me in, though. "How'd you find me?"

"Your mom was going on about how happy you were up here."

"So she knows I'm here?"

"No. I don't think so. I told Anwar I was coming to see if I could find you, but I asked him not to tell the mothers."

She moved aside and allowed me to enter. I immediately pulled her into a backbreaking hug and inhaled her smell. Body odour, ashes, and a faint hint of jasmine. Weirdly enough, it was the best, most incredible thing I'd ever smelled. Other than Anwar, of course. When I let her go, I discovered she was crying. I could also see that her skin was covered in a thin sheen of sweat. It was hot next to the fireplace.

"You're soaking wet," she mumbled.

I moved away and took off my jacket. "Sorry. This coat isn't as waterproof as I thought."

She gestured toward a row of coat hooks on the wall, meaning I should hang it up to dry. I removed my muddy boots as well, uncertain what to say now that I'd actually found her. "Everyone's been so worried."

She chewed on an already stubby nail.

"Sorry. I didn't mean to—I'm a shitty friend," I said. "You needed support and I wasn't there for you. I want you to tell me everything. No more secrets."

"You can't deal with my shit on top of your own," she said, tapping her own chest to indicate my heart. Her voice sounded so profoundly depressed that it made my heart race and thump weirdly. Hugging her again would help me calm down. That was all I wanted to do. Hold on to her and never let her go. Transfer all my relief and joy about finding her safe into her body. Fill her up with love.

"That's where you're wrong. I'm stronger than you realize. I had no idea how hard things were for you. Don't worry, I'm not going to lecture you. How did you get in, by the way?"

"Key under the mat," she said.

A laugh burst out of me. "No way."

She grinned weakly. "Yep. I wanted to stay at our old place, but it's locked."

"Not tightly enough," I quipped.

Her grin widened. "I disappear for a few days and suddenly you're a B and E specialist?"

I winked and crossed the room to warm myself in front of the wood stove. The heat was bliss, though lighting it had been a huge risk. The other cottages I'd seen were closed down for the winter, but there must be a few people who came out here year-round.

"Charlene and Mom have been tearing the city apart, searching for you. They checked all the morgues and hospitals. The police thought you just ran away."

She tossed her hands in the air. "Maybe they'll stop looking. I'm never going back."

"I know you were planning on going to LA," I said, trying to keep my voice light. "Anton went without you."

"Seriously? Good riddance. I wasn't running away, Michie, I swear. I was running to something. My big chance. The show's producers liked my audition video. Getting on a reality dance show has always been my dream—you know that." She dropped her head into her hands for a moment. "I'd convinced myself I was in love with Anton and that he loved me, but then things got really bad and I just ..."

"Is that because Cal found out you were dealing at the club?"

She nodded and rubbed her face, smearing her mascara even more. "That was my last sale. I'm out of the business. Never again."

"You know what? I don't care. I'm just glad you're safe. From now on, I'm going to be a better friend. You can stop protecting me for once and let me help you. We need to tell Charlene you're alive. It's killing her, thinking you might be dead. The police searched the house twice and dragged all of us down to the station to be interviewed. They even went to Club Jelly and tore it apart, arrested a couple people. God, they charged my mother with trafficking, and your mom's in the hospital."

I paused for a breath, but Trissa looked so alarmed that I immediately added, "Charlene is fine. Don't worry. I guess I should have led with that. She'd been drinking a lot since you went missing and not hydrating or eating any food. And Franklyn's working to get Mom's charges dropped."

"Wait. If the cops searched my room, did they find—"

"Nope. But I did." I took out her burner phone and handed it to her. "I flushed your pills down the toilet."

She made a sound that was halfway between a giggle and a gasp. "You really are Parkdale's answer to Nancy Drew."

I laughed. "One more thing. I slept with Anwar yesterday."

She squealed. "What? Was it awesome? I bet he's really good in bed. He's a babe."

I grinned. "You'll never know."

Smiling proudly, she poked my shoulder. "Look at you, bitch. But I don't think I can go back to Parkdale. It was getting so bad. I couldn't stop my life from imploding."

"I get it. At least I think I do. I'm hoping you'll tell me."

"Anton was …" she paused.

"Forcing you to sell the pills at the club," I said for her.

Her eyes widened. "How did you figure that out?"

"I'm smarter than I look."

"Shit. Did you tell the cops and my mom?"

I shook my head. "No way. She was worried enough, and they were bullies." Suddenly, my chest felt tight. "Is it okay if I stay with you? I can't go home tonight. It's too dark out there."

She gestured to the sofa. I sat down and she flopped down beside me, putting her head in my lap. "I've been clean for four days now, Michie. No pills, no weed. It's been hell, but I think the worst is over."

"You look awful," I said.

"Thanks." She snorted. "You hungry? I have water and apples. I burned through the owners' emergency stash of tuna, pasta, and tomato sauce and had to go into town to do some shopping. But most of that's gone now too."

"You spent all my money."

"I'll pay you back. I also had to get a new phone. It was the cheapest one I could find."

"It's okay. The withdrawals from my account were the first clue about where you'd gone."

"I had no choice, I swear. I couldn't get my knapsack back after Jellybean kicked me out." She closed her eyes and fell silent for a bit. "I messaged Anton when I realized Cal was going to tell on me to Jellybean, but then I lost it and—"

"I heard about the cage," I said gently.

She squeezed her eyes shut for a few seconds. "I don't think I really wanted to kill myself, but I was devastated. The club had become everything to me. I was failing my classes, and you felt so distant. It was the only place where I felt good about myself. Then I messed that up, too. I never wanted to start selling to strangers, but Anton pressured me." She paused, but it looked like she wanted to continue speaking, so I stayed silent. After a moment, she said, "Did you know one time he forced me to give him a blowjob by threatening to poison Tink and Tonk?"

"You didn't tell me," I whispered, grabbing her hand. "That's sexual assault."

"I guess I wanted to pretend it was no big deal. Besides, it would have really upset you."

"Who cares if I get upset?" I'd missed so much of what she'd been dealing with. It broke my heart. "I wish you'd told me. I would have kicked his ass."

She sniffled, reached over, and tapped my chest. "I care, Michie. You're tough, but your heart isn't. And I was so scared he'd do something bad if I stopped selling."

"He better not come back from LA."

She barked out a hard laugh, but tears were rolling down her cheeks. "The worst part about that night is that I actually messaged Anton after Cal left me alone in the bathroom. He showed up in time to save me from a beating, but he was furious that I got caught and paranoid that I'd told Cal where I got the drugs. He refused to believe I hadn't said anything. I legit thought he was going to kill me. So I ran. Stopped at home to grab a couple things, like your bank card. Your money got me here."

"I don't care about the money," I said, standing up. I found a paper towel and moistened it with some of her drinking water. "At least Anton interrupted Jellybean's security team. All that matters is you're alive and safe." I cleaned her face. When I was finished, the paper towel was streaked with dirt and mascara, but she'd stopped crying.

I tossed the napkin into a bag she'd been using for garbage, took out two plates and two mugs from a cupboard, and checked them for dead bugs—a cottage tip. I poured out the rest of my lukewarm hot chocolate and served up the last two cheese and tomato sandwiches.

Trissa accepted my offering. She dug into the sandwich so ravenously that I wondered exactly what she'd been eating for the past three days. After we finished, I carried the plates to the sink and washed them with a little more bottled water. I opened up the package of chocolate chip cookies and carried them over to share.

"I've missed you, Michie," Trissa said, before biting into a cookie. Her bottom lip quivered. She pulled her feet up beneath her and rested her chin on her knees.

There would be time to talk later. "I need to tell the mothers you're okay. They must be panicking double with both of us missing."

Trissa made me promise I wouldn't do that until the morning. She wanted one more night before facing the real world. I agreed and pulled her to her feet, then led her into the bedroom, where she lay down. I lay down next to her, playing gently with her tangled hair the way she liked when we were kids. Eventually, her breathing deepened, and she fell asleep. I wished she could be this peaceful while she was awake, but it wasn't in her nature. Never had been. I couldn't change her. I could only try to keep her safe in the future.

I slipped my phone out of my bag and checked the time. It was almost eleven. The messages from Mom and Anwar had progressed from anger to fear to stony silence. A pox on my deeply ingrained guilt complex! It was the only truly Jewish thing I'd inherited from Mom other than my frizzy hair. I glanced at Trissa to make sure she was really asleep and then wrote both Mom and Anwar to let them know I was safe. I also told them I'd found Trissa and that she was upset but mostly unharmed, and I asked Mom to let Charlene know. I added another text saying that I would try to bring her home tomorrow, but it might be hard to update them if my phone died.

Trissa's burner still had most of its power. Anwar knew about that phone, but he wouldn't have memorized the number.

I tiptoed over to the window, lifted the curtain, and saw that the slushy rain had stopped. The mist on the lake had dissipated, and a sliver of the moon was reflected in the lake's surface. Around the edges of the water were the suggestions of trees and bushes. It called to me. I loved it out here. I wrapped myself back up in my jacket, slipped my boots on, and opened the door. Out on the porch, I let the noise of raindrops rolling off the trees and rustling leaves fill me with a sense of calm, the way it used to when we were kids. Trissa would be all right. I'd found her. I'd figure out how to bring her back home.

I carefully tromped down to the beach and followed it to the long wooden dock. Everything was peaceful. For the first time in days, I felt relaxed. I peeled off my boots and socks, sat down on the end, and let my feet dangle into the lake. When my feet got cold, I had to lift them out of the water. I was taller than I'd been the last time we were here; back then my toes had only skimmed the surface. I would have to work at getting Trissa to confide in me like she used to. She might act tough, but she was the most vulnerable of anyone I cared about.

I must have sat there a long time, because eventually Trissa came outside, wrapped in a wool blanket. She sank down on the dock, and my hand immediately reached for hers. She held out one arm so I could huddle under the blanket, pressed against her side, sharing body heat.

"I'm sorry," she said.

I turned to stared at her in profile: lush lips, round nose, curly red halo of hair. "Why are you sorry?"

"For scaring everyone and thinking you'd judge me. I was convinced you'd be disappointed in me."

"Never. You're my sister. I love you."

"I love you too, Michie." She hesitated, then added, "I need to stay away from those pills. They're poison. My body still wants them so badly. Anton is on something all the time. He's a monster, but I just ... needed to be out of my mind. They helped me deal. I don't want to escape that way anymore."

I nodded, hoping it would encourage her to keep speaking.

"I used to love dancing, but even that became a chore after Jellybean started pushing me to be in the cage every night. I was always exhausted afterward, and there was no way I could go to school the next day. I want dancing to bring me joy again. I'm not good at anything else. It was the same with the videos. You had the phone, so I'm sure you already know about them. At first, I felt powerful. Men wanted me. I got money for doing next to nothing and could save up for the trip. Then Anton found out and held it over me—he threatened to tell my mom and demanded I help him sell. It wasn't so bad at first. I got a cut."

"Did Jellybean ever hurt you?" I asked, remembering how he'd watched me change.

Her eyebrows raised momentarily, but she shook her head. "No. Not really. He just kept showing up in the changeroom when I was changing, pretending he'd just forgotten to knock."

"He's so gross," I said. "I'm kind of glad you got fired."

"I really wanted to figure out a way to get on that plane to LA." She looked at me sadly. "I wasn't running from you or my mom. You know being on a dance show is my dream. I probably would have told you before I left, but I was a mess. I only started taking pills because I'd agreed to dance two nights in a row. I don't think Anton meant to get me hooked ... or maybe he did."

"Men like Anton and Jellybean need to have power over people."

"Truth. I'm done with men. It's only women for me from now on."

I burst out laughing. "Sure. We're not always better."

"Burns me up that asshole is in Hollywood right now, living my dream," she said.

I hugged her and laughed into her hair. "Come home. I promise I'll be with you when you explain it all to your mom. She'll understand. We'll help you handle everything."

"I'll think about it, Michie." She rested her head on my shoulder, the way Mom had with Franklyn. It felt amazing. It meant she was starting to relax. I didn't want to pull away, but my ass was freezing after sitting on damp wood for so long.

"We need to go inside," I said. "I'm getting cold and my heart's a piece of shit."

"Don't say that. It's kept you alive all these years even though the doctors thought you'd be dead by now, though I think some of that was your mom's sheer willpower." We headed back inside the cabin. "Did you bring your pills?"

"Yeah."

"Good. Take them and lie down until you feel better. I'm going to build up the fire and boil some water for tea. It's pretty much all I have left."

"What did you spend all my money on?" I joked.

She grimaced. "Let's see. Bus tickets, a ride to and from town for supplies, takeout meals, groceries, a couple sweaters, T-shirts, socks, and underwear. Uh, a pay-as-you-go phone." She groaned and pulled on her unruly curls. "My life is a disaster."

I draped my wet clothing over a wooden chair in front of the stove, turned a sheet that smelled like mothballs into an awkward nightgown, and slid into the bed beneath an extreme pile of blankets that Trissa assured me we'd need when the fire died out and the damp chill crept in. Trissa got in too. I curled around her back and held her lightly, half afraid that if I let go, she'd disappear again.

For the first time since the detectives had shown up at our front door early Saturday morning, my sleep was untroubled. I hadn't lost Trissa. I still had her.

CHAPTER 18

Knowing When to Retire from the Life

Trissa and I were startled awake by honking out on the dirt road near the cabin. The room was blazing with sunshine, but I had no idea what time it was. I leapt to my feet, confused about where I was, then squealed and dove back into bed and pulled the covers up to my chin.

"It's freezing!" I yelped. "That floor is a literal block of ice."

Trissa didn't respond. She looked scared, listening intently to the noises outside. "Nobody has driven down that road in the entire time I've been here, Michie. It's a dead end."

"Uh-oh." Worst-case scenarios paraded through my mind: the owners had found out about the break-in, local cops were here to arrest us, those Toronto detectives had driven all the way here just to take me down.

Trissa had left her clothes next to the bed. She managed to get dressed without exposing a single body part to the cold air. On her way over to the front window, she paused to grab my crusty but dry socks and toss them at my head. My face caught them. Nice.

She lifted a corner of the lacy white curtain, hoping to see who was there, then made a frustrated noise and let it drop. I could tell she was trying to decide whether to go see what was happening or to run away. Her face was tight, and she was chewing on her bottom lip.

"It's definitely not Anton," I reassured her as I pulled on the gross socks. "I saw him at the airport two days ago."

She relaxed a fraction. "Should we go see who it is?"

"Guess so." The second time I put my feet on the floor was slightly less jarring than the first but still resulted in my teeth chattering like the skeleton from health class whenever the teacher carried it around. "It can't be more than a few degrees above freezing."

I practically leapt across the room to get my bag and ripped it open to take out the clean shirt I'd packed. I stuffed yesterday's shirt inside. My pants had slipped off the back of the chair were I left them to dry and now lay in a crumpled heap, cold and stiff, but no longer soggy.

I put on my boots, wrestled with the multiple locks on the front door, and opened it, heedless of how dishevelled I must look. It had to be the police. Anwar must have told my mom where I'd gone, and she must have called the police. It was my fault for bringing them down on us. At least I could be the one to confront them. Alone. I turned to Trissa. "Hide. Anywhere. Don't tell me where you're going so I can't lead them to you."

Then I hurtled up the path. Well, not hurtled, but walked quickly. My chest was tight from sleeping in a smoky cabin that probably had mould on the walls, and my heart was skipping uncomfortably. The honking—accompanied by shouting—got louder as I emerged onto the dirt road. Trissa ignored my command and followed a few steps behind me. I should have taken my pill because my heart felt like it was going to burst. Trissa overtook me when I had to stop and lean against the damp trunk of a barren maple tree for support.

That was when I recognized the voices. And the sound of the car horn. An instant later, my mom's old red hatchback came into view. She stopped the car abruptly, causing the wheels to do a drunken wiggle on the muddy road, then hit the gas and sped toward us, splashing dirt everywhere. Charlene was hanging out of the passenger side, wearing a coat over her hospital scrubs, clutching a cigarette between the fingers of her good arm, and waving wildly. She was yelling something I couldn't make out. Her voice sounded hoarse.

Trissa giggled in her frenetic way. "Just like when we were kids, Michie. When I wiped out on my bike. Remember that day?"

"Oh yeah. I'm still haunted by the memory. Except that time, Charlene was smoking two cigarettes at once. I can still picture it. She must have forgotten she already had one between her lips and lit another, then let both of them burn out without even really inhaling."

When the car got closer, I could see that Anwar and Franklyn were in the back, holding on to the seats in front of them for dear life. Their faces were frozen in identical expressions of horror, like they'd been riding a roller coaster.

Trissa stood still, her mouth agape. All my memories of her bike accident in the park rushed into my head. There was the wipeout, her bleeding and crying, me pedalling madly to get home, confessing what happened, and sitting in the back of our previous car, trying to keep my heart calm as we sped through the streets. Cigarette smoke choking me. Charlene smashing through the wooden barricade barring cars from entering the park and speeding around until we finally found Trissa, limping down the street, alone.

This time, I could do things differently. I shoved off from the tree and staggered out into the road, arms wide in front of Trissa. If they were pissed, they'd have to go through me. Mom hit the brakes. The passenger door flew open before she'd even fully stopped, and Charlene was flying toward her daughter, cigarette butt tossed carelessly onto the muddy road.

"Wait," I said, stepping between the two of them. "Why are you here? I won't let you upset Trissa."

Charlene had shoved her wild hair into a knitted hat, which actually made it look worse, with tufts pushing out from underneath. The sling holding her dislocated shoulder had a coffee stain on it. "Get out of the way, Michelle," she growled. "I need to hug my daughter."

"Y—you're not mad?" asked Trissa, sounding so nervous and small.

"Of course I am, you little asshole." Charlene sidestepped me and pulled Trissa into her working arm. She rocked her from side to side, kissed her face, and started to cry. Together, they crumpled on the road, sitting in the mud and gravel. I almost burst into tears myself, watching them.

Mom and Anwar were out of the car now. Anwar held his ribs, but he was walking all right. They'd probably tied him to a chair and tortured the information out of him.

Mom grabbed my shoulders and shook me kind of hard. "How the hell could you just leave like that!" She sighed and pulled me into a hug. "Michie, you found her. I'm so thankful. But don't you ever try something like this again. If you plan on going anywhere I can't reach you—anywhere—you have to let me know why, where, and for how long."

"I wasn't positive she'd be here," I said. "And if she wasn't, I would have just turned around and come home."

She squeezed me tighter and mumbled into my hair, "But you're my daughter."

"I'm not a baby, Mom. I can take care of myself."

"Oh Michie, I know that. You found our Trissa when none of the adults in her life could. But it's still my job to keep you safe. I'm not always the best mother, but that's the contract I signed the second you were born."

She sounded weirdly like the mom version of the voice in my head when I thought about Trissa. I wanted to say that Trissa was the one who'd really needed protecting all these years, and we'd failed terribly at it. All of us. All the people who loved her. But instead, I sighed and relaxed into her arms. "You're a good mom. I wouldn't want anyone else as my parent. But you had enough going on."

"Don't make excuses," she chided. "I always have time when it comes to your safety."

"How did Charlene get out of the hospital?"

"The minute Anwar told us you'd come up here, she ripped off all the wires, pulled out the IV herself, got out of bed, and walked right out the door. She demanded I drive her here immediately. It was all I could do to make her wait until morning. She refused to sleep, so we left at five."

"Is she going to be okay?"

"She's a survivor. If it had been you who was missing, well, I'd tear a hole in the space-time continuum to get to you."

Tears filled my eyes. "I love you, Mama Bear."

"Oh, sweetie. I love you too. Always and forever."

When she finally took a step back and released her stranglehold of a hug, she continued to hold on to my hand. I felt like a small child tethered to her mother, but it was comforting.

Nearby, Anwar and Franklyn's eyes were locked on Trissa and Charlene, who were still sitting in the mud, sobbing loudly. They both looked like they'd been through the wash.

Anwar glanced at me and shrugged, as if to say *I had to tell them and I don't regret it.*

I smiled and nodded, tugged my hand away from Mom, and went over to Franklyn. "Thank you for everything. For responding when I called. And having my mother's back. She needs people like you on her side."

He looked over at my mom with a certain softness in his eyes. "Your mother doesn't play by anyone else's rules, but she's quite a woman."

Mom gave him a kiss on the cheek and went over to sit down beside Trissa and Charlene. Charlene's face was now buried in her daughter's hair. My mother wrapped her arms around Trissa on the other side, forming the other half of a shell.

"You love my mom, don't you?" I asked Franklyn.

He raised an eyebrow. "How are you so wise?"

I decided he needed a hug too, so I gave him one. "What's going to happen with Trissa?"

"I called the detectives first thing this morning to let them know she'd been found safely and that we were on our way to retrieve her from an empty cottage. They threatened to charge her with breaking and entering—"

"You should have seen him," interjected Anwar. "It was awesome. He was on the phone for two hours while we were driving. He's some kind of lawyer superhero. I bet he could negotiate anybody into doing anything."

"She just needed a place to sleep for a few nights," I said.

Franklyn nodded. "I managed to reach the cabin's owners and explained her history with this area. They agreed that if she hasn't damaged anything, they won't press charges. She will have to give them some money to replace anything she's used, make a formal apology, and do some community service. They made a request that she volunteer at the food bank."

"Want to hear the best part?" asked Anwar. "He convinced the police to drop the charges against Charlene, your mom, and Trissa, so they can use this as a PR opportunity. Missing girl found safe—that kind of thing."

"Lord knows they need some good publicity," said Franklyn, grinning. He had a small gap between his two front teeth. I sure hoped my mother understood how lucky she was. "Telling the public about a happy family reunited is a hell of a lot more pleasant than their usual press conferences."

"Which normally involve making excuses for cops' bad behaviour," said Anwar grimly.

"Or releasing the name of another Strangler victim," I added.

I shuddered at the thought of the Strangler and how worried I'd been that Trissa would be the next face in the news stories. "Great.

We helped them put a nice, pretty bow on their racism, carding, and shoot-first policies."

"ACAB," muttered Anwar, pumping a fist in the air.

I laughed and shoulder bumped him. Would I ever find a more perfect guy for me? Not now, maybe not ever. We did fit like the pieces of a puzzle.

Trissa and Charlene were finally getting to their feet. It must have sunk in that they'd been sitting in mud, because they were trying to wipe their faces and unstick their clothing from the backs of their legs while still clinging to each other. Without discussing it, we all started to walk down the path in the direction of the beach and the dock. When we passed the cabin, Mom insisted that Charlene and Trissa needed some time to talk, so they went to the dock and the rest of us went inside. I took my morning pills, then helped the others to tidy up the cabin as best we could. Mom shovelled out the stove, I packed up Trissa's and my stuff and stowed it in the trunk of mom's car, and then I stripped off the dirty sheets and tossed them in a laundry hamper. There was no way to wash them without electricity and running water. Meanwhile, Anwar and Franklyn wiped down the kitchen and living room and swept the floor.

By the time we were done, my stomach was rumbling, but it was another twenty minutes before Trissa and Charlene wandered up to find us. They looked like they were no longer carrying the world on their shoulders. My heart fluttered—this time with happiness. I hoped this meant Trissa had told her mother everything and that Charlene had listened supportively.

Back at the car, Trissa took Charlene's cigarettes, broke them all in half, and dropped them into the dregs of her mother's half-finished